DANANN CONQUEST

GARY CULLEN

Special thanks to my wife Kathleen who saw the Irish hare
that led her to the site of the White Horse of Binn and
who encouraged me to stay an extra week in Ireland to
explore the countryside.

CONTENTS

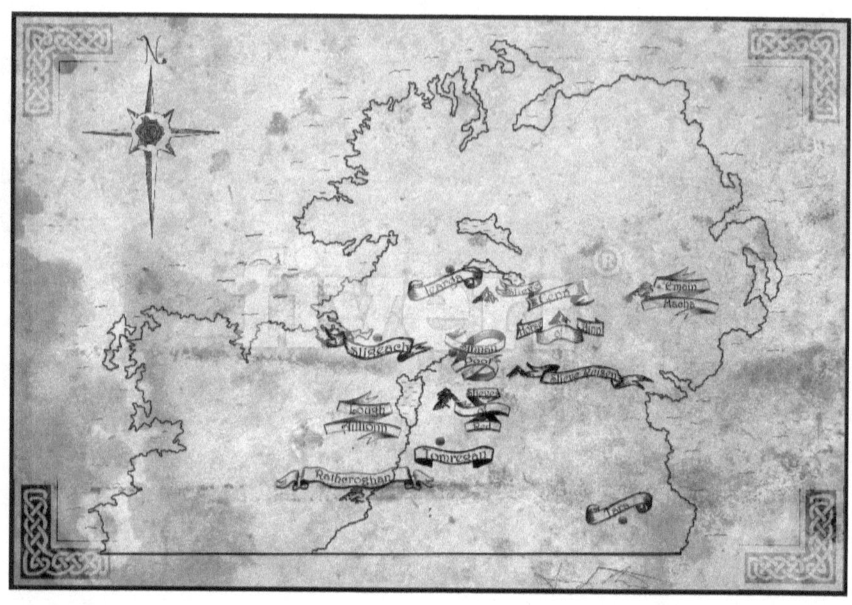

The year 1159 marked a point in time of catastrophic events in the world. It began in the summer of 1159 BC and lasted 18 years. Tree ring data from ancient oak trees recovered from Irish bogs identify this event with a series of very narrow tree growth rings. Our story begins at this point of time with the coming of the Tuatha De' Danann to Ireland.

Elsewhere in the world, the Shang dynasty fell in China, the Mycenaean and Hittite civilizations collapsed. The Egyptian New Kingdom went into decline and eventual collapse. This timeframe marked the transition from the Late Bronze Age to the Early Iron Age

CHAPTER ONE

THE BEARDED STAR

Since the Beltane festival last year, the bearded star has grown until it appears as a small moon in the sky. Peering at it now, the bright orb is even larger than last night, sending a quiver of expectation and excitement, mingled with fear, deep into my soul. Brilliant wisps of hair pulsate from the head of the star, then trail behind in the night sky.

There is much talk among the elders of its location in the star cluster An Scairp. Their readings indicate an ominous sign of trouble and death.

Staring into the sky, I try to fathom how this interpretation is determined. During training, they tell me to look at the moving stars and view their placement relative to the bearded star. Perhaps what they are observing is the morning star, Lugh, moving into An Scairp? Or is it the bright one, Dagda, positioned in Tragan, the star cluster representing good fortune? There is much to learn.

Progress through ominous An Scairp is slow. By my estimation, the bearded star will leave An Scairp and enter the star cluster Bradan, a most fortuitous position, before this year's Beltane, which is six months away. The elders talk about these positions and their meanings during our lessons, but never provide all their insights. It is for us to take their teachings and learn how to consider details and make interpretations. Perhaps the White Horse oracle at Slieve Binn will provide answers. The White Horse is located about a day's walk north of here and on our year-end festival, Samhain, the Tomregan elders send two or three of their most advanced students to camp near its mouth to hear from the oracle. I hope to be among this group.

Time between first and second sleep is only about an hour and I must be well-rested for all our preparations tomorrow for the Samhain festival. But movement, reflecting off the light of the full moon and bearded star, catches my eye on the far side of the rath enclosure where the elders hold their teaching sessions. Two figures are being met by another who has opened the gate and led them into the teaching area. I try to see their faces, but cannot.

Fatigue flows through my body and soon I enter second sleep.

CHAPTER TWO

SAMHAIN EVE

As the sun rises, glints of golden light cascade across the valley from the high upper edges of Slieve Ruisen. Silhouetted forms of my friends and family, already hard at work in these early morning hours, emerge from the shadows.

I glance toward the slieve summit, appreciating the warmth the rays of sunlight provide, and am startled to see a giant hare sitting on its haunches, staring at me. The hare is no more than five feet away and shows no intention of moving. I stop working and kneel, facing the creature. The hare rubs its nose with one of its paws, but does not otherwise move, appearing to examine me as much as I examine in return. After several long moments, the hare drops to all fours, gives me a sideways glance, then hops away. What might this encounter portend?

I hurry to meet my fellow villagers of Tomregan. We are all busily preparing for our year-end, two-day festival of Samhain, the time of year where we give thanks for the harvests from our fields and the production from our herds and flocks. Samhain marks the end of the current year and the beginning of the new.

As I work, I discern movement near the learning center. Father is escorting a dark-haired, brown-skinned woman, clad in furs, along with a tall, muscular, dark-colored warrior through the rath grounds. These two must be who I saw in the early morning hours between my first and second sleep. I have never seen any of the Formorri who live in the village of Sligeach, which is about two days' journey northwest of Tomregan, but from their appearance I surmise they must be from there.

The woman's darker coloring is much different than my light-colored skin. The heads of the men, even the boys of our village, swivel to watch as Father shows the man and the woman the way to a roundhouse. The woman's head is held high and her dark features glow as light from the gold torc about her neck radiates upward. She carries a bronze single-edged sgian, secured in a leather sleeve strapped around her ankle.

My friends, too, watch the visitors. I wonder if the man is her servant. As I move closer to my friends, they whisper in admiration that the woman is the warrior queen of the Formorri, a tribe that occupies the trading village of Sligeach, located along the seashore to the west. The man is her warrior escort. One of my older friends, Una, appears to know much about the queen. She tells me the woman received her dark features from her father, who was the Formorri King of Sligeach before her. Her mother was the daughter of King Ailill of Rathcroghan, whose royal rath lies two-day's journey to the south of Sligeach. This woman before us is named Sianna, after the flowers growing wild along the marshes near Sligeach. Gazing back toward where Sianna, the warrior, and my father have disappeared into the guest roundhouse, I wonder what this sudden appearance foretells. Recent days seem filled with signs.

Preparation for Samhain takes much work and soon I am lost in performing my chores. Morning has nearly passed when I see Father, Sianna, and her warrior escort coming towards me. In the middle of their conversation, Father looks up, as if remembering something, and glances about before he spots me. He touches

Sianna's arm and whispers in her ear while both look toward me.

"Keelen, come meet Sianna of the Formorri," Father calls.

As I approach, Father speaks again. "Sianna, the Queen of Sligeach, comes to learn more about the meaning of the bearded star."

Sianna's deep brown eyes search my face. She must approve of what she finds, for she gives me a warm smile and says, "It is my honor to meet the oldest daughter of Fearghus, the esteemed bard of Tomregan. I have stopped here for a night on my way home to Sligeach after meeting with the High King at Tara. The bearded star's appearance has everyone in Inis Elga anxious, so I wanted to meet with your father to gain his understanding. He tells me I could learn much from you and your family before the end of this Samhain season. Unfortunately, I must return to Sligeach tomorrow morning. Perhaps we can meet and talk sometime in the future?"

Puzzled, I look toward my father. What does she mean?

Father doesn't acknowledge me, so I give a slight bow and say, "It is I who am privileged to meet such an honored person. I don't know how I could tell you more than Father could, though it would be my pleasure to share all I know."

Father smiles at me and says, "I will tell you all about this in more detail after the fast is broken at sundown. Now go catch up with your friends. There is much to do to prepare for our feast."

I bid Sianna and Father leave and return to my friends.

Visitors are not unusual. Our village is the center of learning for all Inis Elga. Our learning center is for teaching upcoming bards and druis. Nearby lies the sacred stone circle dedicated to Cenn. Cenn is a high spirit from our most ancient times who helps us understand how we as individuals are part of the universe and how each of us is an important component of this universe in our unique way. We honor Cenn for helping us gain this understanding and offer him gifts of thanks at Samhain. Both the learning center and the stone circle of Cenn bring visitors, but having a queen arrive in the depth of night with father, the leading elder and most respected bard of Tomregan, waiting for her is unusual.

I can speculate on these things later. The fragrant aroma of honeyed roasting pig on the cooking stones reaches my hunger-strained belly and memories of the taste drive me to help prepare for the feast.

Smoke from the many fires fills the air with the scent of burning wood tangled with the aromas of cooking. My first chore is to heat cooking stones to red-hot. These will be dropped into the fulacht fiadh, our water-filled cooking pits. After the stones are dropped into the pits, the water comes to a boil. Fresh meat from the slaughtered hogs and cattle is wrapped in cooking skins and, as the water reaches boiling, the cooking skins are weighted and placed in the fulacht fiadh. Cooking takes several hours. Once we drop the meat into the fulacht fiadh, the cooking skins will stay until after the sun sets and it's time to break our fast.

The Samhain feasts I remember have all been festive. Father tells of the grand Samhain feasts he knew before the coming of the cold, twelve Samhains past, when the lands were warmer, our crops more plentiful, and herds numerous. We did not need to rely so heavily on acorn meal and wild game as we do today.

When dusk arrives in a few hours, we will extinguish our fires and wait for my father, Fearghus, to create the fire for the New Year within the stone circle of Cenn. This New Year's fire is used to light all the fires in the village. Once lit, our fast can be broken and the Samhain feasting days can begin.

My friends and I are apprentices learning the ways of the drui and bard. When not in training, each of us attends to the daily chores of tending our fields of barley, flax, and wheat, herding our cattle and pigs, cooking, and keeping our homes in good repair. Our great love is the time we spend learning ancient stories and songs, developing the skills to read the stars, acquiring mind-power secrets, delving into the knowledge of the power held by plants and animals, and enjoying the beauty of playing the harp and listening to the harp music from the elder drui and bards.

Much preparation for Samhain still needs to be completed. I am filled with anticipation. Father has promised to entrust my twin brother, Flann, my younger sister, Laragh, and I with an important undertaking.

My afternoon duties include helping prepare the bread for the Samhain feasting and the ground meal that will be used throughout the winter. To make sufficient bread for Samhain and the winter, we must mix barley, flax seed, and wheat, with acorn meal. Preparing the acorn meal takes considerable effort. The acorns must be sorted, cracked, peeled, and crushed.

My friends and I chat among ourselves while working. Although my brother, sister, and I have no special status beyond being apprentices, we each exhibit unique skills which set us apart. My friends have whispered that they know Flann, Laragh, and I will be undertaking some important task. The new Samhain launches the beginning of the thirteenth year since our troubled times began, and should be a time of revelation and change, yet the mystery behind my friends' suggestions and my father's promise cause me to feel unsettled. As I help prepare the acorn meal, my friends and I speculate further on what my father may ask of me, my brother, and my sister. Will it be a journey to the rath of one of the northern kings, perhaps even to Tara, for counsel with the High King? That would undoubtedly be exciting. I've heard the golden splendor of Tara is remarkable to behold.

Our talk dwindles as we take the final step in creating the flour. We work together to crush the wheat, flax, and barley, mixing it with the crushed acorn meats, then blending in blood. We begin this blending with each of us unsheathing our sgians and placing them against our left palm. I join the others and curl my fingers around the blade, giving a quick squeeze. Blood drips from my hand and I ceremonially shake the blood onto the grain meal. One of the other girls brings a container of blood from the slaughtered cows and I help blend it into this mixture. After all is blended, we quickly spread this combination onto blankets for drying. The bright, mid-day sun will soon dry the mixture.

Before long, the last chores of the day have wound down. Those of us who have prepared the blood meal take a portion of the dried meal and deliver it to those preparing the Samhain bread.

The sun begins to dip in the west. Samhain is about to arrive and soon the bounty of the festival will erase my feelings of hunger. Perhaps, too, my questions will be answered.

CHAPTER THREE

SAMHAIN

As dusk descends, we extinguish all fires in the village. The moan of bronze horns echoes through the oak groves and beckons us to the nearby circle of stones. Gathering the village children, my friends and I move along the path through the sacred oaks to the stone circle. Enough light remains to determine our way, but even in the darkest of night, our long familiarity with the path, and the sound of the beckoning horns, would enable us to find our route.

The energy of the massive stones emanates strongly this Samhain. I hold Laragh's hand. She appears deep in thought. Fearghus and the other bards and drui emerge as shadows around the sacrificial center stone. From within their group comes the bleating cry of a frightened calf. Bundles of grain lie on the ground to the sides of the sacrificial stone. A few feet away are stacks of oak and hazel. The horns go silent, and no sound—outside of the whisper of the wind through the oaks and stones—can be heard.

In the depth of darkness, the faint rhythmic pulse of drums begins. The resonance builds, but never becomes loud. The sounds echo off the stones and I feel possessed by this muted, rhythmic beat, and drift into semi-consciousness. I am aware of the sound and everyone about me, as well as the ancestors now with us. Mother appears and communes with me. The drum beat continues. I feel a sense of closeness, of comfort, from those who have passed. Then, as the sounds fade, the visions of my ancestors begin to fade as well. I smile at them, and they smile in return as they melt away into the darkness, for we know we will meet again next Samhain.

As silence again wraps about me, I hear movement coming from within the group of elders. Though too dark to recognize who is moving, I know Father is preparing to create the fire for the New Year. The new fire must be kindled, as tradition dictates, by rubbing wood on wood. Near the wood stacks, a whirling hum is heard. This familiar sound tells me his spindle is at work. Flickers of flame illuminate Father's long, thin face. His graying red hair glints in the firelight. Soon flames leap into the air, illuminating the stone circle and revealing the gathering of people paying homage to Cenn and welcoming the New Year. The bronze-clad outer stones and the gold-clad inner stone shimmer in the firelight.

Father selects each bundle of grain, taps them lightly, one by one on the sacrificial stone, then places them reverently into the fire. With every bundle added, flames spike, consuming the contents. Once the bundles are sacrificed, the calf is brought forward and laid down as sacrifice. A gleaming bronze blade is drawn high in the air over the calf's neck and in the next instant blood flows down and around the stone. Father draws the blade across his open palm, drawing blood. He sprinkles it into the pool flowing from the calf.

The slain calf is placed in a large water-soaked wicker basket. This is hoisted over the fire with the ends resting on supports to keep it above the flames. More wood is added and soon the calf's body begins to be consumed by the fire. The drying wicker basket bursts into flames, dropping what is left of the calf into the sacrificial fire. Each family will carry embers back to Tomregan to relight all the hearths within the village.

With the offering complete, I raise my voice with the roars of those around me as we welcome Samhain. The bronze horns again moan in the night.

The feast begins.

I join my friends as we all gather about the central village fire. On wooden planks, the roasted and boiled meats are laid out for serving, along with freshly baked bread.

Laragh and I take small portions of the succulent meat and place them on cuts of bread. In our wooden trenchers, we place our favorite food: quail roasted in a covering of mud. The hardened clay balls holding the roasted quail are stacked at the end of the food plank. They are still warm to the touch and Laragh and I eagerly grab two each, taking them with our other food back to the fire.

We sit near one of the many skins holding mead. Each of us grabs a skin and take a swallow, washing down our roasted meat and bread. Then we each attack our servings of quail. We crack open the clay on a rock and let the juices flow out. The feathers are glued to the clay and come away as we pull the hardened clay from the birds. With relish, I tug off a leg and thigh, which falls easily away from the roasted birds. The taste is magnificent.

Sounds of music erupt from the harpists. Ceili dancing begins. The intricate footwork is beautiful to watch.

The dancing takes me, even though I was but a child, back to the days of warm nights before the arrival of the dust and cold, twelve Samhains past.

Father and the other elder bards and drui return from the stone circle. They settle on the far side of the central fire and begin eating their fill. Father catches my eye and indicates with a nod, a look toward Laragh, and another nod toward our roundhouse, that he wants to meet with us. Lightly touching Laragh's arm, I tell her Father wishes to speak to us. Once inside the roundhouse, we wait by our hearth.

While waiting, Laragh and I gaze out upon the festivities. I wrap my arms about my little sister, pulling her close. She snuggles against me. Glancing down at her, I wonder what Father wants. Whatever it is, it cannot be about our important task, since Flann was not beckoned.

Weariness comes over me, along with a sense of melancholy. I begin to think about my mother. She died when Flann and I were young, while giving birth to Laragh. When she died, the cloud of dust from the east besieged us and cast our land into overwhelming darkness, lasting for what seemed forever. Those days are profoundly etched in my mind as if they were only yesterday. I clearly recall the smell of sulfur and brimstone; the powdery coating on our clothes, our hair, and the ground; the screams of my mother calling in pain; then the wail of my new sister, Laragh, who was not expected to come for another moon. I wrap Laragh more tightly in my arms.

I sense Laragh has similar thoughts. She is a quiet girl with remarkable beauty emerging. She glances up at me. Her eyes are a gentle green, with a hint of gray, and her complexion is clear and fresh. "Tell me about her," she whispers, and I know she is referring to our mother.

Even though she is young, Laragh carries herself with grace and with the manner of someone wise and mature. Father says Laragh is an old soul who gained much wisdom in past lives. All in our family have the ability of "sight" to some degree, but Laragh can perceive more of the future than the rest of us and can also relate stories of a past long before her time.

Recounting my memories of our mother evokes a smile from Laragh. I hear Father approach. Laragh says, "Mother visits me from time to time to comfort me. I know of her memories and her love for you. I cherish knowing her in this way with my visions and hearing about her from you, but wish I would have known her when she lived, as you did."

As Father enters the roundhouse, Laragh shifts to a sitting position next to me. I see he has a woolen sack the color of red ochre, the top drawn shut by a belt of woven horsehair. A spiral motif in deep blue adorns its sides. It is a striking and obviously special sack that I have faint memories of seeing once, long ago. Father holds the sack with reverence. His face appears sad until the moment our eyes meet, then he breaks into a warm smile.

The memory of when I saw the sack becomes clearer. It was Mother's. She kept within it prized adornments she wore only for the festivals. The gold and amber of these objects heightened and showcased her lush reddish-blonde hair, blue eyes, and milky-white skin. Though I was only a small girl when I last saw her wear them, I remember gazing at her in wonder. Seeing the ochre-colored sack sweeps precious memories through my mind. Could this sack still hold these treasures?

"Laragh, Keelen," Father says softly. "I have items to give you, items that are precious to me."

"Yes, Father," Laragh and I both respond. I don't know quite what to think, but neither of us take our eyes off the ochre-colored sack. I try to remember exactly what my mother kept inside. Father spreads a cloak and places the sack on it between him and us.

Laragh glances toward me, her face gleaming with anticipation and uncertainty. I am sure my face looks much the same.

"Keelen," Father begins, "I sense from your expression you recognize this sack. Laragh," he continues, "this holds many belongings your mother treasured. She received these from her mother, and she from hers. Often, when pregnant with you, she would talk of the time when these precious possessions would be passed to her daughters. She always knew the child she carried was a girl. She told me she sensed your strength and power. Gazing at these objects, she would say, 'This will be perfect for Laragh, the child I carry. She will have green eyes to complement her coal-dark-hair.' Or, she'd say, 'This will look lovely around Keelen's neck, highlighting her hair that is so much like mine.'" He sighs. "If only she were here to pass these on to you tonight."

Father draws open the sack and his fingers linger on each item, as he lovingly lays each one on the cloak between us. The objects are exceptionally beautiful. Firelight dances off the gold and amber.

First, Father selects two gold cloak fasteners and hands one to each of us. "Your mother used these on her finest cloaks. They will draw the eyes of admirers up to your faces and your eyes will mesmerize them." We each take a fastener, holding them tight.

Father continues. "These long, gold hairpins and clasps were used to decorate and hold your mother's hair. With these, her hair would glow with fire and her beauty would radiate for all to behold."

Fingering the pins and clasps, Laragh and I cannot resist decorating each other's hair. We eagerly help each other pull our hair back, set it in place with the pins and clasps, then use the remaining pins to curl and wave our hair in the back. Father watches with glistening and pleased eyes. He seems to be viewing us as much as looking at a vision from long ago.

"These objects," he continues, picking out rings and bracelets, "adorned your mother's fingers and wrists. Keelen, your mother wanted you to have these spiral finger rings to accent your slender hands and long fingers. Laragh, she wished you to have these gold and bronze bracelets to highlight your delicate hands and long, graceful arms.

"These last two items were her most treasured. One she wore not only to highlight her beauty, but also to represent her position of high druis. This, she wanted for you, Keelen."

The neck torc is striking, made of a twisted strand of solid gold. Power and elegance seem to radiate from its golden curves. Placing it around my neck, the warm metal lays light and delicate upon my skin. My mother is close, and I can sense her spirit watching, clapping her hands in delight at our reactions. This truly is a magical Samhain, a time when we can mingle with the spirits.

Returning my gaze to Father, I see he is gently handling the last object. It is another neck adornment, but this one is made of several strands of amber beads. "Laragh," he begins, "as you know, your mother was blessed with having sight. She knew as you grew in her belly, you too would have sight. She insisted your gift would be even stronger than hers. When she sought to meditate with Cenn to divine what the future might hold, she would wear these. She sensed the amber helped bring her closer to Cenn and aided her understanding of the alternate paths the future held. She knew these beads would assist you as well."

Tears stream down Laragh's cheeks. Her hands tremble as she grasps the amber beads and places them around her neck. Clasping her hands together, she bows her head in deep thought, then looks up, dries her eyes, and reaches to embrace first Father, then me.

Laragh holds me by my shoulders, gazing at me. "Oh Keelen, I have never been happier, and I have never seen you look so lovely." Instinctively, I glance toward the central fire, looking for Flann. He is watching, smiling and nodding his approval. Father must have apprised him that Laragh and I would be receiving remembrances from our mother. Detecting my glance, Father motions for Flann to join us.

As Flann comes inside the roundhouse, he reaches for a new sheathed blade that is attached to his horsehair belt.

"Look what Father gave me. Isn't it magnificent?" He gently fingers a small, double-edged, tanged blade. "It once belonged to grandfather. Mother had it for safe-keeping. It is made of the finest bronze and is sharp enough to easily skin a rabbit. I will wear it always."

Father smiles, then draws us in. "Children," he begins, "now I will tell you what you need do when the sun rises in the morning."

CHAPTER FOUR

THE WHITE HORSE OF BINN

We scurry along the path of worn stones through the groves of oaks and fields of heather, laughing and filled with excitement. Father is sending us to the White Horse of Binn! The day is brisk, and our breath sends clouds of vapor into the air. The path is one of the smaller eskers, the ribbons of worn stones that provide an avenue through the gorse and heather. Our gray cloaks are brightly trimmed with designs of intertwined knots of deep blues and dark reds. We pull the wraps close around us so they will not obstruct our travels.

Far ahead on the trail, an elk with mighty antlers, twice as wide as I am tall, is startled by our rapid approach. Elk are rare since the coming of the cold. Food is scarce and wolves prey on these mighty beasts. The elk stares long at us before turning its back and walking away down a branching esker. It is as if he knew which way we would be going.

"Keelen, Laragh," shouts Flann, "come quick. Over the next rise the Horse will come into view." We scramble up the trail to join Flann. Though we have seen the figure before, the sight is always breathtaking. High on the side of Slieve Benaughlin lies the pure white image of the Horse of Binn, outlined by the surrounding heather and gorse. Seeing the magical Horse again sends a thrill down my spine. Shadows are beginning to fall over the image as the sun sinks low in the sky. We must make haste to reach the cairn of Eachon near the mouth of the figure and build the Samhain bonfire, marking the second day of the festival, before darkness falls.

Eachon lived many Samhains ago when the Horse was first etched from the white stone of the slieve. He was one of our people's greatest bards and, to honor him, his cairn was built near the mouth of the Horse of Binn. His spirit is released during Samhain when we build a bonfire on his cairn and it is through his spirit the Horse speaks to those who tend his fire.

We reach the cairn just as the light of day begins to fade and we swiftly gather firewood. Flann removes the leather pouch strapped across his back, carefully unwrapping the wheel, spindle, and bow needed to start the Samhain fire. The spindle spins and smoke filters up through the dried moss and twigs. Soon, the fire comes to life.

As Flann's fire flairs to full strength, what appears to be a black cloud approaches from the east. It is high above us and moving swiftly. As the cloud passes, I see it is a great conspiracy of ravens. They soar by us as though driven to some important destination. We look at each other, and I wonder what the ravens signify. Perhaps they foreshadow death coming to lands to our west. I shudder at the thought, but as the birds disappear into the darkening sky, all of us return to our chores.

Across the darkening sky, I gaze upon the many fires still aflame from last night's Samhain feast. Faintly, in the far distance, we hear horns proclaiming the second evening of Samhain. To the west, high up the summit of the Slieve of Cenn, we see a massive bonfire flaring into the northern sky in honor of Cenn. To the south, we take in the glow from the many fires surrounding Tomregan, where we began our journey. To the north, we spot the reflections of fires coming from the myriad loughs in that direction.

A sense of magic envelopes me. I am flushed with expectations.

Flann takes out his harp and begins to play. Laragh and I spring to our feet to perform ceili dances to the music. Later, we will have flatbread, fish, dried meats, and mead for our feasting. I miss our friends at Tomregan, but know the importance and honor of being selected to come light the Samhain fire for the Horse of Binn.

Our elders teach that since the beginning of the cold, those who tend the fire at the cairn of Eachon experience strange visions, revealing both our deepest past and events about to unfold. These visions are said to come abruptly. At one moment, the tenders of the fire will be chatting or storytelling. In the next, their eyes become heavy. The slow, rhythmic sound of a hum or chant will fill their minds, sending them into a stupor.

The visions from last Samhain counseled that one gifted with the sight must be among those who mind this year's fire in order to understand the upcoming revelations regarding the alternate paths and decisions our people will face in this, the critical thirteenth year. No absolute answer or path will be shown, but the potential pitfalls, as well as the benefits, of each choice will be revealed.

I am convinced Laragh is the gifted one who will receive these revelations. Laragh, though young, is empowered with sight far beyond anyone else at Tomregan.

From her traveling pouch, Laragh retrieves the golden amber necklace she received last night, placing it around her neck. I reach out and hold Laragh's hand for reassurance. Her face is flushed with excitement.

As the midpoint of night approaches, streaks of light begin pouring from the sky over the east horizon. I gaze at this approaching spectacle, knowing it's the bearded star. The howling of wolves in the distance couples with the emerging trail of fire, intensifying my own exhilaration. Despite my excitement, an immediate exhaustion overwhelms me, and I lay down and curl up beside the fire, just as I see Laragh and Flann both tumble to the ground. Sleep welcomes me.

The sound of drums reverberates, filling my entire being. I stir and open my eyes. Feeling lightheaded, I gaze down and am taken aback. I seem to be floating above my body, which is sitting upright, staring straight ahead. This must be the trance state others have described.

I catch sight of movement from the cairn. Emerging from the shadows is the tall, white-haired form of Eachon and beside him, a white stallion. Eachon welcomes me with a slight bow.

Gazing about, I see both Laragh and Flann nearby. They, too, watch Eachon and the White Horse.

CHAPTER FIVE

THE STORIES FROM EACHON

Eachon gazes at each of us, as though addressing us individually. The stallion appears anxious for the evening tales to unfold. Each time Eachon pauses, the stallion shakes his head and stamps his foot, as though telling Eachon to hurry up.

After his welcoming comments, Eachon lowers his eyes, seemingly in deep thought. With prodding from the stallion, he looks up and says, "The White Horse of Binn wishes me to inform you that before the next Beltane, foreigners will be arriving near the reddish slieves bordering Lough Aillionn. They will arrive in strange craft, soaring in the air. They hope to come in peace and live among you as brothers. These strangers have nowhere else to go, as their own homeland is being destroyed.

"Long ago, these foreigners lived here with your ancestors. The god Cenn is the twin soul of Danu, their goddess. Danu and Cenn were once venerated together here in Inis Elga, before Danu led some of the people to new lands across the sea to the west. These ancient ancestors are now known as the Tuatha de Danann, the people of Danu, and under Danu's guidance, they achieved wondrous things."

What does he mean by wondrous things? I turn to ask Laragh and Flan, but find they cannot hear me.

Eachon continues. "Their numbers are now few, after suffering difficult times and the loss of most of their homeland. You and your Tomregan brethren must assist and welcome them to our land. They are learned and can teach you much.

"The times are hard in our land and the peoples of Inis Elga will be tempted to drive them away, or worse. Help our people accept them as brothers. Listen to their stories and learn the wisdom they gained under Danu's guidance.

"Laragh will know the exact place of their arrival and she should lead a group of bards and drui from Tomregan to meet them."

As Eachon continues to tell how Laragh will help us in our early encounters with the people of Danu, I discern a form in the mist near the White Horse. The image is hard to make out, but there appears to be a girl about my age, dressed in a gown of an unfamiliar style. Her clothing is of purest white, and her form glows within its folds. She, too, appears puzzled, as though seeing me as a vision as well, but she smiles and nods before disappearing into the mist. She feels familiar, but how could I experience closeness to someone I have never seen before?

The trance grips me. Eachon now sits on a rock near his cairn. The fire flickers across his lined face. His long white hair is drawn together and tied in the back. He leans against his staff as he speaks. The White Horse nibbles on grass near Eachon's feet. With the vision of the girl gone, I continue to listen to Eachon's tale.

Eachon looks thoughtfully outward. The White Horse impatiently whinnies. Eachon stares at me. "Keelen," he says, "you are the most gifted of all the apprentices in the ways of the drui. Flann is becoming a learned bard and leader. Laragh can see the future and read the thoughts of others. You, Flann, and Laragh must help our people to accept the Danann. Alliances must be formed with these newcomers. You and your Danann friends will meet resistance from the northern kings.

"A joining with the people of Danu will bring new skills to finally lead us from these troubled times. If we accept them, the people of Cenn will come to honor their arrival and regard many of the Danann as gods. Hear me, as I tell you how our people and the people of Danu were once one."

Again, I look over toward Flann and Laragh. They continue looking in the direction of the images of Eachon and the White Horse, but are unmoving.

Eachon begins his account. "In the beginning, we lived in a land to the east, across what is now a sea. We held our ceremonies in deep caves, sheltered from the cold and winds. Our artists drew magnificent pictures of the hunted beasts as an offering to their spirits and their gift of life to us. These images were also drawn to honor Danu and Cenn, the twin souls of our first ancestors.

"Danu and Cenn are from the stars, coming to earth to procreate with those beings already present. Their children are the peoples of Inis Elga and Aletea. Others like them begot peoples throughout the world.

"From these unions with Cenn and Danu, our ancestors received souls. Though all souls are individual entities, each originates from a single, universal soul. The universal soul wishes to expand cognizance through sharing itself among many beings, forming a collective consciousness. Each individual soul follows a journey of growth and understanding that may last many lifetimes, until reaching the comprehension of oneness among us all. Rebirth is no longer needed once this understanding is achieved. The universal soul is enhanced by the knowledge gained from each soul in its journeys.

"We call Danu and Cenn gods, but they too have souls like our own. Their souls have reached the comprehension of oneness. They are helping guide our souls toward achieving this oneness and enhancing the collective consciousness."

Eachon glances towards the Horse, who continues to graze upon the last grasses of the season. He rubs his hands together, seemingly to warm them, then continues. "During our times in the cold lands to the east, Danu and Cenn informed our ancestors times would improve. The unending ice would thaw, the sun would grow strong, and game would be plentiful. However, before the ice disappeared, we needed to journey west.

"The trip was hard," Eachon continues. "Although the weather was warming, our path was still often blocked by ice or water. After many weeks, we came to a place where we could no longer continue. To the west was an angry sea, and to our north, cliffs of ice crumbled under a warm sun.

"Many years passed. The sun continued to provide its warmth and the new land grew green and thick with game. Despite life being good, Danu and Cenn were being pulled apart. Though their spirits were intertwined as twin souls, they were still separate entities with independent thought. Each perceived potentially rewarding but different paths.

"The path Cenn believed best was through learning the universal secrets gradually with limited guidance. He reasoned this approach would lead to more complete understanding and acceptance of the wisdom. Cenn would provide visions at key moments but, ultimately, the people would need to decide for themselves their own future and direction.

"Danu believed Cenn's preferred path to be wise, but wished to follow a path with more direct intervention by providing advanced knowledge and power. By doing so, she foresaw the possibility of rapid advancement toward achieving oneness with the universal soul.

"The two agreed to try both paths. The people would be offered the choice of following the lower-risk path of Cenn or to leave and follow Danu's path."

The fire flickers low as the night grows long. I understand why Danu and Cenn took different paths, but do not understand what is meant by Danu giving more knowledge and power.

I also puzzle about the girl who appeared through the mists. Does she fit into this story? Is that why she appeared? Is she one of the people of Danu who followed the different path? Has something gone terribly wrong with this path?

These thoughts turn about in my mind as I continue to listen.

Eachon continues with his story. "Many years passed before the people of Danu left to pursue their new way in land to the west. We called our home Tomregan. At Tomregan, three major esker paths intersect, making travel across the land simple. One path leads to the west, toward the Kingdom Rathcroghan. The second leads east toward the Kingdom of Ulaidh and the rath of their King at Emain Macha. The third leads to the rath of the High King near the hill of Tara, known as the Hill of Kings, in the midlands of Inis Elga."

My eyes fix on the old man as he bends over the fire. The White Horse settles on the ground near his feet.

Rubbing his hands, Eachon looks up and says, "In the days right before the people of Danu sailed west, a bearded star appeared, flaring as a fiery dragon. From the stone circle near Tomregan, our drui noted the star's appearance over the standing stone marking the An Trogan constellation, the family of stars that honor the goddess Danu. The drui understood this position denoted the time had come for our people to split into two groups: those following Danu to the west and those staying with Cenn. The dragon star strode slowly across the sky for many moons with its long, flowing tail draping far behind its blazing head.

"The star appeared in our people's dreams, revealing to each who would stay or leave. Instructions were provided on how to build a fleet of seaworthy craft. Called curaughs, they were made of skins stretched over a frame of hazel wicker. The people assembled the fleet along the shores of Lough Aillionn. The river Sinann flows from the lough, making its long journey to the sea."

Eachon's new revelations quicken my mind. The girl I sighted earlier in the mists must be of the Danu people, a descendent of those who left so long ago. Seeing her must foreshadow a coming meeting.

Why are they returning? Why must they flee their home? Is this all part of the events that turned our summers cold and brought the dust the night Laragh was born and our mother died?

Eachon continues his story. "The dragon's head revealed the departure would be the morning of Beltane. Those following Danu would board their curaughs, set sail down the river Sinann to the sea, crossing toward the west to their new land.

"The Beltane eve celebrations brought massive bonfires that illuminated the curaughs along the shoreline, with their light darting across the lough into the depths of the night. All joined in dancing and singing as the mead flowed. With darkness, nearly all the young men and women joined as couples, disappearing into the shadows of the forest for their own personal celebrations. These greenwood marriages bore many children, both to those who stayed and those who sailed.

"At dawn, couples streamed from the woodland, filling the curaughs with passengers. Bronze horns moaned all about Lough Aillionn to signal departure. Those who remained pushed the curaughs into the deep water. Sails were set, and paddling commenced. On shore, no one moved until the curaughs disappeared over the horizon."

The White Horse rises, moving to Eachon's side, while nodding his head towards us all. Slowly, the two fade into the night. A cool breeze strokes my cheek as full consciousness returns. Chills run through me. The bonfire still provides warmth, so I move closer. The bearded star now looms ominously overhead. Lightening crackles nearby on Slieve Cenn, its pungent smell wafting to my nose. Looking toward Flann and Laragh, I note they, too, are gazing into the sky. Heaviness overcomes me as I lie down, wrapping my cloak tightly about me.

CHAPTER SIX

HOME TO TOMREGAN

The morning sun greets me on this second day of Samhain, warming my face. Eagerly, I attempt to engage Flann and Laragh in conversation about our visions of Eachon and the White Horse. Laragh reminds me Father wished to be the first to hear of our visions, to ensure we did not taint each other's recollections.

"Besides," Laragh says, "the journey to Tomregan will take much of the day and if we want to participate in the iomáint matches, we need to leave soon."

Iomáint, a game using a hurley stick and a leather ball filled with compacted hair, is our favorite pastime when not studying. Flann is particularly skilled as the báire, the protector of the goal area, while I play lár in the mid-field. Laragh plays a fine game. Her position is up front as the aghaidh where her quickness, fearlessness, and accuracy with her hurley strikes fear into every báire.

Though now daylight, the bearded star is still visible, looming ominously overhead. Despite its presence, we are in good spirits as we hike down the slieve through the oak groves to the esker trail leading back to Tomregan. The air is cool—good traveling weather.

Laragh, who seems anxious to make good time, leads the way with a brisk pace.

After some hours, I can tell we are approaching Tomregan. Wafting in the breeze is the aromatic smell of smoke from cooking fires. Judging from the aroma, the meat must be ready. Good timing on our part, as my stomach grumbles with hunger.

As we top the last hill, we see the clearing where we play iomáint. I hear the boastful shouts of one team to the other. They catch sight of us, encouraging us to join the next match. As we run to reach the clearing, the ground begins shaking violently, knocking us to the ground. Stunned, we all regain our feet. I brush the dirt from my clothes. Looking up, I see the bearded star issuing bursts of flame from what one could think of as its mouth.

The bronze horns echo from the stone circle, summoning all. Laragh and Flann run ahead of me, though another jolt causes me to stumble. Father stands near the offering stone to Cenn, looking tall and strong, his fiery blue eyes scanning all who come. Around him stand elders and others from our village, all with taut expressions on their faces. As we grow close, we can hear him begin to speak loudly so all around may hear his words.

"Friends. In my dreams last night, I glimpsed horrific events taking place in lands far to our west. We elders believe the prophecies provided by the White Horse these past twelve Samhains are now in play. We anxiously await the arrival of my children, who tended the Samhain fire at Eachon's cairn to learn the latest revelations."

Fearghus finally spots us. "I am relieved to see they are here. Please, everyone, return to Tomregan while the elders and I consult with them. Devlyn, Gaeth, and Ultan, please remain, as I may need your services."

Excited whispering blankets the air. Eager faces gaze toward us as the people trickle away.

We move toward the offering stone where Father and the other elders wait. Fearghus calls for servings of meat, along with mead and flatbread.

Flann speaks first. "There are new revelations Eachon relayed from the White Horse during our visions. As instructed, we did not discuss what these visions were among ourselves. But, in the little we did reveal, it is apparent Keelen experienced an unusual vision and Laragh a detailed account of near-term events."

Father regards my sister and says, "Laragh, as we expected, it appears your gift of sight revealed much, and I am most anxious to listen to what you saw and heard. But first, we will hear about the unusual vision Kellen experienced."

I begin. "The initial accounts delivered by Eachon are similar to what we learned in the past. The most revealing new aspects involve the people of the goddess Danu and how we are to expect their arrival by Beltane. In past years, Eachon foretold strangers would come, but now he tells who and when. He predicts they will arrive close to where they originally left our land many Beltanes ago. They will come to the open fields near the base of the slieves of red by the shores of Lough Aillionn. Strangely, they will not come by foot or sail up the river Sinann in curaughs. Instead, flying crafts filled with their people will darken the sky as they circle down to rest in the open fields."

I hear an intake of breath from one of the elders.

"I briefly saw a girl in my vision. She wore a brilliant white gown of an unfamiliar style. It was not like any I've seen from the clans of Inis Elga. The vision was brief but clear. We each gazed at the other through the mists."

Fearghus and the elders nod thanks as I finish. They turn their attention to Laragh. Her green eyes burn brightly as she commences to recount her vision.

"What Keelen heard, I understood as well, though I did not see the girl with the unusual gown," begins Laragh. "After telling us about the people of Danu coming in flying craft, Eachon and the White Horse seemed to turn their full attention toward me. Eachon instructed me to visualize the Danann's V-shaped craft gliding and circling, similar to great soaring Iolair birds. Like the Iolairs, the people who revere Danu could soar into our lives, bringing wisdom and prosperity. However, they will need our help to do so. Eachon revealed several different paths for the future. Some lead to prosperity. Others to death and enslavement."

Gazing across the transfixed faces of the elders, Laragh continues.

"I was given a vision of their arrival. On that day, one of the flying craft, larger than the others, and decorated with gold emblems, came to rest in the center of the landing area. I noted extreme care being taken to unload four objects of apparent high importance, with their unloading being closely overseen by a man given deference by the others. They called him Aesres.

"One object looked to be a slab of rock, which was handled reverently when lifted from the craft. On my seeing it, the name and what powers it held were revealed. The stone is known as the Lia Fáil by the people of Danu. When selecting a new king, candidates each stand on the stone. It roars with approval when the rightful king stands upon it.

"The next item brought from the craft was a long box. Aesres opened this box, bringing from it a sheath of leather ornamented with gold engravings. A sword was drawn with care from this sheath. Aesres examined it closely, lightly sliding his fingers down its shaft. This sword appears much different from the bronze-colored swords we possess. Its name was revealed to be Claíomh Solai, the Sword of Light, and it has the power to slice effortlessly through the armament of anyone who opposes its bearer.

"Claíomh Solai had been forged under the direction of Danu herself from metal rocks sent by her from the heavens. These stones were heated in a fire of immense intensity with the metal beaten out, then folded over and hammered out countless times before its final shaping. The sword is sharper and stronger than any sword known. It will not bend and cannot be scratched or broken."

I see the elders look at each other, shaking their heads in

apparent amazement.

"The third item was a long sleeve of leather with gold ornamentation similar to the sheath for the sword. From this sleeve, Aesres drew a magnificent spear that glinted brightly in the waning sun. He held it high, examining the shaft and pricking his finger on its point. The spear is called Lúin. It was made in the same fashion as the Claíomh Solai, from the metal stones given by Danu. Its holder is always victorious in battle.

"The final item lifted from the flying craft was a small cauldron. It looked unimposing, about the size for cooking enough porridge for three or four people, however, it was shown to me that this cauldron is not for food, but rather, those who drink from it are accorded profound wisdom. All worthy people who imbibe are selfless in their dealings with others and possess insights on how to inspire others to take appropriate actions. Unworthy partakers die in excruciating pain.

"Each of these four treasures was placed in a great tent near the center of the growing encampment. It was Beltane eve and as dark approached, the people of Danu gathered their flying craft into four positions around the encampment, one to the north, one to the south, one to the east, and one to the west.

"A central Beltane fire was kindled near the tent, with flames taken from it to spark new fires at each of these sacred points. Into these fires were fed the flying craft. The flames reached high into the sky, lighting the entire encampment and surrounding grounds. The burning craft were an offering to Danu for delivering them safely to this new home. The old prophecy had been fulfilled."

Fearghus and the other elders listen attentively to Laragh's story. A frown crosses my father's face as he listens. Similar expressions appear on the faces of the other elders. He says, "From what Laragh recounts, it is apparent the people of Danu will be numerous and well supplied. It is also apparent they have powers beyond what the people of Inis Elga possess." Father turns to Laragh. "Was it revealed to you what temperament and intent the people of Danu bring to our land?"

Looking much wiser and more composed than her age of thirteen Samhains seems to justify, she responds in a calm, strong voice. "The people of Danu come from a land of much power, wealth, and wisdom. Some became corrupted by that power and abused it to such an extent that Danu destroyed part of the land twelve Samhains before and is preparing to destroy the remainder. The intense shaking of the earth we experienced earlier was the first of the final shudders before the last of their land sinks beneath the waves.

"These people of Danu know they were chastened and are lucky to be alive. However, they are also a proud people who do not intend to be under the yoke of anyone.

"Their elders will counsel that they should come to our land in peace and hope our people will allow them a place to settle that they may call their own. Their leader, King Nuada, will listen to this counsel and agree with its basic concept. However, he also believes the Danann should be prepared for war and fight if needed. There is no desire to conquer us, but also no intent to be subjugated. They will fight to the last to prevent such a fate and their power would mortally devastate anyone who tries to make them subservient.

"If we accept peace with the Danann, I was shown a path that ends these troubled times and begins a new, long era of prosperity. An alternate path is a war to expel them. Following this path could lead to doom for both the people of Danu and Inis Elga. Going along the path of war will empower the Formorri. If the Formorri gain dominance, they would treat us as slaves. Our troubles would never end. The alternate paths facing us offer perilous options."

As Laragh finishes, Father hastily looks around to the other elders. I see each has the same concerned look he has. I don't even need to look into my father's eyes to know his thoughts. He knows King Ailill of Rathcroghan is of greatest immediate concern. As with the other northern kings, King Ailill and his bard and drui counselors had received updates on the visions from the White Horse each year since the coming of the cold. In these updates, King

Ailill expressed concerns about the coming of strangers. Unlike any other northern king, he has close ties with the Formorri. His own daughter married the Formorri King of Sligeach and his granddaughter is Queen Sianna.

Fearghus confers with the elders and they come to quick agreement on the next course of action.

Turning toward the apprentices, Father commands, "Devlyn, Gaeth, and Ultan, prepare to journey in the morning. Our northern kings must be made aware of the news from the White Horse concerning events about to unfold. They are to be advised that the elders of Tomregan believe the new strangers, the people of Danu, will come in peace if we receive them in peace. Most importantly, King Ailill must be given this news as quickly as possible. His rath is close to where the people of Danu are expected to appear, and this arrival place is within the sphere of his kingdom. Devlyn, you are to deliver this message to King Ailill. Also, inform the king that my children will be coming soon to provide him greater detail."

Father looks to Laragh, Flann, and me and says, "I would like all of you to travel to Sligeach. There, you can recount your visions from the White Horse and answer questions Queen Sianna may have. After briefing Sianna, please proceed to Rathcroghan and inform King Ailill firsthand about the White Horse prophecies. Remain there over the winter, then return here before Beltane. Be watchful of all that happens in Rathcroghan."

Laragh, Flann and I make our way back to Tomregan to prepare for our journey. It is turning dark and the Samhain festivities are commencing again. The weather is becoming cold as clouds flow over the horizon from the west. It appears we could have snow for our journey.

Before returning to our roundhouse, we go to the central fire and procure one of the hardened clay balls holding roasted quail, and a cup of mead. It is Samhain, after all, and we are hungry. We talk for a time with our friends about our upcoming journey. They gather close to learn more about the visions. They glance at each other in wonder as Laragh describes the strange flying craft of the Danann and the treasures taken from them.

The night is turning long, and we are tired from our travels, so we bid our friends goodnight and proceed to our roundhouse. It is too late to organize for the journey and instead we prepare for sleep. As I am about to lie down, I note the ochre sack holding my mother's treasures. I reach out and pull the sack toward me, taking out the golden torc. It catches the light from the central fire and gently glints into my eyes. I regard it, thinking of my mother before replacing the torc in the sack. Laragh is lying near me, watching. "Goodnight," she says. "These are good things to bring with us."

I awake from first sleep and move to the opening of our roundhouse. It is snowing lightly, and the night sky is not visible. I use my study time to review today's events and contemplate what may lie ahead. The time for second sleep comes and I return to my bedding. Soon I am asleep, filled with dreams of the people of Danu and the girl I saw in my vision.

CHAPTER SEVEN

ALETEA

I hear a man's voice say, "Aislinn? Are you all right?"

Feeling dazed and unsure of what is happening, I glance around. Who are these people and why do they call me Aislinn? I am Keelen, daughter of Fearghus. This place appears strange, as does their clothing. The way they speak is different as well. Something is not right.

Softly, another voice says, *Keelen? Is that your name? Everything is okay, I think.* The voice sounds like it is in my head. *I am Aislinn and your spirit appears to be with me in my body. You are the girl I witnessed in my dreams, listening by a fire to stories from an old man who was with a white horse. Do you remember me? Our eyes met for a moment.*

I ask myself, *How can this be? I must be dreaming, but everything appears so real!*

The girl's voice says, "I'm fine," to those who are nearby. "The shaking knocked me off my feet. This quake was stronger than yesterday's. Is everyone okay?"

"We are checking," says the other voice, the voice of a young man. "There's so much damage. You look pale, Aislinn. Why don't you rest while I try to discover what is happening?"

I sense myself kneeling, but the movement isn't mine. Instead, someone else is kneeling and I'm obliged to go along with their body.

This is strange, Aislinn says. *How can you be in my head with me . . . and why?*

I'm as mystified as Aislinn. *This must connect to the stories from Eachon, the old man you saw me talking to two nights ago. Eachon is a spirit from long ago who serves as storyteller for the horse you saw. The horse is the representation of the oracle White Horse Hill figure of Slieve Benaughlin. For the past twelve Samhains, the oracle conveyed stories of our ancient past and how once, long ago, some of our people left our land to follow the promise of the spirit called Danu. Last night, he revealed that the people of Danu are experiencing a massive disaster and soon some of them will be returning to Inis Elga, our home. Are you one of the people of Danu?*

I can somehow listen to Aislinn as she thinks and considers her responses. Her father and the elders have been talking about and preparing to leave their home in Aletea. Her thoughts convey that earthquakes are increasing and the flying stone tears from the bearded star nearly destroyed their home city of Fáilas. She thinks to herself that since I am the girl she observed in her dream, I may be here in her mind to help her and her people through these difficult times.

Finally, she begins to speak deliberately to me again. *As you heard, my name is Aislinn and yes, we are the people of Danu, known as the Danann. I am daughter of King Nuada.*

We have among us a gifted few who have the ability to spirit travel into others. We call their power 'twisping'. You must somehow be twisping into me. Having you here feels queer, but I am most anxious to learn why you have come. Stay with me if you can. I will show what befell us with this last earthquake and hopefully answer any questions you have.

I agree to be an observer in Aislinn's life to learn what I can. Aislinn rises and gazes about. *Over there, up this path,* she says, pointing in the direction of people gathered about a fire, *is my older brother, Cairpre. I will keep your presence secret, but let's join him near the fire and get warm. He is talking with many of our elders. Perhaps he can tell us how things are.*

By the fire a young man with red hair gestures expansively with his hands. The fire is set near the center of a circle of tall stones, much like our own stone circle back in Tomregan. Near the fire, in the center of the circle, is a plain slab of rock, set up high, in a position of prominence and importance. I ask Aislinn, *What is this place?*

Aislinn says, *This is the most sacred spot in all Aletea. The slab set in prominence at the center is what we call the Lia Fáil. Our spirit guide, Danu, stood on this very slab and welcomed us as our curaughs arrived so long ago to these crystal-white shores of Aletea. The stone has been used in our ceremonies for hundreds of Beltanes to help choose the one, from among the different tuatha kings of our land, who will serve as our High King. The High King reigns for a cycle of thirteen Beltanes. When a new High King is to be selected, each tuatha king climbs up on the stone. If he is to be the High King, the Lia Fáil emits a joyful roaring sound like one-hundred men bellowing from deep within their chests.*

I feel the weight of sorrow bearing heavily upon Aislinn. Before continuing to speak, she pauses and gazes across a field toward what appear to be ruins. *We are near our most northern city of Fáilas, named for the Lia Fáil. The stone tears falling from the hair of the bearded star, as well as many earthquakes, laid the city to rubble and most of its thousands of people died.*

Aislinn raises her head to look at the sky. *Keelen, do you see the bearded star? Do you see the same star in your land? Does it drop tears of destruction on your home, as it does here?*

I reply, telling her, *Yes, we also see this bearded star, but no destruction has befallen us.*

She says, *My mother was killed when our family's home was destroyed. Many of my friends are also among the dead. Those of us who survived camp here, near the Lia Fáil, hoping to find protection until the time to leave here forever arrives.*

Although it pains me to tell you these troubles, I sense it is important to do so. I feel Danu nudging me to go on, though in my heart I want to forget. Aislinn wipes tears from her cheeks and slows her pace, but continues.

There are, or were, thirteen important cities in Aletea. The most revered is Fáilas because this is where we first arrived so long ago. Our greatest city lies to the south and surrounds the sacred Slieve of Danu. The Slieve of Danu stands on the southern end of the northern lands. This city is actually three cities that, over time, merged into one. We call them the Cities of Danu. Each began as a port in the three natural harbors surrounding the Slieve of Danu. One city is named Gorias and it faces the sea to the west. The second is Murias and it faces the sea to the east. The final city is Finias and it faces the sea to the south. Over many years, we created interconnecting canals and inner harbors, so our merchant fleets can lie protected in the inner harbors, and small boats can ply the inner canals to any of the three cities.

We are approaching the stone circle. Aislinn catches the eye of her brother and waves.

Continuing, she says, *Across a small sea lie the southern lands. It is from these cities that our troubles began. These nine southern cities of Aletea were destroyed twelve Samhains past when another bearded star appeared over our land. Though I was young, I vividly remember the overpowering presence of this star looming ominously above us each night.*

My father told me many gigantic stone tears from this bearded star struck our southern cities, causing massive destruction. We to the north were spared. Then, on Samhain eve, twelve Samhains ago, a great fiery object swept across our sky from the bearded star's trailing hair. This blazing tear travelled toward our southern lands. In moments, a massive fireball erupted into the air. The ground shook violently. This was followed by a dark cloud of suffocating dust, smelling of fire and brimstone. The sun disappeared behind this cloud for several days, and temperatures became exceedingly cold. Dust, up to a foot thick, covered everything. Many died that Samhain night and for many months after from breathing difficulties. Our land has not been the same since.

I am awestruck by what Aislinn relates. This is the same event which befell our land when my mother died.

Cairpre moves from the fire to greet his sister, telling her, "The others tell me the city is now fully destroyed. Thank Danu no one was seriously hurt in this last series of quakes. Moving our camp near the Lia Fáil appears to have saved us, but we are worried about what may have happened to the south."

Looking through Aislinn's eyes as she peers south, I see massive, ink-colored thunderheads roiling along the horizon. Panic swells within Aislinn. "Where is the Slieve of Danu?" Aislinn exclaims. "There is nothing to see but storm clouds."

"I fear the worst," says her brother. Father was supposed to depart from the cities of Danu yesterday on the first day of Samhain. But there is no sign of him or his entourage."

Despite her growing panic and fear for her father, Aislinn remembers that I am with her and tells me her father, King Nuada of Fáilas, traveled to the cities of Danu to hold council with the High King. Nuada desired to move the three treasures of the people of Danu, held in the cities of Danu, north to where the fourth treasure, the Lia Fáil rests. From the city of Gorias was to come the Claíomh Solai, the Sword of Light, from Finias, the spear, Lúin, and from Murias, the Cauldron of Wisdom.

I've heard of these treasures. Laragh described them in detail from her vision yesterday. I quickly relate this to Aislinn, letting her know all these treasures will be carried to Inis Elga. My sister saw them!

This news greatly relieves Aislinn. "Cairpre, don't ask me how I know, for I don't understand it myself, but I know these treasures will come here to Lia Fáil. We will take them all with us when we finally depart. This must mean Father is still alive."

Cairpre looks at Aislinn in amazement, then quickly turns to the others. "Aislinn is gifted with the sight and now we know our king, my father, is likely alive. We must send search parties toward the south to discover if his aircraft crashed. He and his party may be hurt. The search party can also determine what happened to the cities of Danu."

He points at others as he speaks. "Artgal and Tadgh, gather a search party and provisions and take the road toward the cities of Danu. Spread the party out so a broad swath of ground can be searched as you move. Proceed as far as possible, gathering details on the conditions. If you don't find Father, spread your party further apart to create a greater search fan and return north. This may take many days, so be sure to take sufficient provisions. Aislinn, if you are feeling up to it, come with me and we will assess the condition of the aircraft."

Aircraft? Are these the craft Laragh described as soaring like Iolairs as they bore the people of Danu to Inis Elga?

Aislinn answers my thoughts as we follow her brother. *Yes, Keelen, these are the craft described by your sister. They are among the gifts Danu taught us to make when we came to this land. Let me show them to you.*

CHAPTER EIGHT

GEAL LEACHT

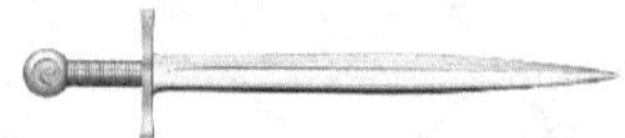

As we walk with Cairpre, Aislinn mentally tells me of the eitilte. *Our flying crafts are in a field not far down this path. We keep them near the stone circle in the hope they will escape being destroyed by the falling tears of stone. Only a few hundred are left,* she tells me, *and all but one of our larger lifting platforms, called vailixi, were destroyed. These are wondrous devices, which we learned to create after Danu showed us the source for their power. The vailixi and eitilte helped bring our people much power.* I feel Aislinn's excitement about sharing information slow as she says with a heavier energy, *This became both a blessing and a curse.*

Aislinn continues. *Soon after our arrival in Aletea, Danu led us to the southern portion where the tall slieve we call the Slieve of Danu stands. This slieve holds caverns and Danu instructed us to go deep inside one of these to where a large chamber opened. Within this chamber, we found a bright silver liquid in a great pool. The liquid is extremely shiny and thick. If you scoop up a small portion and drop it, the fluid breaks into numerous small beads and scatters everywhere. Unlike water, each bead keeps its shape and is not absorbed by the dirt. Danu warned us not to handle this liquid, but said this liquid held incredible power if one learned how to unleash it.*

I am amazed by all Aislinn shares, barely able to take it all in, but she plunges ahead.

We call this liquid 'geal leacht'. Danu taught us that when we place the geal leacht in a container, attach this container to a moveable structure, and manipulate it with power crystals from the slieve, the geal leacht will cause the structure to rise. Levitation by use of the geal leacht is only possible for a limited amount of time and can only be revitalized by returning the liquid to the central pool. The power crystals control both the strength of the geal leacht and how long its powers last.

The path narrows as we cross a small ravine. The stream we cross is merely a rivulet that we step across.

In the beginning, we used the power of the geal leacht to create the vailixi, so we could move massive stone blocks to build our cities. We also moved the huge standing stones to form the sacred circle around the Lia Fáil.

This makes me think of our sacred circle. I wonder how our stones were placed. Surely not so easily.

Over time, our metal smiths and wood artisans learned they could fashion structures with protruding shapes in the form of wings and use these attachments for soaring. The geal leacht and crystals would raise the craft high in the sky, then the crystals could be removed, and the craft would soar like a bird. The crystals can be applied again to regain height. The technique of rising and soaring significantly increases the distance that can be traveled before the geal leacht needs to be returned to the central pool.

This new skill of rising in the air and soaring like a lolair became the realm of an elite group of skilled operators called aracos. They learned the skills of utilizing thermal updrafts and flying techniques to greatly extend the distance one could travel. Eitiltes are made to be lightweight, consisting of skins stretched across frames of wicker to help extend the gliding distance. The geal leacht power is limited and must be conserved as much as possible to achieve flights of significant distance.

I consider this story from Aislinn and try to tie it back to what Eachon taught us at the Horse of Binn. Eachon said Danu led a small group of our brethren from Inis Elga long ago so she could teach them extraordinary secrets and powers. Danu hoped these abilities would hasten her followers along the path of learning the mysteries of the universe. Secrets we who remained on Inis Elga may one day learn as well, but at a slower pace. This geal leacht must be one of these secrets. It sounds like the people of Danu prospered using the geal leacht. However, what does Aislinn mean when she says the geal leacht brings both a blessing and a curse?

Soon we walk onto a vast field covered with strange craft for as far as I can see. We proceed through the field with Cairpre checking the condition of the eitiltes. Aislinn tells me, "This is our fleet. They are being prepared for the time of our departure."

The central portions of these craft look like giant wicker baskets. They are about fifteen to twenty feet long, six-foot wide, and about the height of a man. The sides of these wicker basket-like craft are open, with leather straps attached to the wicker. Inside are a series of small wooden seats. In the center are a series of leather sacks. These are strapped together, and additional straps secure them to the wicker frame. Suspended directly above the leather sacks is another narrow wicker construction that travels nearly the length of the interior. Aislinn tells me the narrow sack above contains crystals. Each end of the structure near the ceiling is secured by a mechanism that can lower or raise the crystals.

Atop all of this are what look like leather wings. Starting just back from the front of the structures, these wings curve out about eight feet on each side, reaching back about one-half the length of the craft. Secured to the back of the structure is a much smaller wing-like affair, curving out about three feet on each side. As we draw closer to one of the eitiltes, I see some of the wing leather is damaged, with bits of broken wicker protruding through. As Aislinn looks about, I see several other damaged craft.

Cairpre says, "It's as I feared, Aislinn. The quake damaged many of the eitiltes. Repair will take weeks. I hope none of the geal leacht sacks or crystals are broken. We cannot afford to lose any. Right now, there are just enough, assuming these damaged eitiltes can be repaired, to carry everyone who is still alive, our supplies, the Lia Fáil, and the other treasures."

Cairpre has a worried look and Aislinn touches his arm to comfort him.

He smiles in gratitude and says, "I am most anxious for Father to return from the cities of Danu with our treasures."

"Can we use one of the undamaged eitiltes to search for him?" Aislinn asks.

"There is only enough power left in the geal leacht to last two, maybe three days. The earthquakes destroyed the caverns within the Slieve of Danu where the geal leacht pool lies and we can no longer re-charge what we have. There is time before we must leave Aletea to search for Father. Artgal and Tadgh are already assembling a search party to head south along our usual flight path from the cities of Danu. This search plan is our only choice." He gives her a questioning look. "You said earlier you are sure he is alive."

Aislinn ponders what I've shared. I had told her the treasures Nuada was bringing from the cities of Danu were in the vision Laragh witnessed. She wonders if this means her father is alive or if it means the search party will merely find the crash site and retrieve the treasures, along with King Nuada's body. "Where are Artgal and Tadgh?" Aislinn asks her brother. "I must go with them and help find Father. I will ride Capall; he is as fast as the wind."

"They are near the Lia Fáil," replies Cairpre, "but do you feel well?"

Aislinn wheels quickly away and heads back along the path to the Lia Fáil. "That was momentary," she replies. "There is no time to waste!"

Soon we are near the bluff where the stone circle, Lia Fáil, overlooks the sea. We spot Artgal and Tadgh packing the last of some supplies in leather bags that fit across the backs of the horses they are outfitting. Many other men are doing the same and everyone seems about ready to leave. The weather is unsettled, looking like a fierce storm is raging to the south and moving our way. The winds pick up and the sea is filled with choppy waves.

"Tadgh," says Aislinn as we arrive, speaking to the closest search party leader, "I am going to take Capall and ride south, ahead of your group. Have your party keep an eye open for a signal fire. If I find him and need help, I will light one to show the location. If you find him, please do the same." Tadgh looks toward Artgal and then both nod to Aislinn. I sense they know it is useless to argue with the daughter of Nuada, especially when Nuada himself is in danger.

Keelen, says Aislinn through our mind-connection, *I still sense your presence. Ride with me for courage. The ride will be dangerous, but Father must be found.*

If I can, I will, I reply. *I don't know how long I will be able to stay, but I know I am here to help and learn. You and I are much alike. I look forward to finally seeing you in the flesh.*

Aislinn moves quickly toward her sleeping shelter near the Lia Fáil. Artgal and Tadgh have cleared their things already, but she gathers her own supplies and places them within her riding pouches. She slings the pouches over her shoulder, then grabs a thick woolen dillat and heads toward a corral where I see a beautiful cream-colored horse pacing about nervously. The horse catches sight of Aislinn and lets out a loud snort and whinny as it rears high on its back legs.

"That is Capall, my stallion," Aislinn tells me. "He is the finest and fastest steed in all Aletea." I can feel the pride and love Aislinn holds for Capall. Even though I know Aislinn's thoughts, she now converses with me as if I were walking with her, except, of course, when others are not nearby. This is more natural and puts both of us at ease. Capall is trotting briskly back and forth in the corral, whinnying loudly as Aislinn approaches.

When we reach the corral, Aislinn rubs Capall's nose. He snorts, shakes his head, and stamps his front hooves on the ground. Aislinn tells me he appears spooked from the last earthquake. I gaze though Aislinn's eyes past the fenced area of the corral and along a well-worn path that leads to piles of rubble that stretch as far as I can see.

Aislinn, I ask, *are those the ruins of Fáilas ahead of us?*

A deep sadness comes over Aislinn.

"Yes. The city used to be home to thousands, but the quakes and the stone tears destroyed it. Most of the people were killed or fled to the south toward the cities of Danu. We who survived and still hold faith with Danu moved toward the safety of the Lia Fáil. The bearded star's stone tears have not touched the area around the Lia Fáil or the stone circle surrounding it.

"Fáilas contained stunning marble-columned homes, wide avenues, running water, and beautiful works of art. Cairpre said the last quake destroyed the remainder of the buildings. The trail leading south skirts the edge of Fáilas. You will be able to take in firsthand the wrath of Danu."

Aislinn opens the corral and leads Capall out.

"Capall, I have with me another soul. Her name is Keelen and she comes from the land of our ancestors."

Capall nods his head and paws at the dirt to show he understands. He gazes at Aislinn, but appears to stare straight through her toward me. He nods his head again.

"We must be on our way. There is a good half-day of sunlight still with us." Aislinn covers Capall's backside with the dillat. Toward the front of it, she slings the pair of pouches. She fits a bridle of soft leather around Capall's nose, brings the reins up around his head, and rests the upper ends on the dillat. She swings herself up, grabs the reigns, and urges Capall forward into a trot.

The winds are increasingly strong, and the sky grows darker to the far south. There is a bite of chill in the air. Soon we are at the edge of what remains of Fáilas. Capall slows to a walk. I stare across the bleak landscape of ruins, trying to visualize a vibrant city with a teaming population. The wind whips through the ruins, causing swirls of dust to dance like mini tornadoes through the ruble. Every few moments, small streaks of light race across the sky from what we know are the tears from the bearded star, now hidden by the sun and approaching clouds. Some of the streaks of light vanish into the air while others strike what remains of Fáilas.

Although it only takes a short while to pass the edge of Fáilas, the time feels interminable. The destruction is inconceivable and the sadness I feel from Aislinn causes my heart to twist. As soon as we are past, Capall breaks into a gallop and I see the rear of the search party. Artgal and Tadgh are deploying the searchers in such a manner that sight and communication can be maintained while still covering as much ground as possible. Artgal goes with a group to the left of the main path and Tadgh to the right. They move slowly south through the difficult terrain. Aislinn whips by and hails them as we push south into the on-coming storm at a galloping pace.

Chapter Nine

The Search Begins

After leaving the core search party behind, Aislinn brings Capall to a trot. I serve as a second pair of eyes in the search. Aislinn focuses on the far horizon, while I scan the nearby terrain. The light of the day is drawing to a close, hastened by the dark storm that is nearly upon us.

Aislinn spots a protected shelter in the rocks and cliffs up ahead. She brings Capall to a stop and we prepare for the night and the approaching storm. The leather carrying satchels and woolen dillat are taken from Capall's back. Near our shelter is a grassy glade and Capall is given leave to eat. Aislinn prepares a small fire, positions the dillat in a protected part of the shelter, and wraps her cloak about her. From the pouch, she retrieves mead and a container holding a mixture of dried meat, berries, bone marrow, and fat. She eats in silence, then laughs and says, "I'd offer you some if you were here in the flesh. I am grateful for your presence. This storm frightens me."

The storm is almost upon us. Capall returns, enters the shelter, and settles near Aislinn. The sky is the color of dark pitch, broken by brilliant flashes of light probing the darkness. The sounds outside remind me of ocean waves crashing on a rocky shore with the mix of thunder and the howling of wind. The air is becoming heavy, laden with particulate, but not as thick of a layer of dust as what accumulated twelve Samhains ago. Aislinn's breathing becomes labored, and there is an odd burnt smell to the air. Aislinn moves next to Capall and leans into him for security and warmth. Capall responds by nudging her with his nose.

"Keelen, our time together will likely end soon. You must be in a trance back at your home, much like I was in a trance when I first spotted you with the old man and the White Horse."

That's true, I reply. *I was settling in for the night just before I found myself with you. It must be near morning or later now.*

"With the little time you have left with me, let me tell you what I remember from when our troubled times began. It will help keep me from worrying about Father too much."

Please tell me what you can.

Aislinn begins. "Although young at the time, I still remember clearly. I had just joined my brother, Cairpre, as an apprentice with the family of High King Conall. Cairpre had gone before me to the cities of Danu. He was excited about having me join him and eagerly showed me the city.

"Preparation for Samhain was frenetic with bustling activity at each turn of our exploration of the city. Since Beltane, a bearded star had appeared in our northern skies. As the months passed, this star became larger, and streaks of light would stream from it toward the south. I was too young to know what this star presaged, but my father often seemed disturbed and would meet regularly with the druis to discuss this omen. He frequently went deep into the cities of Danu to hold counsel with the other tuatha kings and with High King Conall. Later, I learned about how the southern king, King Belial, broke our covenant with Danu.

"Word came of Formorri vessels arriving in the harbor and Cairpre grabbed my hand, pulling me along as he ran. 'You must meet Breas,' he told me. He seemed so excited about his friend. 'He is dark, not light skinned as we are, and he is my good friend. His father is a Formorri king and his mother is the daughter of our High King Conall.'

"I had no idea what he was talking about, but it sounded exciting. We entered the docks as the ships tied up. I found the vessels frightening. Their bright red color looked like the ships had been painted in blood. The parchment-colored sails seemed like skin. These ships caused me to shudder, as I had a vision of our people's blood flowing from wounds in our white skin.

"I put this vision aside as Cairpre waved wildly at a small, darkish-colored boy at the railing of the largest ship. 'Breas! Breas!' shouted Cairpre. The boy heard our voices and found us in the crowds on the docks. Who could miss Cairpre with his flaming red hair? The gangplank went down and soon Breas joined us on the dock.

"Cairpre hardly contained his excitement. He said, 'How was your visit to your father's homeland? What did you see? How was the sailing? Did you get seasick?'

"Breas just watched him, then gave him a hug. He appeared smaller than Cairpre, more my size, though the same age as my brother. His skin looked darker than ours, though not as swarthy as that of the Formorri crew. His hair looked more chocolate in color than black, and hung nearly straight.

'Cairpre, I've missed you and there is so much to tell,' said Breas. 'Is this your sister?' he asked.

'Yes, this is Aislinn and we must show her our haunts,' replied Cairpre.

"Soon we had all climbed high above the harbor to reach a small cave. From this vantage point, we watched the celebrations of Samhain unfold. Though still daylight, the bearded star loomed hauntingly in the sky above the city. The streaming hair from the head was not yet visible, nor were there any of the usual streaks of light heading toward the south.

"Too young to participate in the Samhain ceremonies, we peered down on the festivities from our vantage point. Twilight descended, and we observed the preparation for the central square bonfire. The bronze horns echoed the start of the celebrations and this bonfire soon blazed. Torches were lit from this fire and more blazes were set as the torches moved further and further out. Before long, fires appeared all about us, reaching to the far horizon. Above us, the light from the bearded star, the Samhain moon, and all the bonfires lit up the sky and illuminated the eitiltes with their long flowing streamers in many bright colors as they soared down over the crowds. The eitiltes did intricate in-and-out knotting maneuvers, much to the thrill and delight of the throngs.

"Harp music reverberated all around, with arm pipes accompanying them. On the pathway adjacent to the central square, two additional bonfires, one on each side, were lit. The cattle from all the nearby herds had been gathered earlier in the day into our northern pens. Those herds were driven between the fires and directed to the southern holding pens in a ceremonial sacrifice to Danu. To a four-year-old like me, all this activity appeared magical.

"Cairpre and Breas chatted, with first Breas telling Cairpre of his adventures, then Cairpre filling him in on changes and events in the cities since he left. After the last Beltane, Breas and his parents had left to visit his father's homeland. Though Breas is half Formorri and half Danann, he had known primarily the Danann ways. He told us of a much simpler and more disciplined life in the Formorri homeland.

"I learned the Formorri are a sea people who have few wants. Instead of massive stone cities or elaborate homes, they live in simple huts of wood and thatch. They can be either traders or violent raiders, depending on the strength of the peoples they encounter. At an early age, they learn the ways of the seaman and the disciplines of the warrior. Skills for fishing are taught in the early afternoons with the day finishing with training in use of the sword, spear, and sling. No time is given to learn the skills of the mind, to memorize the stories of the past, or to understand the rules of law. These proveniences are considered of limited value by the Formorri, in contrast to learning the abilities needed for day-to-day life.

"As the Samhain bonfires flickered, we fell fast asleep, all pressed together for warmth. Late that night, our eyes were shocked open by a brilliant streak of light from the bearded star, more intense than anything we had ever seen. Soon, the light disappeared over the horizon. Just after losing sight of the light, a dazzling but ominous flash erupted in the south, followed by a booming reverberation. The earth shook violently, knocking all of us to the floor of the cave. When we recovered our balance and went outside to look out over the city, we felt objects assailing our heads and it became difficult to breathe. The city below began to fade from sight. The three of us retreated and huddled far back in the cave. We used our sleeves to cover our noses and mouths. Panic gripped us and we all began to weep and wonder if we would ever see our families again.

"The dust and debris blotted out the sun. We had been huddled together for many hours, afraid to move. But, hunger began to overtake our fear. A dull lightening of the sky slowly began to spread, allowing us to at least be able to peer a few feet in front of us. We moved to the edge of our hideaway and discovered the ground was covered with ash and small, lightweight rocks. The debris measured about as deep as my hand. Only the rough contours of the trail leading to our hideaway were discernible.

"We worked our way down the Slieve, hoping the contours we followed would lead us to the city. Before long, we heard people calling our names. Breas recognized one of the voices as his mother's. We raised our voices as one, shouting for help and she soon reached us, folding us all within her arms. Tears streamed down her dust-streaked face as she examined each of us to be sure we were uninjured. The adults carried us down the hillside. Soon we arrived at the palace of the High King and could eat and bathe."

Aislinn's story takes me back to the same fateful night when we also experienced the cloud of dust and the coming of the cold. My thoughts trail to these distant memories of my mother, who I beheld for the last time that night. If I could cry, I would. Aislinn detects my sadness and stops. "Do you wish me to end my story?" she asks.

No, I say, *it's just that the story brings back the sad memories I have from that same Samhain. Please continue.*

Aislinn begins again. "High King Conall's palace sat on the lower flanks of the Slieve of Danu, which typically provided a breathtaking view of the cities and harbor below. On that day, only vague shadows of the cities were visible, and the harbor couldn't be seen at all. An eerie stillness surrounded us, but through the shadows, we saw movement. People were moving toward the assembly hall.

"A passageway led from High King Connell's palace straight to the assembly hall. Breas' mother gathered the three of us up, along with some warm robes and blankets, and led us down the corridor. We settled not far from the speaking platform. Conversations filled the hall with a buzzing sound. A hush came over those assembled as High King Conall mounted the speaking platform and began to address us.

"He told us, 'Not long ago, after some clearing of the air, I sent a fleet of our eitiltes toward the south to discover what happened. As they left the cities of Danu, they found expansive destruction within the lowlands and harbors of our cities from a wall of water that came from the south. Many people in these low-lying areas have died. After passing this destruction, the eitiltes proceeded south across the strait of water separating our northern from our southern lands. They flew a far distance and searched widely, but at no time did they ever find land. The waters themselves were covered with debris. I can only conclude our southern lands have been destroyed, and in fact, no longer exist.

'Danu unleashed her wrath and only spared our northern lands. I have consulted with our druis and they say this is our final warning. Danu has slain most of those who have broken the covenant. She gives the remainder of us twelve more Beltanes to renew our pledge. If we fail her, she will let us know with the appearance of another bearded star. Either we renew the covenant in that time or the northern lands will be destroyed like our southern lands.

'If a bearded star appears, the land of Aletea will remain for one more year, giving a small group of us who have remained faithful time to prepare and then escape. The druis say our weather will change and become much colder. Life will be harder and our spirits severely tested.'

"Cries of disbelief and despair erupted from the crowd. Many fell to their knees, beating their breasts, asking forgiveness from Danu. Other, smaller groups, assembled. Those people had grim, angry, and determined looks. They did not appear repentant, but rather like a group who had fallen back in retreat, but who would now muster courage and conviction to fight what they believed was a wrong. They whispered among themselves and glanced about to see if anyone watched. I learned later that they were what was left of the Sons of Belial, followers of King Belial of our southern lands."

I interrupt Aislinn. *These times of cold and hard times also affected us on Inis Elga. You say these troubled times are a warning for your people, the Danann. Why did we suffer as well? Why did my mother have to die because of what your people did?*

Aislinn is silent. She can sense my anguish and grief. But, I sense pain from her, too. After several moments, she speaks again. I perceive she is sincerely sorry for me and the people of Inis Elga, but helpless to provide a good reason.

"Keelen, I too lost my mother when the city of Fáilas was first being destroyed by the tears from the bearded star. Thinking of losing her is still unbearable. She was the person I was closest to in this life. I know your sadness. Why you and your people also suffered is a mystery. Maybe someday we will be able to ask Danu and Cenn this same question."

I recover from my sadness and feelings of resentment and realize Aislinn had nothing to do with this. She and her companions are as innocent as I am. Those who have broken this covenant are apparently dead or about to perish before the next Beltane. *Aislinn, I* ask, *tell me about this pledge.*

She begins telling me the story of her people again. "Our legends say, long ago the goddess Danu led us to this land from your homeland. Here she was to teach us many things, but before she would, a covenant was struck between her and the Danann. The promise was a simple one. We agreed that with the powers she would show and teach us, we would strive to always help each other as a people and to revere all others we met in this world. We were also instructed to keep the secrets she taught us to only those of the people of Danu.

"This was long ago and for hundreds of years our people kept this covenant. We prospered, and our civilization shone above others we encountered. Several of these cultures, especially within the inland sea, emulated, where they could, many of our ways. In our covenant, we were warned if we broke the promise and let pride and power become our guides, this land would cease to exist. We would be warned of impending doom by the appearance of a bearded star.

"If we did not return to the ways of the covenant, we would know our time as a people was over by the second appearance of a bearded star. This second coming would be through the ominous star cluster of An Scairp, occurring near the time of the Beltane feast. Over the year following this arrival, the bearded star would grow to be as bright and large as the moon, spawning fiery children that would streak through our skies, striking fear and destruction.

"In the days before the final Beltane, one of these flaming children would strike what is left of the cities of Danu and eliminate them. The seas would raise colossal waves and swallow the land where the slieve and cities of Danu stood. Some of the people, who Danu knew to still be true to the covenant, would survive in the lands to the north near the Lai Fáil. Those to the north would be the select few being allowed to return to Inis Elga, the land from where our ancestors came. All this would come to fruition by Beltane. The day after Beltane, all the remaining evidence of Aletea would disappear under the waves."

CHAPTER TEN

THE SONS OF BELIAL

How was the covenant broken? I ask.

Aislinn replies, "Our people followed the covenant for centuries. Danu taught our druis the secrets of the mind and powers of geal leacht. Our people developed a system of laws and customs that kept with the covenant of Danu and became the basis for our civilization. Personal honor and fairness to all, both human and animal, have remained our guiding principles. From the High King to our most humble brother, we are all subject uniformly to our system of laws and customs. No one has special privileges, though some of us may achieve more. Accomplishments add to our honor, not to any privilege.

"All learning is oral. True meaning cannot be conveyed by the written word, which we only use for commonplace, simple transactions. Subtleties and shades of meaning are lost when only reading.

"The danger of writing is that issues become fixed and simplified. They become like a flat board of wood, losing the texture and complexity of the whole tree. Issues and ideas can easily become misunderstood and potentially misused. Only years of training provide the necessary insight to properly recount a history, interpret a sign, or fairly judge a situation.

"I'm sorry for wandering away from answering your question," apologizes Aislinn. "As time passed and our power and strength grew, some of our people became obsessed with power and the material world. In time, the Danann became fractured into two distinct groups: the 'people of the law of Danu' and those we call 'Sons of Belial'. Belial was the king of our southern lands until being slain twelve Samhains ago during the destruction of those southern lands.

"My mother was high druis of Aletea. After the destruction of our southern lands, Danu communed with her. The goddess told her about the final months and moments of King Belial and his followers. Danu also revealed the possible future paths for our people, including the one that is now unfolding. Mother relayed what she learned to High King Conall, as well as the remaining tuatha kings, and of course, to her children.

"From Mother's stories, I learned King Belial had initiated contact with a people far to our west called the Brahm. He gained much wealth and power through these dealings. The Brahm, subservient to King Belial, treated him like a god. King Belial began to believe this treatment appropriate.

"King Belial and many of his subjects became lax in the ways of Danu and eventually abandoned belief in her as their spirit guide. They deemed the Brahm inferior and not worthy of equal treatment. They also began to rely on the Brahm for many things. This reliance led to several of the secrets being taught to them. King Belial had his druis teach the Brahm elders some of the mind powers. He also had his aracos instruct a few of the Brahm in how to operate and soar an eitilte, rationalizing he was only teaching them enough to further cement his power and wealth. He thought the Brahm had inferior minds and would never grasp the significance of what they learned.

"From what my mother told him, and from his own

observations, High King Conall appreciated the dangers presented by King Belial and his followers. He attempted to reign in the abuses, but Belial had become powerful with many followers in the cities of Danu and the court of High King Conall. "As a result, on the northern island our people carried on the spiritual traditions of our ancestors and followed the law of Danu, while the Sons of Belial on the southern island became engrossed with satisfying their physical appetites and desires."

A strong gust of wind slams what sounds like a tree against the rocks near the opening of our shelter. The crunching sound of wood on rock explodes through the cave. Aislinn stops recounting her story and leaps to her feet. Capall is rousted and clambers up. Aislinn pats Capall's neck to reassure him, then checks the cavern's opening. A large oak has succumbed to the powerful winds, but it does not block our entrance. Aislinn again pats Capall's neck, telling him all is fine. Capall settles to the ground once more and Aislinn sits again and continues with her story.

"After a time, the Brahm came to realize they weren't serving gods. As this realization grew, indignation spread and the Brahm no longer willingly served the Sons of Belial.

"King Belial became incensed that the lowly Brahm would no longer serve him or his followers. A brutal battle ensued where Belial deployed his forces in a fleet of eitiltes and vailixi. The Sons of Belial had discovered that the crystals used to empower the geal leacht could also be used to create an intense beam of energy. When focused on a target, the beam would vaporize it. The Sons of Belial used these energy beams against the Brahm.

"The battle waged but two days. Massive destruction and death befell the Brahm, however, the crystal-powered energy beam could only be launched from the larger vailixi, of which there were but a few. The beams laid waste to many villages and the eitiltes swooped down from the sky, giving chase and killing survivors. The Brahm used the mind powers they had learned and created a dense fog, hiding their remaining villages and armies. The eitiltes and vailixi of the Sons of Belial cruised just outside of the fog, searching for ways to penetrate. They shot energy beams into the fog in the hopes of vaporizing it enough to discover their enemy, but the fog speedily enveloped the gaps created.

"Meanwhile, the Brahm captured several eitiltes, which they commandeered and outfitted with their finest weapons and warriors. In these eitiltes, they lay in wait inside the fog bank. When a crystal energy beam discharged, the vailixi momentarily became powerless and vulnerable. The Sons of Belial didn't consider this a danger. Because the vailixi hovered high above the ground, neither armed guards nor eitiltes had been assigned to provide protection.

"Knowing this, the Brahm, in their seized eitiltes, swept from the cover of fog the moment an energy beam discharged, rapidly landing on the platforms and dispatching the vailixi crew. After killing the crew, the Brahm slit open the bags of geal leacht. As the geal leacht spilled, the vailixi would list, and fall to the earth. Just as the vailixi began to list heavily, the Brahm warriors would leap back onto their eitiltes and scamper back to the protection of the fog. They destroyed all the vailixi."

I mentally shake my head as I visualize the battle. I have to admire the Brahm's actions against King Belial.

"The loss of the vailixi devastated King Belial's forces. With no vailixi and with their eitiltes at low power, the Sons of Belial had little choice but to return to their homeland. They had succeeded in destroying the key forces of the Brahm, but their own forces had been severely crippled.

"At the precise moment the battle began, a bearded star appeared in the sky. Growing as the days of the battle progressed, many flashes of light streaked from the hair of the beard, rocketing toward the southern cities. Stones flew from the light streaks, crushing into these cities, inflicting destruction and death."

This is the star that eventually destroyed the southern lands?

"Yes," Aislinn responds.

"King Belial's rage toward the Brahm became uncontrollable. Believing himself truly a god, he swore he would deal with the blasphemous Brahm. He thought the shower of stones from the sky to be merely an annoyance engineered by Danu to help the Brahm, and vowed he would deal with that issue as well, once finished with the Brahm.

"King Belial ordered the southern cities evacuated and told his followers to find safety in the many caverns underlying the southern lands. The caverns, he said, would protect them from the shower of stones and enable his followers to work on building new vailixi.

"Despite the order to evacuate to the caverns, chaos reigned in the southern lands. Not everyone had forgotten the ways and teachings of Danu and they told all who would listen that King Belial was a false god and only by keeping their ancient covenant with Danu could survival be possible. Danu, they said, was punishing the Sons of Belial for their attack on the Brahm and their breaking of the covenant. They were being given one last warning. But the Sons of Belial would not listen, and those who still followed Danu struggled in their efforts to relocate to the north island where the covenant was maintained.

"Emissaries from King Belial also went north to the court of High King Conall. They reminded the High King those of the southern and northern lands are one people and each had the right to share in the treasures from the Slieve of Danu, especially the geal leacht. High King Conall regarded King Belial and the Sons of Belial as grave dangers, convinced Danu was displaying her wrath and providing warning. If King Belial continued his war with the Brahm, the southern lands would be lost and perhaps even all the lands of Aletea would be destroyed.

"King Belial had warned his emissaries High King Conall might need reassurances that the new supplies of geal leacht would not be used against the Brahm. They were to tell the king the geal leacht was needed to replace that lost during the destruction of their vailixi.

"Many followers of the southern king were part of the court of

High King Conall. They advised to grant Belial's request, saying the appeal was reasonable. Others advised that King Belial could not be trusted and no geal leacht should be provided. After much consideration, High King Conall granted the request to recharge the existing stockpile, but refused to allow for any new supplies. The emissaries protested the decision, but they also hurriedly recharged their stocks of geal leacht and returned to the southern lands.

"After several moon cycles, the completion of the vailixi drew near, however King Belial was unable to make them all operational because of the lack of sufficient supplies of geal leacht. He consolidated his forces to support two of the new vailixi, estimating that by the next Samhain eve, everything would be ready for a new attack against the Brahm.

"The vailixi would again serve as King Belial's foremost weapon. This time each vailixi platform would include an armed guard of elite warriors and each would be escorted by a half dozen eitiltes. They would not be taken by surprise again.

"Despite the damage to their cities from the bearded star's fiery tears, the Sons of Belial brimmed with confidence. They defied Danu and again prepared for battle. They believe the festival time of Samhain would bring their ultimate victory over both the Brahm and Danu.

"Danu spoke to our elders and said she held no hope King Belial or his followers would stop in their efforts to subjugate the Brahm. She said, however, she would only mete out the final destruction if the Sons of Belial deployed their new weapons. If deployed, the destruction would be swift and complete. Her greatest fear was that even if she destroyed the southern lands and the northern lands remained, the contamination of thought from the followers of King Belial would infect many in the northern lands."

Again, we are distracted from the story by the howling wind and the sounds of another object crashing into stones near our shelter. Capall only raises his head and looks toward Aislinn. She smiles at her horse and he settles his head back down.

"The bombardment of stones from the bearded star continued

unabated until the day before Samhain eve. Then the tears of the bearded star ceased. Danu would put King Belial and his followers to the final test during Samhain. She wanted to see if they would mount an attack against the Brahm. She knew their new vailixi were complete and their forces appeared to be readying for an assault.

"The ceasing of the fiery tears elated King Belial, as he believed that showed a weakening of the strength of Danu. He ordered his two battle groups of vailixi and eitiltes to prepare for deployment, this time to begin the attack as soon as the sun rose on Samhain. Preparations went forward the whole of Samhain eve. Excitement filled the Sons of Belial as they thought finally they would attain their revenge, regain their rightful position of authority over the Brahm, teach Danu not to interfere with their ways, rebuild their cities, and resume their daily lives.

"The vailixi and eitilte battle groups were taken from their caverns just before sunrise. It was a beautiful morning with a gentle warm breeze greeting the Sons of Belial. Excitement and enthusiasm abounded. King Belial mounted the platform of the lead vailixi, raised his right arm with his fist clenched in triumph. He ordered the crystals to be placed into position for the aircraft to rise. When lowered into position, the entire fleet began to float from the ground, to the deafening cheers of the crowds below.

"As the fleet began to rise, Belial and his followers spotted a glowing ball of fire on the far northern horizon, growing ever larger and streaking toward them. It came fast, and soon the object became larger and brighter than the sun itself. The eitiltes stationed on the north side of the fleet burst into flames. There was no time to escape, nor time to even scream in horror. The entire fleet exploded into a conflagration of fire, and then the fireball burned deep into the earth, creating a massive crater in the heart of the southern lands, where once the fleet and crowds of people stood. The thin walls on the sides of the crater could not hold back the surging sea. Each wall collapsed. Nothing of the southern lands remained. The sea boiled over what was once the domain of King Belial and his followers."

CHAPTER ELEVEN

NUADA IS FOUND

Although Aislinn could have communicated the story regarding the Sons of Belial instantly through the connection between our minds, she preferred telling the story verbally in the tradition of bards. Hearing the story unfold in this way allows me to sense the emotions and not simply the facts of the story. It also helps me understand the significance of this betrayal by the Sons of Belial and the profound sadness the Danann endure regarding the loss of their way of life. Those dark days of the past have re-emerged and, again, my people will be drawn into the consequences. The White Horse warns of different possible futures, depending on how my people respond to the Danann coming to our land.

Telling the story also helps pass the time inside the cave and keeps our minds away from the fury and noise of the storm outside. Shadows, cast by the flickering of our fire, dance off the walls. I sense Aislinn is about to fall asleep when Capall raises his head, perks his ears, and snorts. Aislinn tenses. We catch the muffled sound of a man's voice. It sounds as though someone is calling out.

Capall rises, stamps his front hoof, shakes his head and whinnies.

Aislinn draws her sgian and moves cautiously toward the cave opening. The sound comes again. This time it is a little louder. Aislinn recognizes the voice and shouts, "Father!" She slips the sgian back into its sleeve and bounds from the cave entrance. The storm is fierce, and the wind knocks her to her knees. She recovers, and through the blowing dust, she hazily makes out the figure of her father struggling against the wind. Aislinn again shouts "Father!" and is soon by his side.

Aislinn takes his arm and labors against the wind, helping Nuada reach the cave. On entering, Nuada collapses to his knees in exhaustion and whispers his thanks. Aislinn drops beside him, wrapping her arms about him. Through tears, she keeps repeating, "Father! Father!"

Capall moves forward, nudges Nuada gently, and nickers. Nuada grasps Capall's neck, gives him a gentle pat, and pulls himself to his feet. Aislinn gets a drink of mead and some dried meat for her father, which he gratefully accepts.

Clasping Aislinn's arm, he smiles, and says, "I questioned whether I would ever lay eyes on you again, Aisy."

"Father," begins Aislinn, "what happened in the south? What of the cities of Danu?"

Nuada looks down and I can see the sorrow in his eyes as he says, "All is lost. The cities of Danu and the Slieve of Danu have all vanished beneath the waves. Only your uncle Aesres and I escaped in my eitilte. A handful of the traitorous Sons of Belial who'd been in the cities of Danu when their own land was destroyed tried to escape in a Formorri vessel as the cities and Slieve were destroyed. Aesres and I crash-landed on the other side of the valley from your cave. While inspecting the damage to the eitilte and ensuring Aesres' wounds were properly treated, I caught sight of your movement in the distance. I could not tell who it was, but detected preparation to camp for the night. I thought it best to place Aesres in a sheltered area with some provisions and try to make camp before the storm hit. Unfortunately, the winds swept in rapidly when I was only part way across the valley. The going was difficult, and I only found this shelter based on an occasional glimpse of firelight through the storm.

"Aesres should be fine until this storm loses its strength. Tell me of the further damage in Fáilas and any injuries from the latest earthquakes."

Aislinn clutches her father's hand and says, "No one was hurt by the earthquakes. Some of our eitiltes became damaged, but they should be repairable. The last of the buildings in Fáilas have collapsed. What happened while you were in the cities of Danu? Have our treasures been saved? What of High King Conall and his family?"

"I am afraid High King Conall and his family are gone. As to the three treasures, they are safe but only after difficulty, and only with the help of Aesres," he replies. We will be able to bring them and the Lai Fáil with us when we travel to the land of our ancestors.

"The cities were in turmoil when I arrived," Nuada tells her. "The people knew the end to be near, with no chance of escape. Many spent their last hours trying to make their peace with Danu. Others were in denial, saying the bearded star would soon fade away and life would return to normal. How they could say this after our cities were destroyed once before shocks me."

Nuada reaches for the bag of mead, taking a long drink before he continues. "The remaining Sons of Belial, however, knew the end neared for the cities of Danu. Instead of trying to come to terms with Danu, they plotted their escape. They had maintained contact with the few remaining Formorri traders, making plans for passage. They dearly wanted to take the sacred treasures with them.

"High King Conall was a beaten man. All his efforts to lead the people back to the ways of Danu and re-establish the covenant had failed. He told me many of the people wanted to return to the old ways, but the surviving Sons of Belial, though few, were well organized and they convinced many who heard them that the old ways should be abandoned. They argued no people are as strong, or as learned in the secrets of nature as the Danann, that if given the opportunity, the Sons of Belial would lead the Danann to a position where all people would become their servants. They told those who would listen that wealth and power would be shared among all the Danann, securing their rightful place as masters of all.

"These were alluring ideas to some. They had always been taught to use their powers to help all men, but the idea of total domination and immeasurable wealth proved tempting."

Nuada shifts his sitting position, his face grimacing.

"The Sons of Belial prepared for their departure in secret.

"High King Conall had his attendants keep close watch on their actions. Their transcribing of the ancient teachings and preparations to leave the cities of Danu on a Formorri ship did not overly concern him. Protecting the Sword of Light, the spear, Lúin, and the Cauldron of Wisdom were what concerned him. He, and the keeper of the ancient treasures, your uncle Aesres, proved diligent in maintaining the secrecy of their locations and made plans for their movement north to Fáilas."

Aislinn describes her uncle Aesres to me. *He is a tall, dark-haired, muscular man in his middle years who devotes his life to protecting the ancient treasures. When Aesres enters a room, all know he is a man of wisdom and power. His sheer presence demands respect. He wears simple clothes, the only adornment being a gold ring with the sacred knot symbols of Danu. His eyes are kindly in nature, a soft green-brown that rarely flare in anger.*

As Nuada finishes his story, Aislinn notes a lessening in the storm's intensity. Nuada says it is time to leave so they can tend to Aesres. Dawn approaches as Aislinn breaks camp. She follows Nuada. Dust coats the ground halfway up our sandals, but the wind has subsided, and the air is clearing. The air has a cloaked dullness, making it difficult to see.

Soon we arrive at Aesres' shelter. Inside, he is fast asleep. He awakens with a start and immediately moves into a defensive position, holding the Claíomh Solai. Recognition shows in his face and he lowers the sword.

Aesres expresses his joy to see us, but I note the sadness in his face.

"How are you, my brother?" inquires Nuada.

"My wounds are much better."

He looks away for a moment, then says, "Teagan visited me in my dreams. It is still hard for me to accept that my wife is dead. The touch of her hair and the softness of her voice seem much more than only a memory. I often ask myself why she died instead of me when the fiery tears first shed on Fáilas. In my dream, she reminded me that death is only the passing through the universe's door, merely a transition between the physical and spiritual worlds.

"Teagan transported me to the land of green where we will travel with our eitiltes after escaping the final destruction of Aletea. In the dream, I am unloading the sacred treasures. Through the bonfire light, Teagan points out a figure at the edge of the darkness and light who thinks she is hidden by the shadows. It is a woman who looks like no other I have seen. Teagan tells me this woman will play an important part in my future and I should take note of her features.

"Why did she tell me this? I will never have thoughts for anyone but her. Gazing at this woman, I wondered what future role Teagan thinks the woman will play. Teagan tells me I knew this woman in a previous life, and our lives were intertwined then, as they will be intertwined again in this lifetime. I stared at my wife and said, 'No, this is not possible.' The eddies and currents of souls traveling through time have always kept me close to Teagan, not this unknown woman.

"Though she was crouching in her effort to conceal herself, I could see the woman was beautiful. She had a dark complexion and wore a gold torc about her neck, highlighting an oval face with high cheekbones. The bonfire light glinted off her gold adornments. She appeared to gaze my way as I looked towards her and I felt her eyes burn into my soul. Teagan tells me the reason the goddess Danu struck her down with one of the stone tears was so this future destiny with this dark-skinned woman would occur. I refuse to believe this!"

The woman he saw sounds to me like Queen Sianna. I feel sadness for Aesres and wish he wouldn't dwell on this dream any longer. I suggest to Aislinn that she ask him about their escape from the cities of Danu.

Aislinn agrees and says, "Uncle Aesres, can you tell how you and Father escaped from the cities of Danu? Father was nearing this part when the storm subsided, and we came for you."

Aesres appears deep in thought when Aislinn makes this request, but he recovers, smiles, and says it will be his pleasure. "High King Conall summoned your father to come to the cities of Danu under the guise of needing to meet with him concerning the shortages of food.

"The true reason was to help me take our treasures north as soon as possible. Soon after your father landed, I joined him, and we met with the High King.

"I urged High King Conall to come with us and make the trip to Inis Elga, but he refused, saying he had no right to leave, given everything that happened under his reign. We clasped each other's shoulders, then your father and I set off to where I had secreted the treasures.

"We were starting to secure the treasures in the eitilte when we heard people on the path. I knew it was the Sons of Belial. I instructed your father to prepare the eitilte for ascent while I retrieved the Sword of Light.

"As I ran toward where I had hidden the sword, I could hear one of the approaching men say, 'Quick, they are getting away with the treasures. You three, take command of the eitilte while the rest of us go after Aesres!'

"I noted each had their sword drawn as they moved towards us. I saw my brother set his crystals in place and his eitilte rose to a secure height above the charging men. Reaching the Sword of Light, I wheeled about and prepared to use it against the set of attackers who were intent on wrenching it away. Wielding the sword, the blade slashed through each attacking man. Blood flowed freely, but they would not desist. Soon, a heap of broken swords and bodies piled high. Knowing their efforts doomed, two survivors ran back toward the harbor.

"Nuada lowered his eitilte and helped me aboard. Despite my victory, I had been wounded. My brother raised the eitilte into a hovering position and attended to my wounds. Fortunately, they are only shallow flesh wounds and easily bound. After attending me, Nuada set the crystals in position to guide the eitilte up to soaring height for the return trip to Fáilas. As we rose, the outline of a Formorri ship leaving the harbor could be detected in the light cast by the moon and the bearded star. The remaining Sons of Belial were escaping.

"As we reached soaring height, a flare of light appeared from the bearded star. Nuada released the eitilte for soaring as the flash of light streamed toward us. The air became hot when it flashed by, before slamming into the Slieve of Danu. A thunderous blast exploded below us, followed by an immense rush of air. I firmly clutched the sides of the eitilte while Nuada mustered all his araco skills to keep it in control.

"We were swept like a tidal wave toward the north. While being pummeled about in the air, I looked down to where the ground once was, as well as toward where I last observed the Formorri ship. The sky had become bright as day with the blast. Below me, I discovered the Slieve of Danu no longer existed. The waves of the sea washed over the area where the cities and slieve once stood. To the east, I spotted the crest of a mighty wave. At the top of the crest rode the Formorri ship, making good its escape toward the inland sea.

"The turbulence buffeted the eitilte mercilessly. Your father had difficulty keeping control. The wind pushed us further north and I nearly passed out from the pain. We were being pushed down at a rapid pace. With fortune, your father found some relatively flat ground. The turbulence would not permit a controlled descent, so we came down hard into a sliding stop.

"The eitilte was heavily damaged, its wings sheared in the slide and crystals scattered. My wounds had broken open. After collecting our wits, Nuada attended my injuries and built a shelter. While gathering the materials for the shelter, he told me he noted movement on the other side of the valley. Despite the approaching storm, your father commenced to cross the valley. I succumbed to sleep as the storm hit."

As this story unfolds, I feel myself begin to slip away. I am being called back to my own world, sensing my brother Flann saying, "Keelen, please wake up. Are you all right?" Slowly I transition from the land of Aletea to Inis Elga. I feel I have been asleep a long time.

The last remnants of the people of Danu are coming to Inis Elga and it is up to me and my brethren at Tomregan to ensure they are welcomed and not treated as invaders.

Flann, I do hear you—and I am awakening.

CHAPTER TWELVE

JOURNEY TO SLIGEACH

Through a fog, I begin to distinguish Flann's features. He is peering down and talking to me, looking worried. My vision is murky, as if I had taken a potion, but my mind is beginning to clear. How strange I feel. Looking up at him, I do my best to smile. Relief sweeps across his face and he glances toward two figures standing nearby. I adjust my focus to discover Father is here, looking relieved, and Laragh, who looks at me knowingly.

"Keelen," Flann begins, "you would not awaken, and it is well past midday. Laragh told us you were in a trance, that you had twisped to visit another. She told us not to worry, but Father and I felt so helpless."

I lift myself to a sitting position. Fatigue grips me, but my strength is returning. "I am sorry for being away so long. It must be too late to begin our journey to Sligeach. Perhaps wait until tomorrow morning? There is much I need to tell you."

When everyone nods, I tell them of my experience. "Laragh correctly understood that my spirit left my body and was with another. I have been with the girl I glimpsed in my visions at the

Horse of Binn. She is one of the people of Danu, a people called the Tuatha de Danann. I learned much about the Danann, including why their land is being destroyed and why only a few thousand will survive and come to Inis Elga."

I tell of their power and wealth and how a group of Danann in their southern lands, known as the Sons of Belial, angered the goddess Danu, how the goddess destroyed their land twelve Samhains ago when our own times of trouble began. I tell of the continued treachery of the few surviving Sons of Belial and how Danu is now meting out her final punishment, this being the complete destruction of Aletea. I tell of Aislinn and her family, and that they will be among the surviving people of Danu who will be coming to Inis Elga.

Fearghus and Flann hang onto my every word. Laragh smiles with knowing.

As I finish my story, dusk is settling in and a light snow begins to fall. The Samhain feast continues, and we join for a last evening of festivity before we leave for Sligeach. I brim with excitement and anticipation. Much is about to transpire and each of us will play a vital role. If my visions are correct, our world will be transformed by next Samhain.

* * *

Morning comes with the ground blanketed by a light dusting of snow. The sky is clearing. The day will be cold and crisp for our trip to visit Queen Sianna. We strap our leather pouches with our belongings across our backs, secure our cloaks about us, and begin our journey. Father walks with us to the head of the primary esker that leads up through the gap between Slieve Cenn to the north, and the slieves of red to the south. The esker is wide and well worn, rising about a foot above the surrounding landscape. He bids us farewell as the sun breaks through the morning clouds.

The climb is steep as we travel toward the gap between the slieves. We hope to reach the sacred pool that marks the beginning of the river Sinann by nightfall. The sun and our brisk pace keep us warm. The snow is only about half a finger deep and the dusting acts as a cushion as we walk. The climb is tranquil with no sound but that of our feet crunching in the snow. No one speaks.

My mind drifts aimlessly as I let my body take hold of the task at hand. It is a refreshing experience to think of nothing and simply enjoy the physical exertion of one's journey.

Hours pass, and by midday we complete the climb up the steep terrain to the high plateau. The number of trees have thinned considerably as we distance ourselves from Tomregan. We quicken our pace as we know we are close to the sacred pool. After a few more hours, we see a thickening in the number of trees, which indicates we are approaching the pool.

The esker winds into the trees and skirts the northern edge of the pool. The waters are dark and appear deep. The pool's spring creates a light surge near the middle with the water escaping on the south side to form a stream. I know this small stream flows into Lough Aillionn, gathers strength, and emerges from the other end as the river Sinann.

Small strips of cloth dangle from many of the branches overhanging the pool. These are offerings left by other travelers to the goddess Danu, the same goddess honored by the Danann. For our offering, we each brought a sprig of mistletoe from the sacred oaks near Tomregan. We suspend our offerings from the branches above the pool.

Flann takes out his spindle and bow for lighting a fire and soon one is roaring near the bank of the sacred pool. Flatbreads and dried meat are secured from our travel pouches. After relieving our hunger, we gather pine boughs that we spread about near the fire on top of the snow for our bedding. Darkness is soon upon us. To the east, the bearded star makes its nightly appearance. The moon is near full and light from the moon and bearded star casts murky shadows among the trees nearby. Wolves howl in the distance.

We chat for a short while about what we may find at Sligeach, but fatigue overtakes us, and another full day's journey lies ahead. Flann stokes the fire, and as it flames we huddle closely for warmth and wrap our cloaks about us. Sleep comes swiftly.

In the early morning half-light, I awake with a start as I hear a rustling noise. I feel Flann and Laragh are also awake, lying still. None of us move. I am sure there was a muffled crunch in the brush not far from where we lie. I slowly reach for my sgian. Flann always sleeps with his staff at his side, so I'm sure he is ready, too. I continue to lie still, feigning sleep, listening for any additional sounds. Nothing more is heard.

As the sun rises, I rouse myself, acting as though nothing occurred in case we are still being watched. Glancing at Laragh, I know she's wise to my behavior and is mirroring it, as is Flann. Flann re-kindles the fire and we eat our morning meal. We chat about Sligeach and what lies ahead.

Although nothing further is heard, I still have the sensation of being watched.

We gather our things and move along the esker leading to Sligeach. Leaving the woodland surrounding the sacred pool, the trees again become thin as we move upwards toward the final gap between the slieves. The sense of being watched leaves as we travel. We stop briefly to discuss what happened and agree keeping our watcher or watchers unaware was our best tactic. Reaching the crest of the gap, our good spirits return. Most of our remaining journey will be downhill.

Time passes briskly as we make timely progress toward Sligeach. The snow disappears and by late afternoon, the heavy atmosphere and salty smell of sea air engulfs our senses. Our trail snakes through dense forests of oak, elm, and hazel.

Rounding a corner, we are startled to encounter numerous Formorri warriors blocking the trail. A coal-dark, bejeweled woman sitting in a chair seems to be their leader. The woman steps down from her chair to greet us.

"Welcome to Sligeach," she says. "I am Trista, high counselor for Queen Sianna. We have been expecting you since our scouts returned from the sacred pool of the Sinann telling us of your approach. You must be Keelen, you Flann, and you Laragh. My scouts overheard you talking at the pool and noted your names and appearance. I am most interested to learn why three young emissaries come from Tomregan so soon after Queen Sianna returned from there herself."

We give each other a look. *So, this is Trista,* I think. *She is high counselor, but she is not Sianna and Trista is full Formorri, the representative of her brother, the Formorri High King. Father warned us to only trust Sianna in our visit to Sligeach.*

Though the Formorri village has existed for many years and relations between the people of Inis Elga and Queen Sianna have been civil, we of Inis Elga maintain a degree of distrust regarding the Formorri. Though we have not battled for many years, there has been bloodshed. I have to wonder why Trista's scouts did not make themselves known to us. Knowing Trista had us spied upon makes me uncomfortable.

Trista returns to her riding chair and beckons. She ignores the fact we did not answer her question and says, "Come, accompany me. I am too old to walk comfortably anymore. We can talk during our journey to Sligeach."

"Kellen, please come along beside me."

There is but room for Trista in her riding chair and one other person beside her on the path. The riding chair is held low, leaving me at about the same height as Trista. Flann and Laragh follow close behind.

Once I am alongside, Trista says, "My queen wished she could have stayed longer in Tomregan to learn about the Samhain visions from the White Horse. I understand the three of you were honored to light the Samhain fire at the cairn of Eachon and see the revelations."

I do my best to be friendly with Trista, but only speak in generalities concerning the White Horse and its revelations. I don't divulge details and certainly do not speak about my spirit visit with Aislinn. I sense Trista suspects I am not entirely forthcoming, and she probes gently but persistently. I sidestep the issues and we are soon within the grounds of Sianna's rath.

Her rath overlooks the bay at Sligeach and the roundhouses that make up the village below. Sianna's roundhouse, Trista's, and those of the council are surrounded by the protective rath, yet there is still an expansive view of all activity both in the bay, and the village itself, which lies along the shoreline. A great Formorri ship rests at anchor. Smaller vessels are darting to and from it, off-loading and loading goods. I remember Aislinn's description of the Formorri ship she viewed as a child and recall how it frightened her. This ship, too, is painted the color of blood, with an eye adorning its bow. Chills race down my spine.

When we arrive at Sianna's roundhouse she greets us as old friends, though she only met me but once and has never met Flann or Laragh. "Welcome to Sligeach!" she says. "I am honored the children of Fearghus come visit so soon after my time in Tomregan. The news from the White Horse must be noteworthy. Please, make yourself comfortable by the hearth. I was informed of your approach and arranged food and drink for you."

I had told Flann of her exceptional beauty, which he had dismissed up to this point. It is now difficult for him to not stare and takes him some time to regain his composure. The sight of an uncomfortable Flann is amusing.

My impression of Sianna is only from one meeting. Father has provided us background concerning her. He says Sianna has a true love for the land of Inis Elga. Her mother, who was the daughter of King Ailill of Rathcroghan, died giving birth. Sianna's Formorri father, King of Sligeach, died when she was little more than a child. He never recovered from the grief of losing his wife. Growing up, Rathcroghan was as much Sianna's home as Sligeach.

Before he died, Sianna's father anointed her Queen of Sligeach. Being a true Formorri and speculating her mixed blood might lead to mixed loyalties, he also appointed his sister, Trista, to be Sianna's high counselor and the court representative for the Formorri High King, Elotha. Father told me Sianna had welcomed Trista as her high counselor and they became close, with Trista hovering like a mother.

Sianna addresses us, saying, "I have been anticipating your coming since my consultations with Fearghus. He revealed to me much about the meaning of the bearded star and the recent earthquakes. We spoke about the White Horse visions. Your father said this Samhain would be particularly important with this being the thirteenth since the coming of the cold. Please, warm yourselves and eat your meal."

The food is welcome and Sianna visits as we eat. It is a seafood stew, nothing like anything I have ever tasted at home. As we eat, we ask about the Formorri ship, what it carries, and what it will carry when it leaves. Sianna says the cargo being unloaded includes wine, olive oil, salt, amber, and the precious metals of gold, tin, and copper. The metalworkers of Inis Elga are renowned for the finest quality gold and bronze work and their finished products are among the items the Formorri trade. The people of Inis Elga also trade leather, furs, salted fish, and meat. The Formorri take this cargo to the inland sea to complete the trade route before returning to their homeland.

We are revived by our meal. Sianna is eager to listen to what news we bring.

Shortly after we arrived, I found an opportunity to discretely remind Sianna what Father instructed regarding the information we would be providing her.

Customarily, Trista would be present for meetings, but Sianna informs Trista of the meeting conditions. She protests, saying her role as chief advisor requires her presence. She reminds Sianna her grandfather, the Formorri High King, wants Trista to know everything connected to dealings with the people of Inis Elga. For some reason, Trista looks my way as she says this. Does she distrust me? Why does she look at me and not Flann or Laragh?

Sianna's voice acquires an edge as her discussions with Trista continue. Sianna reminds Trista sternly she is queen and she intends to follow the wishes of Fearghus. Trista's jaw sets, but she bows to Sianna and acknowledges that as queen, she makes the final decisions.

I decide to test my mind powers with Trista, as I am uncertain of her true loyalty. Is it to Sianna or to the High King of the Formorri? Having only practiced these powers in our training exercises at the Tomregan learning center, I am uncertain if I will succeed. My challenge is to enter Trista's mind and be aware of her thoughts while still participating in our meeting with Sianna. We are taken to the royal council room of the rath for the meeting.

As Trista departs, I focus my thoughts and enter her mind. I sense that she takes her duties of high counselor, as defined by the Formorri High King, seriously. In earlier years, her brother had revealed a secret passageway leading from a hidden entrance within Trista's roundhouse to a chamber located below the council room. Sianna is unaware of this chamber.

Within this chamber, all that is said in the council room can be heard. Trista had never used this hidden chamber before, but feels compelled to use it now. She excuses herself from her servants, saying she is tired and does not wish to be disturbed. She then enters the passageway, making her way to the hidden chamber.

This is disturbing, but I know of no alternative. The council room is the appropriate spot for our discussions and I cannot reveal to Sianna possible treachery by her high counselor. This will indeed reveal Trista's ultimate loyalty.

With trepidation, I commence recounting our night with Eachon and the White Horse. Sianna understands much of the initial story from her discussions with Fearghus. As I describe seeing the girl in the mist, she asks what I learned from her. I tell Sianna nothing more happened during this vision, but that I learned more from this girl later. I will share this information after Laragh recounts what she visualized.

Laragh begins by saying she envisioned the coming of the Danann to an area near the shores of Lough Aillionn. Sianna is keenly interested in learning more. This site is near Sligeach, being only a day's journey away.

Laragh speaks about the landing of the Danann aircraft and the unloading of the four special treasures. Sianna asks detailed questions regarding the treasures, and questions her about the individual called Aesres who oversaw their unloading. Laragh explains about the powers of the treasures, but confesses she knows little about Aesres. Of course, I know about Aesres from my time with Aislinn, but for the moment keep this to myself.

The manner of how Sianna states her questions reveals to me she, too, knows of this vision in some way. Finally, I ask her how she is so knowledgeable about the arrival of the Danann. Sianna confesses she had this same vision in a dream the night of Samhain, the same night as Laragh's vision. It appears Sianna somehow experienced part of Laragh's vision at the same time as Laragh.

Laragh completes her account and I begin sharing my experience of being with the Danann girl, Aislinn. My time with Aislinn and the stories she conveyed cover many different areas. These include describing the devastation to their land, Aislinn's family, and the history of the Danann. Additionally, I describe the storm, the finding of her father during the storm, and his narrow escape from the cities of Danu. My story includes telling how her father and uncle rescued the treasures from the doomed cities of Danu, the escape in the eitilte, and the crash landing. I describe the eitiltes and how they will be used to bring the people of Danu to Inis Elga.

Telling these stories takes us deep into the night. When we finish, Sianna expresses her gratitude that we travelled to Sligeach to provide her with this information in person. She says as queen she intends to welcome the people of Danu and will help in any way to ensure their arrival is peaceful. She will also speak with her grandfather, King Ailill of Rathcroghan, who she suspects may be opposed to their arrival.

Wishing us goodnight, she indicates where we will find the sleeping furs. Sianna draws a thick woolen curtain across the opening and disappears toward her roundhouse.

All during our meeting, Trista listened. I need to stay awake to listen to her thoughts and discover what she intends to do with this information. I sense Trista truly loves Sianna and regards her as a daughter, however she believes there is danger with this coming of the people of Danu. She suspects the High King of the Formorri intends to increase the Formorri presence in Inis Elga. The presence of such a formidable people as the Danann would complicate these plans.

Trista ponders these issues and resolves on a course of action. Never has she withheld anything from Sianna, but her ultimate loyalty and allegiance is to Trista's Formorri grandfather, High King Elotha. Trista departs the chamber and returns to her sleeping quarters.

The Formorri vessel we saw earlier is scheduled to leave at high tide in the morning. I hear Trista awaken her handmaiden and instruct her to proceed to the shoreline with a message for the captain. The ship's captain is to be summoned to immediately report to Trista on a matter of major importance.

Once the captain arrives, I sense Trista rising, and I listen to her offer the captain food and drink. The captain thanks her but declines, saying he hopes to return to his ship quickly to finish preparations. Trista sits again, and I sense her stretching out her hand toward the captain, so her signet ring is clearly visible in the firelight. "Captain," Trista begins, "do you see the design on my signet ring and know what it means?" When he nods, she says, "What I am to tell you is for Elotha's ears only and you must meet with him as soon as possible. I know you are scheduled to first deliver your goods before returning home, but the urgency of this message requires that you must first return home and meet with the High King." I am aware Trista is scrutinizing the captains' face and experience her satisfaction as he focuses on the signet ring. He answers, "What message do I carry?"

Trista recounts the major points about the coming of the Danann people and that they will arrive by Beltane. She tells him to tell Elotha how she thinks Sianna might not be fully trustworthy if the Formorri were to oppose this arrival, but she, Trista, will be his eyes and ears. Once Trista finishes giving the captain her message, she has him recount it to ensure he understands everything accurately. Satisfied, she allows the captain to return to his ship.

* * *

The next morning breaks bright and clear, a perfect day to take in the sights of Sligeach before we begin the journey towards Rathcroghan tomorrow. Sianna greets us warmly and provides us with both food to eat now, as well as food to take on our journey tomorrow. Gazing toward the harbor, we note the Formorri ship preparing to set sail when the tide changes. The ship is an ominous sight that again sends a chill down my spine.

Moving close to my siblings, I share what I overheard when I went into Trista's mind. This information is disconcerting, but perhaps it is only Trista fulfilling her duties as representative of High King Elotha. We agree to wait and see and not inform Sianna.

After preparing our travel sacks for tomorrow's trip, Sianna guides us on a tour. She takes us along a long path up a hill overlooking Sligeach and its harbor. At the top of the hill rests a large old cairn, positioned to provide a panoramic view of the village and harbor.

Sianna says, "Not many people know of this cairn or are knowledgeable about what it represents. My father brought me here as a child and recounted its legend. It is the site of the last struggle between the peoples of Inis Elga and the Formorri and it represents the integrity associated with this last battle. My mother was a native of Inis Elga while my father was Formorri. I am honored to have my dual heritage and I often visit this sight to remind me that peace needs to be maintained and at what price this peace was originally gained."

Sianna informs us the cairn holds the remains of two champions who once fought here to the death. She tells their story. "When the Formorri first came to Inis Elga, fierce battles raged. Many deaths were endured on both sides. The Formorri could not secure a firm, secure landholding but the people of Inis Elga could not drive them away. After nearly a year of battle, the leaders from both sides agreed to end the bloodshed by having a champion from each side do battle to the death. If the champion for the people of Inis Elga was victorious, the Formorri would leave and never return. If the Formorri champion won, the Formorri would be allowed to establish a settlement and use it as a trading center between the Formorri and the people of Inis Elga. The names of the champions have long been forgotten, but both were the strongest, most courageous, and skilled from each side. This battle to the death was without weapons and without protective armament or clothing.

"Warriors from both sides worked together to clear the hilltop of trees and brush in preparation for the battle. Boundaries were set so the fight would only occur in full view of everyone. Warriors from each side intermingled and surrounded the hilltop just outside of the boundaries. No cheering took place, for the moment was solemn.

"The two champions and all who were to watch gathered in the grey darkness just before sunrise. The two warriors sat side by side, facing toward where the sun would rise, and silently waited for the first streaks of sunlight to strike their faces. As the sun for the new day struck, the men rose to their feet, turned to each other, and embraced before positioning for battle. The repeated sounds of striking fists and blows to the bodies from leg thrusts filled the air for hours. The atmosphere was silent except for these sounds of battle. The surrounding warriors watched intently, entranced as blood flowed freely from each champion.

"At the top of the hill a red cloth had been placed. Upon it sat a large stone. This stone was to be used for the final blow once one of the champions was no longer able to fight. As dusk approached, both champions were nearing their end. Finally, the champion for the people of Inis Elga collapsed and did not rise. The Formorri champion staggered to the stone and lifted it from the cloth. He moved to where the other champion lay, then crushed his skull with a blow from the stone. The Formorri champion stood over the fallen and now dead champion from Inis Elga for a long while, breathing intensely before he too collapsed and died.

"Bonfires were lit all about this hilltop and stones gathered for the cairn. This cairn was erected directly over the bodies of the two champions at the spot where they died. After the cairn was finished, the warriors from Inis Elga retired to the south and left the Formorri alone. The Formorri returned to the shoreline at the base of this hill and created the village of Sligeach."

As we sit on an edge of the cairn, listening to this story from Sianna, I haven't noticed the hours go by. When she finishes, the sun is already well past the high point of the day. Far out from the harbor, we see the Formorri vessel coursing at full sail in the open sea. We watch it rise and fall on the ocean swells.

We are to have a formal dinner tonight with Sienna and Trista. Our time in Sligeach is drawing to a close. We fulfilled our father's wish to inform Sienna about our experiences with the White Horse before we go to winter in Rathcroghan. Having the Formorri receptive to the coming of the Danann is critical for the long-term survival of the people of Danu. With Sienna, I believe they have a strong friend. Trista is the problem.

CHAPTER THIRTEEN

JOURNEY TO RATHCROGHAN

I awake to the din of bustling activity coming from the direction of Queen Sianna's roundhouse. Rays of sunlight flow through the opening created as I draw back the woolen curtain. Flann stirs the embers from the remains of last evening's fire, adds new fuel, and soon a roaring fire blazes again.

Sianna calls out "hello", then enters the council chambers. "I heard you moving about," she says. "I'm sorry our commotion woke you. Last night, after we parted, I began to think of my grandfather and believe it's vital to go with you and meet with him as well. Do you mind having another traveler accompany you?"

Glancing toward Flann, I see his eyes brighten. I suspect he would like nothing better than to have the striking Queen Sianna accompany us to Rathcroghan. The idea pleases me as well, and I see a smile cross Laragh's face. We each regard this young queen highly and welcome the notion of having her journey with us. I say, "Speaking for us all, we would be most pleased to have your company."

"Perfect!" Sianna replies. "Let us eat a morning meal and be on our way. I've collected a few things to take and am ready."

Some meat and blooded bread are brought to us, which we quickly eat, hoping to start this adventure as soon as possible.

Trista joins us for the morning meal. As we eat, she and Sianna discuss the village duties that need attention during her absence. I note Laragh is listening intently to their conversation. A small crease crosses her forehead.

When the two finish discussing arrangements, Trista turns and wishes us well on our journey. Laragh gazes deeply at her, weighing Trista's words. Then she gives a slight shake to her head and turns towards us as we leave Sianna's roundhouse. I bump slightly into Laragh and ask in a whisper if anything is wrong.

"I am uncertain," she replies. "Something is there, but I don't know what. I feel a sense of conflicted loyalties. Given your story from last night, we can't be too careful."

With our travel satchels ready, the four of us proceed toward the village edge where the esker leading south begins. Sianna is traveling alone. I assume she's chosen to do so because she wants time alone with us for added discussions. Sianna and I take the lead. The weather is cool and clear. It should take us two days to reach Rathcroghan.

Sianna and I exchange meaningless pleasantries as we begin the journey. We also banter with Laragh and Flann. After a while, we fall into the pleasant silence of physical exertion. By mid-morning, we come to a split in the esker. One branch is the direct route to Rathcroghan. The other also leads to Rathcroghan, but indirectly, along the edge of Lough Aillionn. It is at Lough Aillionn, on the plain near its eastern shore, where the Danann are to arrive in Inis Elga by the next Beltane. Sianna and I glance at each other when Laragh says, "Though it will add an extra day to our travel, I think we should go this longer way." We all nod affirmatively and proceed toward the shores of Lough Aillionn.

The sun is beginning to descend below the western horizon, signaling the time for us to stop for the evening. Finding flat ground, we gather pine boughs for our bedding and wood for our fire. But before we light the fire, I see a wisp of smoke from another fire and point it out to the others. This fire is just down the lakeshore on a promontory that provides a sweeping view of the opposite shore and particularly the flat plain at the foot of the slieves of red that drop down to the lake. I look at the others and ask, "Who could be there, and why?" Sianna motions for us to gather to discuss the situation in whispers.

We decide, with the remaining light, to circle behind the location of the fire to a position above the promontory. From this vantage point, we catch the sound of the voices of maybe three or four men. Slowly we creep forward until we are close enough to take in the surroundings. Sianna indicates she recognizes the men.

The conversation among them reveals little, but we see they have built a sturdy shelter. It is obvious they intend to stay here for an extended time. We watch for a while longer, but their conversations simply revolve around the food they are eating, what they are going to eat tomorrow, and the good luck they had at fishing. There is only a partial moon tonight, but the bearded star provides enough light for us to creep gradually away from the fire and back to where we left our satchels.

Sianna whispers, "Those men are from the court of Grandfather Ailill. His son, my uncle Eoghan, is leading them. I am uncertain why they are here, but it appears they are to provide reconnaissance of activities around this lough. Given what your father told me regarding my grandfather's uncertain response to the coming of the Danann, we must not let anyone in my grandfather's court know we have seen them."

We decide it would be unsafe to venture further down this path as well as unsafe to stay until morning. We scatter our gathered firewood and pine boughs to eliminate evidence of our presence and use the light of the bearded star to lead us back up the esker. After travelling half the night, we near the esker fork we passed earlier. We stop and curl up in our cloaks for a few moments of rest.

The early morning sunlight awakens me. Although my brother and sister still sleep, I find Sianna sitting with her cloak tightly wrapped about her and arms clenched around her knees. She is staring straight ahead, apparently deep in thought. I don't wish to disturb her, so I lie still and let Sianna be with her thoughts. Before long, Laragh and Flann stir, and their sounds take Sianna out of her reverie. She sees I am looking toward her and gives me a sad smile.

We retrieve a meal of dried berries and dried meat from our satchels. Sianna, still looking sad, says, "It appears my grandfather distrusts the intentions of the Danann despite the counsel of those from Tomregan. I wonder what potential allies he has enlisted. One would think possibly the Formorri, but he has not consulted me. Perhaps he thinks I listen too closely to the counsel from Tomregan. Our visit should be interesting, and your stay over the winter revealing. Let us not mention we went along the esker toward Lough Aillionn."

Each of us agree with Sianna's counsel. Father has always been wary that King Ailill may feel threatened by this upcoming arrival of strangers.

By late afternoon, Rathcroghan comes into view. The seat of King Ailill is impressive. Remnants of the old city fortifications appear on the left. To the right lie the many roundhouses of the village inhabitants. The village marketplace is further to our right. We see several hundred people milling about the many stands, inspecting and trading goods. Directly in front of us are the rath earthworks that surround several impressive roundhouses, including those for King Ailill and his sons. Our path leads directly to the rath gates. Attendants to King Ailill spot our arrival and lead us toward his rath. They say, "We have been expecting you. Your father, Fearghus, sent a message regarding your coming. But we are surprised to see you, Queen Sianna."

Sianna, of course, knows these attendants well and immediately engages in conversation regarding how things are in Sligeach, about our trip, and about the goings on in Rathcroghan.

The attendants seem to be trying to subtly draw information from us about anything unusual we may have seen on our journey and Sianna is correspondingly as persistent but subtle in asking questions about her grandfather and about her uncles. The attendants learn nothing of our side trip to Lough Aillionn, but we do learn that Ruairi, King Ailill's eldest son, is gone to Tomregan to spend the winter consulting with Fearghus and the elders, while his second son is also gone, though the attendants are uncertain where.

The four of us enter the grounds of King Ailill's rath and are led into his council chamber. Within, we find a great hearth holding a roaring fire. There are elk skins to sit upon. Blooded bread and mead are brought as we settle on several of the comfortable elk skins near the hearth.

Soon, King Ailill joins us and greets Sianna warmly. "How was your journey, granddaughter? It is a most pleasurable surprise to see you. What brings you to Rathcroghan?"

"I have come to offer support for the children of Fearghus. What they learned from the White Horse portends great change ahead."

Turning to us, King Ailill says, "I have been eagerly anticipating your arrival since receiving word from your father that you were on your way. Having my granddaughter with you enhances your arrival."

We bow, extend our gratitude for his warm reception, and offer greetings from our father. We tell King Ailill it is our father's wish for us to not only provide him the latest account from the White Horse, but stay the winter and be available for further counsel.

I say, "The recent earthquakes, the foreboding bearded star, and the latest revelations from the White Horse about coming events will make our presence useful to you. Father wished for you to learn all we know, as your decisions will shape our future."

King Ailill agrees, saying we will stay in the roundhouse of his eldest son, Ruairi, who so happens to be staying the winter at Tomregan. He turns to Sianna and asks how long she is to stay and tells her she is welcome to stay in Eoghan's roundhouse. Eoghan, he says, is away on a hunting expedition.

"I only intend to stay a few days," says Sianna. "My decision to come to Rathcroghan was at the last minute. Unfortunately, other duties in Sligeach press and I cannot visit longer."

"Your presence is always a pleasure, granddaughter. I am only happy you decided to come, even if only for a short time."

King Ailill tells his attendants, "Prepare the roundhouses of Ruairi and Eoghan for our visitors." Turning toward us, he says, "Please make yourself comfortable and rest. We will talk tonight after our evening meal."

This is the first time I have met King Ailill and I must admit I find him to be pleasant, and with what I perceive to be a kind and high regard for his granddaughter, Queen Sianna. Perhaps Sianna's uncertainties about him are unfounded.

As he leaves the council chambers, King Ailill gives us a slight bow. When the hanging woolen blanket is swept aside as he leaves, I observe a man with dark skin standing back from the entrance, trying to avoid being seen. He is a Formorri and appears to have been listening to our conversation. Luckily, he does not notice me watching him. Quickly turning to Flann, I inquire if there is more mead. Seeing the Formorri man is strange. Why would a Formorri man need to hide when the Formorri Queen of Sligeach is present? I am sure Sianna is not aware of his presence.

I wash and change into more presentable clothing and prepare for the evening meal and the discussion to follow. Entering the council chambers, I see the attendants finishing with arrangements. The smell tantalizes my appetite. I see my favorite dish—quail covered in clay—will be served. A stack of them sets at one end of the eating area near the flatbread and other sliced meats. Mead is available in clay jars every few feet across the center of the eating area.

As the last of the food and drink is arrayed, King Ailill and his advisors enter the council chambers and sit at various spaces around the eating area. The four of us join them and Sianna sits next to her grandfather.

Sianna remarks, "Where is your high advisor, Trevor?"

King Ailill replies, "Trevor accompanied Ruairi to Tomregan and will stay with him for the winter. I imagine they are sitting down with Fearghus for their evening meal as we speak. It is important for them to learn all they can from Fearghus of the prophesies and what we need to know of these people of Danu. First, let us eat, and then the children of Feargus can tell me what they learned at the White Horse."

The meal is wonderful, equally as good as the food at our last Samhain feast.

King Ailill tells stories of Sianna's mother. He recounts her childhood and how she met Sianna's father.

"Sianna's mother's name was Caoimhe, which means beauty and grace," says King Ailill. "She was tall, slender, and graceful, with long, light red hair. Sianna has many of her features, but with the darker skin and hair from her father. Sadly, Caoimhe died soon after Sianna's birth."

I sense his love and longing for her even after these many years.

Continuing, King Ailill says, "Sianna was a mischievous child, knowing no matter what she did, I would always forgive her. I cherished the time she spent with me in Rathcroghan." He smiles at Sianna and she returns his loving look.

"Her mother became curious about the dark-skinned people who lived in the village to the north along the sea. Whenever I went to visit this village of Sligeach, she would beg to come along.

"Caoimhe would say, 'Their ways are so different from ours and they look so strong and powerful. I always look forward to learning more about them when we visit Sligeach.'

"Morca, the son of the Formorri King of Sligeach, took interest in Caoimhe. He was older than she, but he enjoyed her company and she never tired of his stories. As years passed, they became fast friends and when Caoimhe came of age, it seemed natural they should wed.

"Morca's older brother, Elotha, had become High King of the Formorri and Morca became King of Sligeach. Elotha encouraged this union between his brother and the daughter of the King of Rathcroghan. Elotha thought highly of the lands of Inis Elga and wanted to ensure the Formorri foothold in Sligeach remained strong."

As King Ailill tells the story of Sianna's mother, I see tears swelling in his eyes. Recounting how his daughter Caoimhe died giving birth to Sianna, Sianna reaches out and comforts him. King Ailill regains his composure and says, "The hour is late, and my mood is now wrong for listening to the stories from the Horse of Binn. Let me wait to hear them another time."

To this, we of course all agree. Flann, Laragh, and I retire to Ruairi's nearby roundhouse and Sianna to her uncle Eoghan's. It has been a long and eventful journey from Sligeach. I am sure our upcoming stay this winter with King Ailill will give us the opportunity to learn much about him.

CHAPTER FOURTEEN

THE RETURN TO ALETEA

The winter passes uneventfully at Rathcroghan. Flann, Laragh, and I look forward to returning home. Beltane is coming soon, and I have had no recent contact with Aislinn or the people of Danu. At this moment, King Ailill appears unconcerned about the Danann, apparently taking a wait-and-see attitude. We will return home tomorrow. It is late, and I fall asleep quickly.

A thunderous clap far in the distance awakens me. As my eyes open, a streak of light illuminates the grey, early morning skies. I gaze about, but cannot recognize where I am. There are makeshift shelters all about, and a field nearby is blanketed with strange objects. Suddenly, I sense myself getting up, but with no sensation of control.

I start to panic, when suddenly my movement freezes. "Keelen," I hear a voice say, "is that you?"

Now I understand. *Aislinn! I am so glad to hear your voice! I was becoming anxious, not sure what was happening. It has been a long time since my last time with you. You must be near the end of your preparations to leave. Beltane comes soon.*

"Many moon cycles have passed and often I wished and hoped you would return. The times have been difficult. The earth trembles continuously, making our last preparations to outfit the eitiltes trying. Those not securely bound to the earth often become damaged. Fortunately, the tears from the bearded star avoid striking where we sleep, the corral area with the horses, or the field where the eitiltes lie."

Aislinn glances toward the field of eitiltes, then continues. "The last explosive sound and streak of light was from one of the larger tears striking our home city of Fáilas. No one ventures there anymore. The tears from the bearded star fall on Fáilas more than any other part of the country around us. Danu appears to want to destroy all that remains of Fáilas, save for the stone circle.

"My father estimates it will take two days to reach Inis Elga with the eitiltes. It is fortunate that Inis Elga is not too far, as there is barely enough power remaining in our geal leacht to travel three, possibly four days. I am anxious for the journey to begin, but fearful and distressed to leave our entire lives behind."

On a hill to the east, I take in the shrill whinnying of a herd of horses. Aislinn senses my question and says, "We released most of our horses over the past few weeks as there is room to only bring a few on the eitiltes. They appreciate their freedom and appear to sense the end is near." I now hear loud whinnying being returned from the corral area.

"They visit each other every morning," Aislinn says. "The whinnying and agitation increases each day. I fear Capall wishes to stay."

We walk toward the corral where Capall and two other horses are being kept. Capall lets out another loud chorus of whinnying, rising high on his back legs, then rearing down to pound the earth with his front hooves. He looks toward Aislinn, and trots towards us. He nudges Aislinn and then seems to peer deep into her eyes. "I believe he senses your presence, Keelen, and he, too, is glad you are back." Capall nods his head and lingers as Aislinn strokes his nose.

After receiving some affectionate stroking, Capall backs slowly away, inhales deeply, then emits a long blustery snort. He looks toward Aislinn, gives one last nod of his head, then starts across the corral area, first in a trot, then at full gallop. The other two horses follow him. On the far hill to the east, the sound of whinnying increases. Capall and his companion horses answer in whinnies of their own. Capall circles back toward Aislinn at full gallop, passing her while nodding his head vigorously. He proceeds, along with the other two horses, at full gallop toward the corral pole fence. In a leap, Capall and his companions are over the fence, galloping toward the other horses.

We see them arrive and mingle in the distance. After they exchange greetings, all the horses turn toward us. There is no movement for many moments, then Capall gives one last whinny, rising high on his hind legs, saying goodbye. After this gesture, he leads the herd away from the encampment, into the wilds of Aletea.

I can feel Aislinn's sadness, but find it best to express nothing.

Cairpre comes up the trail towards where we are standing. "I'm sorry Capall is gone," he says. "He was a close friend. We need to take things we find dear to this new land if we can. Losing him is a tough blow." He wraps his arm around Aislinn and squeezes her shoulders against his strong body. The remnant of a single tear streaks his left cheek.

Aislinn is silent for many moments before finally saying it is best for Capall to be with his own in these final days. She grasps Cairpre's hand and guides him to a log to sit. The ground trembles again, but only mildly. Aislinn says, "Cairpre, do you remember when we found Father and Aesres and brought them back to our encampment? Do you recall me telling you the strange story about the girl from Inis Elga who came to be with me in my body while I was looking for Father?" Cairpre lifts his eyebrows at her. Aislinn continues. "She is with me again."

Cairpre stares at Aislinn in disbelief, then says, "Why is she here? Can she talk with us?"

"Cairpre," I sense myself saying, not with my voice but with Aislinn's. "In my last visit, I came to know your sister well and we have a strong bond between us. Talking with you using Aislinn's voice is strange to me. Please forgive me if this offends. Aislinn believes this is how best to communicate."

Cairpre shakes his head in wonder, staring at Aislinn/me in utter disbelief.

"I don't know why I am here, I was just suddenly here," I say.

Cairpre begins talking in a rush, seemingly wanting to say and ask so much but not knowing where to start. Finally, he seems to collect his thoughts. "After Father returned, Aislinn told me much about you. At first, I found what she said difficult to fathom, but with all that is happening in our world, I began to reason I should listen to everything Aislinn learns from you. Knowing we already have friends among your people helps diminish some fears about the trip we will soon make to Inis Elga."

Cairpre asks questions about all I told Aislinn earlier. These include questions regarding the White Horse of Binn, the visions we received from Eachon over the past thirteen Samhains, and especially this last Samhain when I was informed the people of Danu would arrive near Lough Aillionn. I tell him about my family and our home and the learning center at Tomregan. The remainder of the morning is spent relating these stories and I perceive Aislinn is content to listen and enjoy the stories again.

Finishing these stories, I commence informing both Cairpre and Aislinn about the more recent events and some of our suspicions and concerns. First, I speak of Queen Sianna, the half Formorri queen of Sligeach, telling them Sligeach is not far from where the people of Danu will arrive in the land of Inis Elga. "Sianna is a close friend," I say. "She, too, has visions regarding your people and your coming to Inis Elga. Sianna knows you come as friends and she will welcome you. But her advisor is not to be trusted."

I then talk of King Ailill, Sianna's grandfather, who is the local king with his rath in Rathcroghan, another village near where the

Danann will arrive. "My brother, sister, and I met with King Ailill and conveyed to him what we learned during our last visions. Queen Sianna came with us to lend support to our urgings that the people of Danu be welcomed to Inis Elga."

When I talk about our side trip along the shores of Lough Aillionn and what we witnessed, both Aislinn and Cairpre become even more attentive.

Cairpre says, "Do you think the men you spotted were keeping watch over the area where we are supposed to arrive in our eitiltes? You know these men included the son of King Ailill?"

I answer that we each thought the men were settled in for an extended stay and that Sianna recognized her uncle Eoghan, the son of King Ailill. I also tell them, none of us could be certain, however, what they were doing by the lough. The reason might be as innocent as the hunting trip King Ailill alleged Eoghan was on, or as ominous as a fear of the forthcoming arrival of the Danann. In my heart, I believe Eoghan is positioned to observe the coming of the Danann.

Of course, Aislinn knows all I am thinking, but I add for Cairpre's sake, "There could be danger for the Danann from all this intrigue."

I can sense Aislinn thinking, *Keelen, please tell Cairpre about these feelings. Hearing them from you rather than me would be best.*

I agree and proceed to tell Cairpre of my misgivings. Cairpre does not appear surprised. He says, "It is easy to understand why King Ailill may feel threatened. Thank you for these insights. Could you talk to my father and his brother Aesres, letting them appreciate firsthand all that you have told me? They are nearby, supervising the loading of the remaining eitiltes and the repair of the two damaged in the last earth shaking."

"Of course," I reply.

Aesres, I reflect, is the brother of King Nuada and the man seemingly destined to have a connection with Queen Sianna.

Aislinn rises and begins talking to her brother. "Now you, too, have conversed with someone from Inis Elga. All is not lost. We will find a new life. Keelen tells me there are many in Inis Elga who think as she thinks."

We travel along the trail leading toward the extensive field that nearly bursts with eitiltes. I observe two men conversing and pointing at one of the eitiltes. This eitilte is somewhat larger than the others and stacks of dried grass are being removed from its interior. They turn toward us as we approach and Aislinn's father says, "Aislinn, Cairpre, I'm sorry about Capall and the other horses."

"I am as well, Father," replies Aislinn, "but now at least he is with his family."

"Aesres and I were discussing what to carry in the large eitilte with the horses now gone. We are considering using it to transport the treasures of Aletea, along with an armed contingent of warriors," states Nuada. Without warning, Aesres turns to Aislinn and appears to gaze not at her, but at me.

CHAPTER FIFTEEN

LEAVING RATHCROGHAN

Awakening in Rathcroghan, I still feel the eyes of Aesres burning into me. It must have been his sudden glare that led to my hasty departure from Aislinn's body. Did he sense my presence? I did not have the opportunity to meet with Nuada. Perhaps Danu and Cenn believe it is not yet time for Nuada, Aesres, and me to be in direct contact. Aesres is a man of considerable power and position. Are there things he and I should not know about each other yet?

Looking about, I realize much of the morning is gone. Where is everyone? I spot my sister looking toward me from near the fire.

"I recognized you were off to visit the spirit of Aislinn," says Laragh. "Your face appeared as it did the previous time you went. I told Flann what was happening and that he should go and continue to prepare so we can leave tomorrow."

Though our stay at Rathcroghan has been for the most part uneventful, I feel weary.

King Ailill and his court are difficult to decipher. They have treated my siblings and me with courtesy throughout the winter, but the deference seems too formal. It appears they want to learn all we know, but our perception is they are not telling us all their thoughts or intentions in return.

Laragh's visions during the winter have been foggy. She senses someone may be blocking her powers, keeping her from seeing everything. Through the fog, she did not detect the Danann, but did see faint images of warriors moving in and out of the mists. Nothing she saw helped to conclude King Ailill was up to anything, but when we took a moment to talk among ourselves, each of us confessed uneasy feelings had surfaced.

Shaking myself from my reverie, I say, "Thanks, Laragh, for having Flann continue with our preparations to leave. Yes, I was with Aislinn again. For now, I would like to keep this hidden from anyone but you and Flann. Their preparations to leave are nearing completion. Their time to come is near."

"We have a few hours remaining to complete our preparations. Let us sit and talk for a while," Laragh replies. "I feel an urge to hold mother's amber necklace." She often holds the necklace when she's anxious, so this, more than anything, shows me her concerns. "Much is about to begin and the alternate, diverse paths for our future with the Danann are being set into play," she says. "Which path will be taken is uncertain."

As Laragh reaches for the satchel holding her necklace, Flann returns and inquires about how I am. Laragh tells him I was with Aislinn, as she suspected. Flann turns to me and says, "Are you prepared to face this last council? I understand many of the local drui fear the coming of the Danann, despite all the good portents and the support of the drui in Tomregan. King Ailill's son, Ruairi, and his high advisor arrived late last night from their winter's stay in Tomregan. They, too, will be at this last council."

Laragh carefully removes the necklace from her satchel and places it around her neck. Her face is calmer. But soon, the calm fades and a furrow crosses her brow. She looks startled.

"Laragh, what is happening?" I say, feeling worried. Flann, too, looks alarmed.

"Cenn and Danu have taken me to be with Aesres," she says. "You are right, Keelen, he did sense a presence in Aislinn, but you left, so it was only a momentary concern and he brushed the sensation off. He does not seem to sense I am with him. Mother's necklace must be protecting me from being known to him. There is much commotion and I will describe to you what is transpiring as best I can. I know we do not have much time before we must leave to go to council with King Ailill, so I may need to leap forward in time.

Laragh tells us, "Aesres and Cairpre are about to leave on a scouting mission to Inis Elga. They expect the journey to take at least a day, maybe longer. Many of the Danann have gathered to wish them a good journey. There is anxious chattering, with a sense of both nervousness and excitement.

"Cairpre is finishing loading warm clothing and bedding along with several days' worth of food into the eitilte. Aesres holds a piece of parchment. While talking to King Nuada, he unrolls the parchment and points to it. I see it is a drawing of two land masses, separated by water.

"We are now climbing into the eitilte. Cairpre is lowering a sack that looks filled with stones over another sack that appears to hold a liquid. Aislinn, do these sacks hold the power crystals and geal leacht that power their eitiltes?"

"Yes," I reply.

"We are rising high into the air. It is strange to be so far above the earth. Everything below is becoming so small. Cairpre is lifting the sack of crystals away from the geal leacht and we are starting to move away from the land to soar out over the water. The flight is exhilarating, like nothing I've experienced before."

Laragh tells us she is now going to take a time jump up along the most probable future path to the time Aesres and Cairpre arrive over Inis Elga. She estimates this future time will be sometime in the early afternoon tomorrow.

"I see the top of a tall slieve beginning to come into view and lands are unfolding beneath us. Aesres is pulling the parchment from his pocket, checking land details against what is drawn on the parchment. He is telling Cairpre they have arrived, and the prophesied landing area should be a little further to the east.

"We are now where the parchment indicates should be the landing area, and Aesres is soaring down to a lough that looks like Lough Aillionn. Aesres is pointing to a wisp of smoke coming from the western shore and guides the eitilte towards it. Cairpre hands him a polished crystal. Aesres is putting this crystal up to his eye and I can see though it with him. We see three men cooking food. What were specks in the distance are suddenly close when looking through this crystal."

I ask Laragh how this can be, seeing things up close while being so far away. Is this some sort of magic? Laragh cannot explain the crystal's power.

Laragh continues. "We are still peering through the crystal. One of the men is looking up and pointing towards us. The others are now looking, too. Aesres hands the crystal back to Cairpre and quickly takes us up to a great height. He spots a stone path heading south, which we are now following.

"Cairpre is looking through the crystal now. He is excitedly telling Aesres there are three figures making their way north along the stone path. He hands the crystal back to Aesres and we peer down at the three figures. I think we are seeing *us*! Remember, this is all happening tomorrow. We must be sure to head north along the esker toward Lough Aillionn after we leave Rathcroghan."

Laragh tells us the craft is continuing to soar south above the stone path and they are now coming to a large village. She tells us it is Rathcroghan. She says Aesres remarks to Cairpre that this must be the village of the local king. He points to the large roundhouse dominating the high ground near the center.

Laragh tells us, "Aesres is making a quick scan of the village and we are now proceeding north, following another stone path. It is the esker leading to Sligeach. The etching of the trail of stones through the forest can be seen clearly, moving far to the north.

"The view is breathtaking! Looking down on the earth is like viewing a giant map. The lough lies immediately below and the tops of the slieves of red tower above the lough, though they also seem far below. The different eskers leading to Sligeach, to Rathcroghan, and to Tomregan stand out as a bold white against the forest backdrop.

"I see Sligeach coming into view. It takes such little time to reach Sligeach from Rathcroghan using the eitilte. What a wonderful machine. We are now in a hovering position over the village. Aesres asks for the viewing crystal. We examine the village through it, seeing no sign our presence is noted. I can sense Aesres is particularly interested in the skin color of many he sees below.

"Cairpre is reminding his uncle it is time to return to Aletea. Aesres acknowledges this and is making one last scan of the village. A movement catches his attention and he is now focusing the viewing crystal on a hill above Sligeach. Do you remember the cairn Sianna took us to where the two champions fought and died? It is that one.

"Looking through the crystal with Aesres, we see a young woman with dark skin peering intently up towards us. Aesres lowers the crystal, reflecting to himself *could this be the woman I've seen in my visions? Like in the visions, her skin is dark, but not as dark as a Formorri. Her clothing and gold adornments indicate she is a woman of high importance.* Aesres lifts the viewing crystal to his eyes one last time to watch this woman. She is still there and still gazing up at us.

"Aesres is handing the crystal back to Cairpre, then for some reason, Aesres wiggles the wings of the eitilte before sending it into a deep dive. We are now soaring back across the waters toward Aletea. I can sense Aesres wondering to himself why he did that."

With these last words, Laragh's glazed look disappears. Shaking her head as if to clear it, she says, "That was remarkable. Aislinn, I envy the time you have spent with the Danann. I can't wait for us to see the eitilte tomorrow from the ground."

Just then, the horns sound, calling all who are to attend the council to come. We look at each other, smooth our garments, and proceed towards the council chambers.

We are among the last to arrive. King Ailill is in the center of the chambers in an elevated position on furs near the central fire. To his left are the druis of Rathcroghan as well as druis from many of the outlying villages within the sphere of King Ailill's rule. To his right sits his son, Ruairi, and King Ailill's high advisor, both of whom have recently arrived after their winter stay in Tomregan. As we enter, King Ailill greets us and Ruairi nods his acknowledgement. "Please sit here next to Ruairi. We are sad to have you leave tomorrow, but we know you must. Important times are ahead and by hearing counsel from you and from all who are here, I hope to make the best decision possible."

Ruairi begins. "Your father and friends send their greetings as they anxiously await your return home. I learned much while in Tomregan and am prepared to give my father counsel."

As we settle into place, we thank Ruairi for his kind words and convey that we, too, are most anxious to return home.

King Ailill begins to speak to those gathered around. "Tonight is a special occasion. My eldest son, Ruairi, has returned from his winter's stay at Tomregan. He learned much from Fearghus, the father of Keelen, Flann, and Laragh. We've had the pleasure of having these three with us during Ruairi's absence, but I know Fearghus yearns for the return of his children, just as I did the return of my son.

"We come here tonight, not just to honor the return of my son and my high advisor, nor to say goodbye to the children of Fearghus, but also to discuss one more time the impending coming of the people of Danu. As the nearest king to where they are expected to arrive, I need to be prepared for all possibilities and consequences. We listened to the words of the children of Fearghus, and of my own granddaughter, Queen Sianna. Ruairi and my high advisor listened to the words of Fearghus and the other drui of Tomregan. They tell us the Danann are a broken people whose homeland is being destroyed by their god and that they come in peace. They tell us that the Danann are returning to their original homeland from long ago.

"Although broken in spirit and few in number, they are still proud and have much power. I have been counseled that this power will be used for the good of the people of Inis Elga, but I must confess this strength concerns me. Their intentions may be pure regarding coming in friendship, but once here, perhaps they will decide conquering this land and becoming our masters is preferred, rather than simply becoming our friends. Let us talk further."

With this, the king's high advisor speaks. "Ruairi and I spent the long winter in Tomregan to learn what we could in order to bring wise counsel. Both Ruairi and I are inclined to believe these people of Danu come in peace. Ruairi will speak for himself, but I, like you, King Ailill, confess concern. They have significant strength. Should they decide to become masters, we would have difficulty resisting them."

The other drui of Rathcroghan and the outlying settlements are mixed in their opinion. Many say they look to Tomregan for guidance and the druis of Tomregan advise to greet the Danann with open arms. Others agree with the high advisor. The discussions go late into the night. A notion is emerging that perhaps some power could be conjured to keep the Danann from landing near them. Perhaps, it's suggested, they could be forced to land further east.

The high advisor commands everyone's attention again. "There is one way we may be able to prevent the people of Danu from landing nearby. With all the drui who are present, we could conjure a mighty fog that covers this entire area for days. The Danann would not be able to find where to land their craft and would need to go elsewhere." The other drui react primarily in support of this concept, though a few remain opposed. I glance toward Flann and Laragh who appear as alarmed as I am at these words.

I rise and say, "The White Horse of Binn counseled that we should welcome the people of Danu as friends. We of Inis Elga will prosper with their presence. I can understand fear regarding the arrival of new people, but remember the counsel given by Tomregan and the encouragement to welcome them."

King Ailill rises and everyone grows silent. "I heard much tonight and am gratified to know different strategies can be taken. I am uncertain yet as to what my decision will be, but for now, nothing more can be said. Let us retire for the night and wish our young guests a safe journey tomorrow."

The gathering quickly disperses. My brother, sister, and I return to our sleeping quarters with much to ponder regarding this concept of a great, blocking fog. As nervous as this makes us, we still must sleep in order to leave early in the morning. We want to be on the esker near Lough Aillionn when the Danann eitilte appears. We are also anxious to return home with this news.

* * *

We all awake just before dawn. After eating food we had set aside, we leave the roundhouse and proceed toward the esker leading to Lough Aillionn. Only the sentinels are awake, and they acknowledge our departure. The bearded star lights the path from the west, and the rising sun is beginning to break over the horizon to the east. We speak little as we hasten along.

Despite knowing the eitilte should appear, we still feel compelled to hurry. By mid-morning, Lough Aillionn is near. Laragh says, "This appears to be the terrain I observed through the viewing crystal with Aesres when we were spotted on the esker."

We stop to peer into the sky and before long see a speck coming towards us at high speed. It becomes increasingly large and soon is directly overhead. It is like observing a lolair gliding across the sky, heading towards its prey. The eitilte disappears to the south as quickly as it arrived, but the thrill of seeing it is overwhelming. The stories and visions we have known and seen for so long are actually about to happen. We gaze at each other in excitement, but quickly return to the esker taking us to Tomregan.

CHAPTER SIXTEEN

THE FOG

The sky is darkening, but we know Tomregan is close. The ridge lying ahead should be the one immediately above our village. Approaching the crest, we perceive someone being roused by the sounds of our coming. As we grow closer, we see it is Ultan, Flann's good friend. "Hello!" he cries. "We thought you might arrive today and I couldn't wait to see the three of you. Your father is most anxious to receive you. I will run ahead and advise him of your arrival." Ultan departs as the three of us continue toward the village. Soon, Tomregan is visible and Father moves toward us.

Father embraces us, smiling broadly. Our winter stay in Rathcroghan was the longest we've ever been away from Tomregan. After allowing us a short time to acknowledge our friends, Father beckons us to follow him to our roundhouse.

"I'm sure you are hungry and tired. I suspect you pushed yourself to make it a one-day journey. Food and drink are coming, and you can warm yourselves by the fire. Make yourselves comfortable and tell me the highlights of your trip."

I briefly describe our journey to Sligeach and the visit with Queen

Sianna while Flann and Laragh relieve their hunger. Then I describe our travels from Sligeach to Rathcroghan, including our side trip along Lough Aillionn and the encampment we found.

Flann picks up the story about our winter's stay with King Ailill while I appease my hunger.

Flann passes the story back to me to speak about my spirit-visit with Aislinn.

Laragh finishes by describing her spirit-visit with Aesres and the final council with King Ailill. She includes in her descriptions the suggestions from King Ailill's advisors to conjure a fog to block visibility of the local terrain and thus force the Danann to land somewhere else.

Father listens without interrupting. When Laragh finishes he says, "You are tired and there is much we need to discuss in greater detail. Rest and we will talk again tomorrow."

Father leaves our roundhouse, proceeding to the teaching center where the other village elders wait anxiously for his update regarding our journey.

I am weary. After consuming a few more morsels I curl up on the sleeping skins and fall fast asleep.

* * *

Morning comes with a thick, gloomy fog shrouding the village. Being the first to wake, I peer about, thinking to myself, *Has King Ailill made his final decision regarding the people of Danu, and is he now trying to block their landing? His son and companions will have reported their sighting of the eitilte by now. Maybe that sighting triggered his decision.*

Father enters our bedchamber. After saying good morning, he says, "Perhaps King Ailill indeed followed the words of his high advisor. This fog does not seem natural. I woke early and climbed high on the ridge to be above the fog. I could find no break in any direction.

"The horns will soon sound, calling all the elders for council. Join us then in the council chamber and we will assess the situation."

Once Father leaves, we unpack our traveling satchels, and change into clean clothing. While working, we talk among ourselves about the thick fog. Has King Ailill decided his own fears regarding the Danann are greater than the assurances received from the White Horse of Binn? What can we in Tomregan do? We are still chatting when the horns sound, summoning us.

The council chambers are located near the center of our rath. We arrive first and start to sit in our usual positions to the side in order to allow the elders the more prominent positions, however Father enters the chambers at nearly the same moment and motions us forward to sit next to him. The elders and villagers of Tomregan soon fill the council chambers and Father rises to address them.

"My fellow villagers," he begins, "as you heard, my children have arrived safely from their long journey to Sligeach and a winter's stay in Rathcroghan. My heart is lifted to know they are here again. They not only bring me and their friends joy with their presence, but they also bring news regarding what they have seen and learned during their journey.

"You have all seen the dense fog enveloping our village. After listening to what my children told me last night, I fear this is no ordinary fog. Let us hear from them what they have learned and seen during their journey. Keelen, if I may impose on you to begin."

I recount our journey to Sligeach and how Sianna's high advisor, Trista, met us on the esker just before it entered Sligeach. I tell of our meeting with Sianna and how she had dreams similar to Laragh's concerning the people of Danu.

"Sianna is in agreement about how we should greet the Danann," I say, "but we need to be wary of Trista." I finish my description of our trip to Sligeach and then to Rathcroghan by describing how Sianna had decided to journey with us and what we encountered along the shores of Lough Aillionn.

"Queen Sianna was sure one of the men watching the shoreline was the son of King Ailill?" asks Father. I reply that she was most certain he was her uncle, Eoghan.

"I know this spot you refer to along the lough. This place commands a view of much of the eastern shoreline and little could happen along the shoreline without being seen," says Father.

Flann continues the story. "Our time in Rathcroghan was marked by a feeling that something was afoot, but nothing was obvious. Laragh caught glimpses of dark-skinned warriors in her visions, but they were murky images.

"At the final council with King Ailill, much concern was expressed about the coming of the people of Danu. It was even suggested by King Ailill's high advisor that a fog be conjured to cover this part of Inis Elga with the hope the people of Danu would go to another part of the land."

Much discussion follows about what Flann and I have relayed. Father describes how he went up the ridge earlier in the day to determine if the fog was widespread and confirmed for himself its extensive coverage. The discussion focuses on what can be done about the fog and how it would be difficult to counter a spell conjured by what is likely many drui from both King Ailill's court and the villages near Rathcroghan.

Sadness overwhelms me as I reflect on the difficulties being faced by Aislinn and the Danann. Although there is alarm, no one seems angry with King Ailill. To them, King Ailill's actions are understandable, though unwanted, reactions to uncertainty.

Father rises to speak. "To prevent the people of Danu from arriving near here as prophesied, the fog would need to cover an extensive area. This is a difficult spell to conjure, even by the best of drui, and much effort is needed to maintain the effect. From the stories of the White Horse of Binn and Laragh's visions, the people of Danu will be arriving in their flying craft on the eastern shores of Lough Aillionn in two or three days.

"If we travel to Lough Aillionn, we Tomregan drui could focus a counterspell, burning a hole through the layer of fog immediately above the lough. Hopefully, the Danann will be able to locate this clearing and land. Laragh, last night you mentioned your spirit was transported into the body of one of the leaders of the people of Danu, the one known as Aesres? Please, tell us all about this experience."

"It was the morning of our last full day in Rathcroghan," Laragh begins. "Keelen had just returned from a trance where she was visiting the spirit of the Danann girl, Aislinn. Through her dream, we learned the Danann are nearly ready to depart. We were preparing for the council session when abruptly I sensed being within the spirit and body of Aesres. He was unaware of my presence and was about to leave in an eitilte with Cairpre, the son of the Danann king, on a reconnaissance mission."

"Do you think you could return and be with the spirit of Aesres again if you wanted?" Father asks. "Do you think you might even be able to make him aware of your presence and be able to correspond with him like Keelen does with Aislinn?"

I see Laragh pondering this question. She is inexperienced with this skill and replies, "I did not initiate my visit with Aesres; it just happened. But, now that it has occurred once, perhaps I can instigate such a visit again."

Discussions continue among the elders. A few voice concerns that the drui of Inis Elga should not go against one another, but most believe the drui of Tomregan should help the Danann.

It is noted by some that prophecies and visions are never wholly correct, but rather illustrate what is likely to happen given current conditions and prevailing attitudes. Now that King Ailill has created this fog, perhaps the conditions and attitudes have changed enough to where the coming of the people of Danu may be imperiled.

Agreement is reached to fulfill the wishes of the Horse of Binn and assist the people of Danu. It is decided the best course of action is to travel to Lough Aillionn and create a hole in the fog above the prophesized arrival area. Laragh, Flann, and I will accompany the band of drui travelling to Lough Aillionn. We hope Laragh can again travel to the body of Aesres and somehow communicate with him regarding the break in the fog we intend to create. I am going to potentially convey this same information to Aislinn. Flann will assist with the creation of the counterspell.

We intend to camp at the same location used by King Ailill's son, Eoghan, and his companions. The site is an ideal location across the lough from the anticipated area of arrival. Eoghan and his companions likely returned to Rathcroghan after sighting the eitilte and hopefully have not come back.

The journey to this area is a hard day's travel and the fog will not make the trip easy. Father and the other elders cannot travel as quickly as Laragh, Flann, and I.

The three of us are to push ahead quickly to ensure the camp is unoccupied. If not, Father says we will need to establish ourselves elsewhere. However, the three of us reason, it all depends on how many are there. If only one or two people are there, our thought is to subdue and restrain them, thus ensuring they cannot return to Rathcroghan to alert King Ailill.

We turn to bid Father and the others farewell and assure them we will meet along the trail tomorrow with our report. Father's face holds an expression of concern as he bids us farewell. As we proceed up the esker toward the ridge overlooking Tomregan I sense Father's voice as he tells me, "Your plan is a good one. If you think you can accomplish it without endangering yourselves, do so. It is best King Ailill is not aware of our actions until after the arrival of the people of Danu."

CHAPTER SEVENTEEN

LOUGH AILLIONN

The fog makes our travels toward Lough Aillionn difficult, but we are more than halfway there before dark. Settling in for the night, we talk among ourselves regarding what we will find tomorrow. With an early start, we should reach the site before midday. I am certain King Ailill has the camp occupied. If there are people there, the thick fog will work to our advantage.

We wake early. It has been two days since we spotted the eitilte carrying Aesres on his reconnaissance over Lough Aillionn. In my sleep, I had visited Aislinn, but this time my stay was different. Excited, I tell Flann and Laragh about my dream as we prepare food.

In this dream, instead of my spirit sharing her body and the two of us being able to communicate as we could during my previous visits, I float above Aislinn, surveying all that is happening about her.

Displayed before me across a vast field is frenetic activity of people moving hurriedly to the different eitiltes spread across the field. The fleet forms a diamond, and within the overall diamond are smaller groups of eitilte, also forming diamonds. Each smaller diamond holds four eitilte. The larger diamond is composed of thirteen of these smaller diamonds, arranged in rows of first one diamond, then three diamonds in the next row, five diamonds in the third, then the fourth row goes back to three diamonds, and the last one is a single diamond again. A smaller, single eitilte is in the front of the large diamond by itself.

The Danann are boarding the eitiltes. From my count, each eitilte includes about thirteen Danann. The master diamond formation includes fifty-two eitiltes, meaning nearly 3,000 Danann are journeying to Inis Elga. Aislinn is near the smaller eitilte at the front of the formation. With her are her brother, Cairpre, her uncle, Aesres, and her father, King Nuada. They are surveying the activity, ensuring each of the eitiltes is filled with passengers and aracos. The eitilte at the tail of the last diamond is being loaded with cargo that's being treated with extreme care.

As the final eitilte is filled, Nuada clasps Aesres on the shoulder, then proceeds at a run toward this last eitilte. Aesres watches his brother's progress while Aislinn and Cairpre board the smaller front eitilte. Once Nuada boards the eitilte, Aesres gives one last sweeping glance across the fleet, then enters his craft and sits in the araco position. He releases the lever adjusting the crystal over the geal leacht, and soon his craft lifts high into the sky.

As Aesres' eitilte rises, each succeeding row in the diamond formation also begins to elevate. Once all the craft are high in the air and level, Aesres banks his eitilte into a soaring dive. The fleet, like a flock of birds, follow with their own soaring dives, one row after the other. The people of Danu are on their way to Inis Elga.

I remained floating over the land of Aletea, observing the fleet depart in their wavelike motions of diving and soaring, then diving and soaring once again. On the meadow where the eitiltes once lay, I spot a herd of horses. They flick their heads toward the departing eitiltes, then the lead stallion, which I recognize as Capall, rises on his hind legs, whinnies loudly, and gallops off, the herd following.

The land of Aletea appears bleak and empty. I note the ruins of the once proud city of Fáilas and, nearby, the tottering standing stones of the circle that formerly surrounded the Lia Fáil. The Lia Fáil is heading toward Inis Elga with the remnants of the once mighty people of Danu. The bearded star hangs low and large over the western horizon. Fiery tears still stream from its face, striking the land of Aletea. A massive, blazing burst of light suddenly erupts from the star, coursing towards me before slamming into the ground. An immense plume of debris and dust rise, then I can perceive no more than the ocean, covered with debris.

Laragh and Flann listen intently. As I finish, we know we must hurry toward the encampment. Laragh estimates Aletea is a little over a day's journey by eitilte from Inis Elga. The people of Danu will likely reach the shores of Inis Elga by midday tomorrow. We will need to act quickly to secure the area and prepare to create the counterspell.

Before restarting our journey, Laragh opens her travel satchel and removes a vial and three pieces of cloth that have each been stitched onto a section of leather. Side straps have been sewn on the leather. "These are used to apply the sleeping potion from the vial to the faces of those we want to subdue," Laragh tells us. I remember Laragh saying she had an idea about how to subdue anyone. I am impressed by her creativity.

She hands us the applicators and demonstrates how one strap fits over our thumbs with our hand slipping in under the other strap. She says, "Once the potion is applied to the cloth, you close your hand to keep it from evaporating. When you want to subdue someone, you open your hand and place the cloth over their nose and mouth. Almost immediately, they will collapse into a deep sleep. When we near the camp, we will slip these on and I will apply the potion."

Laragh gathers her satchel and we commence our journey again in deep fog. The esker snakes down the hillside toward the lough and by late morning we come to its southern shoreline. After fording the Sinann, we follow the shoreline until coming to the split in the esker where the path to the south leads to Rathcroghan, and the other path travels along the shoreline leading north towards the camp. We travel in silence and walk lightly to minimize all sound.

We proceed single file, keeping about ten steps between us. The spacing is in the event the lead person should stumble across a sentry. If that happens, only the first in line will be discovered. Secrecy is of utmost importance. Fortunately, no sentries are encountered as we near the rise where the camp is located. Listening closely, nothing is heard.

Our plan to subdue those we find will only work if there are no more than three people. If more, we will need to retreat and select a different site.

Laragh draws from her satchel the vial containing the sleeping potion as well as the three cloth and leather applicators. Securing an applicator to our hands, Laragh applies the potion. We close our gloved hands and noiselessly move up the esker.

As we proceed, the muted glow of a campfire filters through the fog. In front of me, Flann comes to a stop, listening for voices and to determine if there is any stirring. A nod from him tells me he doesn't hear or see any movement. Progressing slowly and peering about to ensure we miss nothing, the fire glow brightens before us. I catch the muffled sound of voices. All of us freeze in our steps as we try to determine how many men are there and what they are doing. Uncertain, Flann creeps closer with Laragh and I follow close behind.

Two men sit by the fire, idly chatting while preparing their morning meal. They do not seem concerned about the possibility of intruders. Sgians are strapped to their thighs and staffs lay near their feet.

Flann approaches the one on my right from behind. I circle behind the one to my left. Laragh remains motionless, keeping watch for anything unexpected. Once in place, I signal my readiness to Flann. He nods and we both rush our targets. My applicator is soon wrapped around my quarry's nose and mouth. His struggle is minimal, and he collapses at my feet. A cry comes from the man

Flann is attacking. He must have spotted Flann's approach. But he, too, soon succumbs to the sleeping potion and crumples to the ground. Laragh remains in the shadows of the fog while Flann and I secure our two captives.

Behind Flann a man rushes toward him from out of the fog, swinging his staff and shrieking a blood-curdling battle cry. Flann avoids the initial lunge. He spots a staff lying on the ground near the man he subdued and seizes it, warding off repeated blows from the attacker. I see another staff near the man I subdued, secure it, and position myself to assist Flann. Meanwhile, Laragh goes unnoticed. She slips behind the attacker, and as he backs off from one of his lunges, she moves forward and wraps the sleeping potion cloth across his face. He quickly joins his companions in sleep.

All three of King Ailill's men are secured. Laragh gives each another smell of the sleeping potion. "This second treatment should keep them asleep until Father and the other drui arrive," she says.

We partake in some of the food our prisoners had been preparing and deliberate our next moves. The Danann may be arriving as soon as tomorrow and we need to complete our preparations before attempting to create the hole in the fog. We decide I will go back to Father's group immediately and inform them the area is secure. Flann and Laragh will stay with King Ailill's men.

It only takes an hour or two before I find Father and the other elders. I inform them the camp is secure and we have three captives. Father is relieved. Within a few hours, our party reaches the campsite. Father approaches the prisoners, who have awakened, and assures them they will not be harmed. He explains we come from Tomregan with the intention of helping the people of Danu by creating a clearing in the fog. The men voice their objections, saying the will of King Ailill should not be ignored. Father again assures them they will not be harmed, telling them that after the Danann land and appear safe, they will be released to return and report matters to King Ailill.

I recount my dream and voice how it is likely the people of Danu will soon approach Inis Elga and confront the bank of fog. Father and the elders discuss how best to employ the counterspell against the shroud of fog.

Father turns to Laragh and me, asking if we could attempt to contact Aislinn and Aesres. We nod acknowledgement and initiate the process by sitting comfortably on the ground, focusing on the fire, and allowing our minds to drift. I am having no success contacting Aislinn but, as with my dream last night, I find myself floating above the fleet of eitiltes, peering down at them.

I tell the others, "The eitiltes are hovering close to the high slieve near the west coastline of Inis Elga. The sky is darkening, and the fleet appears to be pausing for the night. Looking toward where I believe Lough Aillionn should be, I see a thick fog blanketing the land."

My ability to hold this vision is brief. Laragh has been unable to contact Aesres. Night is upon us and with the dense fog, it becomes even darker than usual. Father counsels us to sleep, and suggests the drui rise early to begin conjuring the hole in the fog. By morning, perhaps Laragh and I can make contact with the Danann and guide them to the hole.

* * *

The dim light of morning finds Father gathering the Tomregan drui together to begin the process of conjuring an opening in the fog. He instructs the elders to place themselves in a comfortable sitting position and begin meditating. In the meditation, they are to imagine bright sunshine reflecting off the waters of Lough Aillionn.

I attempt to contact Aislinn or at least hover above the Danann as I did yesterday. Looking toward Laragh, I see she is in a trance. Hopefully, she is having better luck. Soon, Laragh begins talking, saying she is able to coexist within the spirit of Aesres. Aesres is unaware of her presence, but Laragh describes how Aesres is in the scouting eitilte, trying to find an opening in the fog. He is frustrated because he can find no gap. Taking bearings from the high slieve where the fleet of eitiltes waits for his return, he knows approximately where the lough and red slieves should be. However, without a break in the fog, landing the fleet will be impossible.

Father instructs Laragh to try to make mental contact. Laragh does not answer for a period but then says yes, contact is established. Aesres was startled to feel her presence and she needed to explain to him who she is and why she is there.

Laragh tells us he felt this was trickery, but she has assured him she comes as a friend to help and he has accepted this truth.

Father informs Laragh the counterspell is working, and she is to tell Aesres to search for a hole in the fog. Laragh says Aesres is putting his eitilte into a dive down into the hole towards the waters of Lough Aillionn.

With the spell broken, Father and the other elders regain full consciousness. Bright sunshine glistens across their faces and they hear Laragh say, "Look into the sky toward the slieves of red. You will spot the eitilte Aesres is commanding."

Father looks up. "There," he says. "Just to the north." He points at a speck in the sky that's moving swiftly and growing larger.

Aesres is bearing toward us. Soon a rush of wind strikes our faces and a gasp of excitement erupts from all who are there. Aesres has seen the smoke of our fire and brought his eitilte close to the ground. The eitilte is now gaining altitude and returning to the fleet. Laragh tells us Aesres is overwhelmed with excitement at finding this break in the fog. The arrival of the people of Danu is finally at hand!

CHAPTER EIGHTEEN

THE ARRIVAL

Aesres allows Laragh to stay with him as he begins his journey back to the main fleet. I can channel all that Laragh is hearing, but not what she is seeing. Aesres feels energized with anticipation as the path now appears clear for his people to make their landing in Inis Elga. Elation overwhelmed him when he found the hole in the fog and swooped down over the landing site.

Earlier, finding the thick fog was perplexing. The visions and prophesies had told his people they would be welcomed in this new land. The attempt to prevent their landing, however, made it apparent not all the people of Inis Elga welcome the Danann. He and his brother must come to know who created this fog and why they tried to prevent their landing. They must also seek council and assistance from the people who helped them.

Having another entity occupy his body is discomforting. Aesres believes he has found a way to create a mental wall between himself and Laragh so he can maintain some privacy of thought. Laragh now is still able to sense his emotions, look upon all that occurs through his eyes, and still talk with Aesres, though she is no longer able to read his thoughts.

Aesres asks Laragh who is present in the camp. She responds, saying it includes her father, Fearghus, and the leading elders from the village of Tomregan as well as her brother and sister. Laragh tells Aesres Tomregan is the leading learning center of Inis Elga. It is at Tomregan where the stone circle honoring Cenn, the soul twin of his own goddess, Danu, stands.

"No one else is there?" asks Aesres.

"No one else," answers Laragh. She senses in Aesres both an uneasiness and sadness with this reply.

The return trip to the fleet does not take long. Laragh describes Aesres soaring over the mass of hovering eitiltes and rocking his wings to display success. He directs his eitilte toward the last craft in the formation, which holds his brother. As he approaches, Aesres dips his eitilte's tail to reduce speed, then skillfully maneuvers into a hovering position above his brother's craft. Lifting the crystals, he lowers his eitilte.

Aesres positions his eitilte to where the front of his craft touches the front of King Nuada's eitilte. Immediately, Aesres tells Nuada he is accompanied by the spirit of another who helped resolve the problem with the fog. Nuada stares intently at Aesres saying, "Is this the same spirit who visited Aislinn? A girl native to Inis Elga?" Laragh tells Aesres she is the sister of the girl who visited Aislinn, which Aesres conveys to his brother.

Nuada is updated on the reconnaissance flight, including the creation of the hole in the fog. He asks his brother if he knew why the fog appeared. Aesres conveys what Laragh has related.

There are additional discussions regarding the logistics of the final approach to the landing site, after which Aesres bids his brother farewell, lowers the crystal over the geal leacht, lifts to a proper height for a short soar, then returns to the front of the fleet. When in position, he again rises to soaring height with the rest of the fleet following his lead one row at a time. Upon reaching soaring height, he lowers the nose of his eitilte and begins the soaring process back toward the opening in the fog.

Excitement within our camp escalates with the news from Laragh that the fleet is now on its way. Everyone, including the prisoners who were unbound on their word that they would not leave until given permission, keeps watch over the lough and the shoreline on the other side. By late afternoon, Laragh announces the fleet is hovering at the edge of the opening. Aesres wishes to conduct one final sweep before signaling the fleet to make its approach.

She advises us to survey the northwest corner of the fog opening for the first sight of Aesres' eitilte. Everyone is straining to catch a glimpse. Then, one of the prisoners points excitedly to a speck in the sky that's growing increasingly larger. Aesres is making a pass, turning and flying over the landing area, then lifting upward to the fleet.

I sense Aislinn's presence in the eitilte as it streaks by. We watch with anticipation as the eitilte becomes a speck high in the sky. After a short while, we all spot the shape of a huge, dark diamond floating into view: the Danann fleet. As the fleet descends over the lough, the front tip of the diamond bends downward, with the rest of the fleet rippling after, like water over a cliff.

It is an impressive, almost frightening, sight. The massive diamond of Danann eitiltes are following Aesres toward the landing area. The diamond formation moves as one until the entire fleet is hovering over the landing plain. Moving from this formation are two individual eitiltes. The smaller holds Aesres and his party; the larger carries King Nuada and the sacred treasures. They rise over the formation, center themselves side-by-side above the fleet, then begin descending straight down. As these two eitiltes descend, the entire fleet follows. Soon, all the eitiltes are settled on the ground.

From our campsite, we can only see a bustling of activity on the far shore. We rely on the information provided by Laragh as she watches the unfolding scene through Aesres' eyes.

Though night is near, the prisoners inquire if they are free to leave so they can return to Rathcroghan and report to King Ailill the wondrous sight they witnessed. Fearghus grants their request, directing the prisoners to inform King Ailill the Danann have landed with Tomregan assistance. He says to tell King Ailill no rash actions should be taken, especially considering the size of the contingent of Danann who are establishing camp. Father adds that he hopes to meet with the Danann soon and will send word to King Ailill regarding the meeting. The prisoners agree to carry this message and are soon on their way.

Laragh describes the activities of the Danann.

The passengers from each eitilte are quickly unloading the goods they carry. From some come stacks of cloth and clothing. From others, containers of food and drink, from still others ingots of metal and tools for metalworking. The eitiltes near the outside of the diamond primarily contain weapons. Bundles of swords, shields, and spears are brought out and arranged on the ground for quick access. With the unloading of these weapons, the Danann are quickly creating an armed guard around their new camp.

Aesres and King Nuada oversee the activity. The eitilte carrying King Nuada is not unpacked until all the outer eitiltes with their weapons are unloaded and the perimeter secured.

A splendid tent, adorned with spiral symbols in deep red and dark blue, and edged in gold, is erected near Nuada's eitilte. Laragh conveys she is viewing the same scene she envisioned last Samhain during the visit to the White Horse of Binn.

Once the outer perimeter is fully secured, King Nuada and Aesres enter Nuada's eitilte and begin carefully removing its special cargo.

Laragh says she sees Aesres reaching down for a large, flat stone. His brother helps him lift and carry it into the tent, gently resting it near the tent's center. From visions given by the White Horse, she tells us she knows this is the Lia Fáil.

She says Aesres now returns to the eitilte. When inside, he reaches for a long box and takes it into the tent, laying it to the right side of the Lia Fáil. Opening the box, he retrieves a leather sheath with gold engravings. From the sheath, he draws a bright blade and examines it. Laragh says she feels the pride Aesres has for this blade as he puts it back into the sheath and returns it to its box.

"I recognize it," she says. "It's the Claíomh Solai.

"I see Aesres now watching Nuada enter the tent with another long box, which he lays on the other side of the Lia Fáil. Aesres is opening this box as well, retrieving another leather sheath with gold engravings. He is pulling from the sheath a long spear and examining it. It must be the spear, Lúin. This, too, he returns to its box.

"This leaves only the Caldron of Wisdom as the final sacred object missing from the tent," Laragh says.

"Aesres is now looking up after replacing the spear, Lúin, in its box. There is a noise near the front of the tent. It is his brother, carrying in this last treasure.

Laragh tells us Aesres and Nuada return to the eitilte one last time. Aesres retrieves a large bundle of bent hazel wicker and Nuada follows with what appears to be a folded piece of soft leather, which, judging from its size, is comprised of several hides stitched together. These items are also brought into the tent. They are laid out on an open area and arranged in a manner indicating these pieces somehow go together to make something.

Armed sentries are stationed at both the entrance to the tent as well as inside, near the objects. King Nuada and Aesres are taking no chances with these four sacred treasures.

Laragh perceives satisfaction from Aesres with the landing and the securing of the four treasures. She then senses from Aesres a desire to now give thanks for their safe arrival into the land of Inis Elga and to honor their goddess, Danu, along with her twin soul, Cenn, the god of Inis Elga.

Their homeland of Aletea is gone and they find themselves along the same shores their ancestors left so long ago. The day is Beltane eve and dusk is falling. Aesres directs all the bags of geal leacht be taken and brought to the opening of a cavern near where the tent holding the four sacred objects stands. Soon, a mound of geal leacht bags stands high.

Aesres directs all the eitiltes be put in piles at four positions: one to the north, one to the south, one to the east, and one to the west. A Beltane fire is kindled at each of these sacred points and into these fires are fed the flying craft. A massive circle of light radiates around the camp as the people of Danu offer as sacrifice their flying craft in thanks to Danu for delivering them safely from their previous home and to Cenn for guiding them and welcoming them to this new one. Laragh perceives a profound sadness sweeping over Aesres as he surveys the four burning stacks of eitiltes. Aesres reflects that all is now abandoned from his previous life, save the sacred treasures.

King Nuada completes the sacrificial ceremony by slashing open the bags of geal leacht. The silvery liquid pours from each bag, the bright silver streams reflect the light from the Beltane fires as the geal leacht snakes to the cavern opening. The cavern swallows each drop until no more can be seen.

Aesres surveys the activity from his position near the tent. The fires brightly light the sky and all about him he can see everyone is busy eating or preparing bedding for sleep. This has been an eventful, long trip for the Danann and an even longer day for Aesres. Fatigue is overtaking him, and he thinks it best to prepare for sleep.

Laragh informs me that his gaze once more sweeps the darkness now enveloping the sky and the surrounding landscape. All appears to be well, but then Aesres catches a glint of what seems to be a reflection of the firelight on something at the edge of the darkness. He feels someone is watching.

Peering hard into the edge of darkness, he detects the figure of a person standing near a tree and another person crouching behind. Looking more closely, Aesres believes the standing figure is a woman, noting the reflection is from the fire shining on the gold torc she wears about her neck. Though hard to discern, Aesres recognizes this woman. He has been seeing her in his dreams and she is the same woman he saw from his hovering eitilte a few days earlier on the hilltop near the Formorri village to the north. Though a distance apart, he feels their eyes lock. Then, she bows his way and slips into the darkness along with her companion. Aesres stares at the spot where the woman had been for some time. Laragh can sense sadness again overtaking Aesres as his thoughts turn towards his deceased wife. He moves away and begins to prepare a place to sleep.

Laragh leaves Aesres and returns to her body. We sit on the edge of the hill, gazing across the lough. The fires from the burning eitiltes still blaze fiercely and reflect off the water. Laragh and I talk about the woman Aesres saw. We both believe it is Sianna. Looking into the sky, we see a diminished bearded star.

CHAPTER NINETEEN

THE FIRST MEETING

Long after everyone returns to their sleeping areas, Laragh, Flann, and I stay on the hillside, viewing the Beltane fires at the new Danann encampment. It is deep in the night, but each of us keeps talking, watching, and speculating as to what will happen next. It appears everything as we understand it has changed forever. The Danann are relatively few, but their experience, history, knowledge, and power are beyond anything anyone in Inis Elga possesses. No wonder King Ailill is fearful of having them so close to Rathcroghan. Perhaps if I were king, the same decision would be made.

Flann says he will go and retrieve the bedding we laid out earlier so we can stay and view the Beltane fires as we fall asleep. He soon returns, and we huddle together, making ourselves comfortable while maintaining a clear view of the fires.

The Danann keep the fires blazing throughout the night, and the flames reflect hypnotically on the waters of Lough Aillionn. I contemplate the legends that foretold when the people of Danu would leave Inis Elga to find the new land promised by the goddess

Danu. They left Inis Elga in curaughs from the shores of this same lough during another Beltane so many centuries ago. Now they have returned to the same spot during the same festival, but in flying craft and not simple curaughs.

I faintly notice someone calling my name. A familiar woman's voice. The sound is coming from the darkness along the esker, which is just below us. "Keelen, it is Etain and I. We come from watching the landing of the Danann." It is Queen Sianna's and her companion.

"Welcome," I say. "Flann, Laragh, and I are watching the Beltane fires of the Danann. We knew the two of you were there earlier tonight. Laragh's spirit was with the one known as Aesres and through his eyes she spotted you standing near the edge of the firelight."

A brief flash of concern crosses Sianna's eyes. "Yes, we were there. When the thick fog came two days ago, I thought it possessed unusual qualities. I asked my druis about the fog and they informed me it was conjured. We could think of no other reason for it but an attempt by my grandfather to try and prevent the people of Danu from arriving.

"There was nothing we in Sligeach could do to counteract the spell. The expected Danann landing site is not far from Sligeach, so I decided to come to the shores of Lough Aillionn to see if anything would happen. I knew if anyone had the power to counteract the spell, it would be the druis from Tomregan.

"Etain and I arrived along the northern edge of the lough as your spell opened the hole in the fog. We made our way along the esker on the east side of the lough toward the plain at the foot of the slieves of red where the Danann were expected to land. We noticed the single eitilte yesterday as we made our way down the esker. We hid so those in the eitilte would not detect us. We found a favorable vantage point near the edge of the landing area. The landing of the fleet was a remarkable sight, happening nearly on top of us. The eitiltes are as you described, Laragh, from your vision. They did indeed appear like soaring Iolairs, settling to earth as they landed."

We create a spot for Sianna and Etain.

Sleep finally overtakes me and I do not wake until the sun is fully up.

After a drink of water and clean-up in the lough, we all make our way to the camp. We find Father and the other elders deep in discussion. Father notes our arrival, saying, "I trust all of you finally had a good sleep. Queen Sianna and Etain, it is good to see you again. Laragh said she spotted you in her vision last night. I noticed you had arrived when I checked on my children this morning. I trust from your vantage point the arrival of the people of Danu was a spectacle."

"The event was overwhelming," replies Sianna. "The eitiltes were even more impressive than expected. We will need to ask why they burned them and what substance was in the bags they split open."

I know the substance was geal leacht, which was the source of power allowing the eitiltes to rise into the air, but decide to leave questions regarding the eitiltes and the geal leacht for another time. "Father, what do we do now with the Danann here and so near?" I ask.

Father explains he and the other elders had been discussing this specific point. It is their collective thought the next move is in the hands of the Danann.

As he speaks, I sense the presence of another within me. Aislinn is with me. She asks if I will allow her to directly address everyone present through my voice.

I consent and tell the others Aislinn of the Danann is with me and wishes to address them. She begins to speak. "My father, King Nuada, and my uncle, Aesres, want to thank the people of Tomregan for their help which allowed us to land at the spot designated by the goddess Danu. All went well with our arrival and we are nearly settled. We assembled a copy of an ancient watercraft we believe our ancestors used to leave Inis Elga long ago. We built the vessel while still in Aletea from sketches we found etched onto the bottom of the Lai' Fail and practiced sailing with it. The vessel is similar, though larger, to a craft used in Aletea. For the journey, it was disassembled, but we re-assembled it this morning. I, my brother, Cairpre, King Nuada, and Aesres are now outfitting it and are about to set sail to come see you."

Turning towards Sianna, Aislinn continues. "Aesres stated during his reconnaissance flight he saw a Formorri village. Are you of this village?"

Sianna replies she is the queen of this village and is also the granddaughter of King Ailill of Rathcroghan, the local king of this region.

Aislinn continues. "We look forward to meeting your grandfather as well. Our understanding is he may have ordered the fog that almost prevented us from landing. We must gain his confidence and trust if we are all to live together peacefully." With this final statement, I feel Aislinn's presence leave me.

Everyone glances at each other with excitement and anticipation. Their coming will be our first meeting with the Danann! Excitement grips me regarding finally meeting Aislinn and seeing the others whom I have already seen through Aislinn's eyes. The mutual sharing of our spirits and bodies gives us an unbreakable bond of friendship and understanding.

A messenger arrives, gasping for breath. We recognize him as one of King Ailill's men. He gains his composure to announce, "King Ailill and an entourage are in route from Rathcroghan. The scouts who had been your prisoners informed the king of the arrival of the Danann. Since the fog was not successful, King Ailill understands it is vital he come in person to meet with the Danann to assure them he holds no ill will towards them."

I notice the wry expression on my father's face. King Ailill understands he cannot afford to be seen as an enemy of the Danann. Fearghus tells the messenger, "Please, return to King Ailill's party and inform them the Danann king and his family are expected within a few hours." The messenger takes a long drink of water, bows towards Fearghus, and then is off at a run back down the esker. Fearghus turns to us all and says, "Let's prepare a proper welcoming area for the momentous occasion of a new, powerful people coming to our lands, not as invaders, but in peace."

Little can improve the humble surroundings, but we clear away an area where a meeting among royalty can transpire. A spot is prepared for Queen Sianna, another for King Ailill, a third for King Nuada and Aesres, and a fourth for Fearghus. Fearghus ensures his spot is on equal footing with the others.

While in the midst of our preparation, one of the elders calls out that he sees a craft on the lough heading our way. By its size and shape, the vessel appears to be a curaugh.

King Ailill and his entourage arrive. Father greets King Ailill and takes him to the hillside overlooking the lough to point out where the Danann encampment lies and to indicate the curaugh coming across the lough. Father says, "The curaugh holds the Danann delegation, including King Nuada, his brother Aesres, and his two children, Aislinn and Cairpre."

"That is good to hear," a voice exclaims behind them. "I know each of them well and Cairpre is my childhood friend."

We all turn to this voice. King Ailill says, "Please let me introduce Breas and his half-sister, Rayna. They are the children of the Formorri High King Elotha, and Breas's mother was the daughter of the High King of the Danann. Sianna, how good to discover you are here. Breas and Rayna are your cousins."

I peer first at the young man, then Sianna, to observe her reaction. She shows no emotion, but says, "I have heard of you, Breas. Your father was my uncle, whom I did not know well. Rayna, you will need to excuse my ignorance, but I do not know of you. What brings the two of you to Inis Elga at this particular time?"

Both Breas and Rayna appear to be about my age and about five Samhains younger than Sianna. Rayna is dark skinned and is likely full Formorri. Breas is more of a light chocolate color, similar to

Sianna.

I remember the story Aislinn related about when she was a child and came to the cities of Danu to be with her brother, Cairpre, and meeting Breas then.

Sianna speaks again. "Breas, you say you are a childhood friend of one of the Danann? Your mother was a Danann?"

A half smile crosses Breas's face, but he looks a little sad as well. Rayna glances towards Breas, then back to Sianna.

Rayna says, "Yes, Breas's mother, Fiona, was the daughter of the high king of Aletea. She, along with the high king's immediate family, died with the destruction of their main city last Samhain. Breas was living with my family in our homeland at the time of the destruction. We are half brother and sister. My mother was High King Elotha's youngest wife."

Breas adds, "I spent much time in my youth at my mother's home in Aletea. Cairpre was an apprentice, fostering in the family of High King Conall, and we became fast friends. I also met his sister, Aislinn, after she joined Cairpre as an apprentice. The three of us were high up on the Slieve of Danu thirteen Samhains ago when the fiery ball in the sky struck the southern lands of Aletea and destroyed them.

"I have not seen Cairpre or Aislinn for many years, but when I heard the stories of a small group of northern Danann who planned to use their eitiltes to make a final escape, I hoped they would be among them.

"We were on our way to see you, Sianna, but the dense fog kept us from arriving in Sligeach. We had to make landfall farther south, and Rathcroghan was the nearest village. We only arrived yesterday. When the messengers came early this morning with news of the Danann landing, we came immediately."

"They should be here soon," says Father to Breas and Rayna. "Look out over the lough in that direction. Can you spot the approaching curaugh? Let us proceed to the water's edge and greet them."

We gather as a group and follow the winding trail leading from our camp to the water's edge.

The curaugh makes good progress across the waters and is soon near shore. I see King Nuada's and Aesres's faces and deduce they are surveying the surroundings and examining each of us along the shoreline. They both appear satisfied all is well, then we catch a shout from the curaugh. "Breas, is that really you? What a wonderful surprise!" It is Cairpre, leaning out over the edge of the curaugh to get a better look. Breas smiles and waves toward Cairpre in greeting.

The curaugh touches the shoreline and Cairpre leaps from the craft. He and Breas tightly embrace. Fearghus greets the others as they disembark and introduces them first to King Ailill, then to Queen Sianna.

Looking toward Aesres, I sense uneasiness. The last time we nearly had mind contact was in Aletea when I was with Aislinn. At the time, our near-mind engagement was quickly prevented by my leaving Aislinn's consciousness. The gods seemed to prevent our minds meeting at that time. Is it time now?

I concentrate on Aesres and soon I am with him. He does not sense my presence, as his mind appears pre-occupied. I see in his thoughts that as the curaugh approached the shoreline, he spotted Sianna and immediately recognized her as the woman who had been appearing in his dreams and the one he had seen in the shadows the night before. He feels excitement as well as guilt. He now is contemplating his dreams, especially the dream when his wife, Teagan, told him this woman would play an important part in his future.

A feeling of guilt and embarrassment comes over me. I should no longer access the minds of Aesres, or for that matter Aislinn or any of the Danann without their permission. I immediately leave Aesres' consciousness.

Sianna and Aesres exchange formal greetings but both exhibit reserve, as they appear to be appraising each other. Aislinn finishes her formal introductions. We recognize each other immediately. She dashes over to me and we embrace warmly. Though I know Aislinn through my mind visits, I am delighted to meet her in person.

Spirits are high as we move up the hill to the camp. Fearghus shows where everyone should arrange themselves and mead is served for refreshment. Though he is not a king, Fearghus leads and coordinates this first meeting between the peoples of Inis Elga and the Danann. The peace and future prosperity of the land depend on these interactions. He lifts a cup of mead into the air, toasting, "Welcome to our homeland. We of Tomregan will do all in our power to make your arrival a peaceful one and our future relationships fruitful."

All present raise their cups as well and soon drain their contents. The talk among us at first centers on questions to the Danann regarding their homeland, its last days, and their trip to Inis Elga. Everyone is curious about the wondrous aircraft the Danann travelled in. How did they work and why were they all destroyed? It is not until later that the discussion turns to more formal topics and questions are asked about what the Danann wish to do. As these conversations take place, I notice King Ailill, as well as Breas' sister, Rayna, are reserved. They participate in the conversations, but don't actively engage the Danann with direct questions.

CHAPTER TWENTY

DISCUSSIONS

King Nuada rises to address everyone. "Fearghus, King Ailill, and Queen Sianna, my people are grateful to be here among you. I can understand your concerns, King Ailill, with so many of us arriving within the lands you govern. However, I am heartened, despite your efforts to prevent our landing with the dense fog, by the fact you are now among the first to welcome us.

"Queen Sianna, the Formorri have long and prosperous trading relations with our people. Through you, we hope to continue those relationships. We are pleasantly surprised to find Breas here among you. We did not expect to ever see anyone from our past again. Fearghus, I cannot thank you, your children, and your companions from Tomregan enough for your assistance. We would not be here without the efforts from Tomregan. I feel I already know your daughter, Keelen, despite meeting her just now for the first time, as she was with my own daughter, Aislinn, when she found Aesres and I after our eitilte crashed. I am grateful for the friendship the two created and their sharing of knowledge.

"There is much to discuss, and many tough decisions to be made.

We come to Inis Elga in peace, needing to find a permanent home. Destroying our flying eitiltes was not only a sacrifice of thanks to our goddess Danu, but also a sign to all of you who live in Inis Elga that we have no intention of keeping a superior technology that could be construed as a possible weapon. Armaments we have, but only for defensive protection. Our people suffered the devastating loss of our homeland along with the loss of nearly all the Danann people. We are but a small remnant of what once was the mighty kingdom of Aletea. We bitterly weep over our loss, but fully understand the wrath felt by the goddess Danu over our actions and the reason for the destruction she inflicted. We are humbled and wish nothing more than to live in peace and give honor to Danu.

"As I see it, there are three issues to directly consider and hopefully settle. The first concerns the urgent needs of my people. Settling into a location quickly is critical, even if the spot is only temporary. We brought with us supplies that should last for a time, but there is a need to ensure supplies of food for the future. We brought seed from our homeland and hope to trade for horses and cattle.

"King Ailill, it appears the area where we landed is generally uninhabited. The ground is not ideal for raising crops, but we can plant and raise enough for our immediate needs. The terrain offers fine grazing land with nearby forests of oak for gathering acorns when Samhain season comes, and the lough has fish. Your kingdom is the nearest to this land. Does our staying at this location, at least until we all settle on a permanent home, meet with your approval?"

All eyes turn toward King Ailill. The drui of King Ailill's court sit near him, but he does not beckon for their advice. He shifts his weight slightly as he composes his response in his mind. There is silence for several moments, then King Ailill rises to address King Nuada. "Your plan is sound, King Nuada. You are correct, I did not want you to land so near to Rathcroghan, despite the counsel of those from Tomregan." He nods toward Fearghus. "You are a people with a proud and mighty history, perhaps the mightiest the world has ever seen. I feared such a people would want to rule and would not be satisfied with just living in peace among us. Only time will tell if this is the case, but I find what you say encouraging.

"Yes, you and your people are welcome to stay along the shores of Lough Aillionn to plant crops, and to raise cattle and horses. This place is known as Moytura, the plain beneath the high red towers. To meet your requirement in cattle and horses, you may need to travel. A few herds are available for trade at Rathcroghan and I am sure there are more at Sligeach. However, I believe you must travel to Emain Macha and perhaps as far away as Tara. Doing so will provide you the opportunity to meet with King Daire of nearby Emain Macha and the high king of Inis Elga, Cullainn, of Tara, which is many day's journey to the east.

"Through the prophesies and visions recounted to us by those of Tomregan, we have been expecting your coming and preparing for it. It would be my pleasure if my eldest son, Ruairi, accompanies you to Emain Macha and to Tara to meet with King Daire and High King Cullainn. Perhaps Fearghus or another representative of Tomregan would also join you." King Ailill nods towards Father and toward King Nuada as he finishes speaking.

King Nuada rises again to speak. "Your offers and suggestions are received most gratefully, King Ailill. The suggestion I travel to meet King Daire and High King Cullainn is the second issue I wanted to discuss. If we are to settle peacefully and create alliances beneficial to all, I, as king of my people, must meet with the powers of these northern lands. I am honored you would allow your eldest son to join me and I fervently hope Fearghus or another from Tomregan will accompany us as well. I am most anxious to begin this journey, perhaps within the next few days." King Nuada gazes toward King Ailill, who nods his approval, and then looks to Father.

"Fearghus," continues King Nuada, "I would be especially heartened if you or your chosen representative accompanies me on my journey. I suspect my son and daughter may also come. Perhaps your children would join us as well. I feel they are already part of my family and would embrace the opportunity for all of us to become even closer."

Detecting a slight shifting in King Ailill's position while King Nuada speaks, I suspect he too senses this deference toward Father. Is he uneasy with this? Though outwardly King Ailill is expressionless, I feel a tension. Perhaps King Ailill does not want the relationships between King Nuada's family and my family to become too close.

King Nuada glances toward King Ailill, perhaps noting his nearly imperceptible movement as he begins to speak again. "Before Fearghus responds to my request, I believe I should reveal the third issue I wish to address today." Turning toward Queen Sianna, he continues. "Queen Sianna, my people held a long and prosperous relationship with the Formorri in Aletea. Your cousin, Breas, was a close childhood friend of my son, Cairpre. His mother was the daughter of our High King Conall. When my brother, Aesres, informed me he saw a Formorri settlement near where we were to land and shared that he sensed a connection to this settlement, I knew meeting with you and your people should be accomplished swiftly. With your permission, I hope Aesres can initiate this dialog by accompanying you as you return to Sligeach."

Everyone looks toward Queen Sianna, except King Ailill. He is studying Aesres, whose demeaner appears to soften when Queen Sianna is discussed. Does King Ailill see this softening as well?

I glance toward Queen Sianna. She seems surprised. Etain is seated by her side, her expression cold.

Queen Sianna briefly glances toward Aesres as she rises to address the gathering. "King Nuada, I am honored you wish to send your brother so soon to meet with me and travel to my small village. Perhaps King Nuada's daughter, Aislinn, who I have heard much about from Keelen, could come. If this is possible, then Fearghus, I would hope Keelen and Laragh could join us as well."

I look excitedly toward Aislinn and we both turn toward our respective fathers. Each nod their approval.

"It is settled," says Fearghus. "Keelen, Laragh, and Aislinn will join with Aesres to travel to Sligeach with Queen Sianna. I would like my son, Flann, to join King Nuada, Ruairi, and Cairpre on their journey to Tara and Emain Macha. I know High King Cullainn is most anxious to hear first-hand that the prophesies have been fulfilled and the Danann are now among us. King Daire is also most anxious to be updated. I will send a messenger to him to provide the details of your arrival and your intent to travel to Emain Macha after leaving Tara." Father looks around. "I see our meal is prepared. Unless anyone else wishes to speak, let us eat."

Dry grasses have been spread about a flat area of land near where the discussions are being held. Wooden planks, raised slightly above the ground, are arranged in a circle. Roasted meats and breads are spread upon the tables. King Ailill, King Nuada, Queen Sianna, Fearghus, and Aesres enter the inner area of the circle of tables and settle before the food. After they are settled, Laragh, Flann and I join them. The others in attendance settle on the outside of the tables.

Breas and Rayna sit near Cairpre and Aislinn. They are across the table from King Nuada and Queen Sianna. It has been many years since Breas last saw Cairpre and Aislinn. He is no longer a boy, but now a young man. Both he and Rayna wear the clothing and adornments of Formorri royalty. Cairpre talks excitedly with Breas. Breas wishes to learn all that has happened in the doomed land of Aletea since their last meeting. Rayna listens intently while sitting close to Breas.

Aislinn, Laragh, and I also interject our thoughts into their conversation, though generally we talk between ourselves regarding our upcoming trip to Sligeach. Queen Sianna joins our conversation, telling Aislinn about the countryside we will travel through and the sights Aislinn can expect to see.

Aislinn says, "The times on Aletea over the past year have been hard. Being in this new land is already calming, despite the uncertainties. I feel fortunate to already know Keelen, and am looking forward to this trip with you, Queen Sianna."

For Aislinn, this is the beginning of a grand adventure in this wonderful new land. As for me, I am thrilled this is finally happening. The long wait since last Samhain is over.

Aesres is seated on the other side of Queen Sianna and he joins in the conversation with Breas and Cairpre. He appears reserved, talking cordially, but not leading the exchange. He seems more focused on observing what is going on, regarding body movements and expressions. There is one person I note who isn't partaking in the conversation. This is Etain. She is sitting among us, but appears distant.

With the light of day fading, King Nuada indicates it's time for him and his companions to return to their camp. It's agreed that everyone who will soon be traveling will spend the next day in preparation. The Danann will return to this spot late tomorrow, and each party shall embark on their respective journeys the following morning. King Ailill sends a messenger to Rathcroghan to inform Ruairi to prepare for a journey with King Nuada to Tara and Emain Macha.

The Danann all rise and exchange final greetings with their hosts. They make their way down to the shoreline and board their curaugh. All signs of the fog have disappeared, and the glow of the setting sun adds to the surreal ambiance this day has brought.

CHAPTER TWENTY-ONE

EXPLORING THE LANDS OF INIS ELGA

Excitement grips me as Flann, Laragh, and I prepare for our journeys. Queen Sianna and Etain are camped on the far side of us and are engaged in deep conversation. They join us for meals and appear normal, but I sense tension.

During the morning meal, Sianna mentions Etain and most of her entourage are returning to Sligeach. Etain says many preparations need to be made before the traveling group arrives in Sligeach and she wishes to personally oversee these arrangements. Breas and his sister, Rayna, ask if they can journey with Etain to Sligeach. Breas explains Rayna is not feeling well and needs to rest in more comfortable accommodations. Sianna says they're welcome to join Etain and hopes Rayna is soon better. I see Sianna shoot a quick glance toward Etain, who sees, but ignores her.

Soon after the meal, Etain, Breas, Rayna, and those accompanying them depart, moving toward the esker leading to Sligeach. King Ailill's son, Ruairi, arrives about midday. Toward mid-afternoon, I spot two curaughs. The trip across the lough takes about an hour, so an evening meal is prepared for the Danann.

The first curaugh touches shore and King Nuada, Aesres, Aislinn, and Cairpre climb out. They are met by Father and he leads them up the bank to the meal. The second curaugh touches shore and the small entourage accompanying King Nuada disembarks, unloading the supplies for their journey.

Everyone seems animated. King Nuada and his brother, Aesres, try to maintain an aura of calmness and purpose, but even their faces emanate excitement as they are wrapped in these moments of anticipation. A new era is dawning, not only for the Danann, but also for us in Inis Elga.

Aislinn sits next to me. She is engaged in lively conversation with Sianna, asking about Sligeach and what to expect. She then turns to Laragh and me, asking if the fabled White Horse of Binn is nearby or near the path leading to Sligeach. I shake my head and tell her the White Horse is near Tomregan, which is the wrong direction from Sligeach. Aislinn's face shows disappointment, but Sianna says, "I am in no hurry to return to Sligeach. If Aesres is amenable, we could travel first to Tomregan and the White Horse of Binn before proceeding to Sligeach. I have never seen this famous site either. Though it's not Samhain, the time when Eachon and the White Horse appear, perhaps Eachon might visit us since we include in our midst members of the long-awaited people of Danu."

Aislinn's face brightens and she eagerly turns toward her uncle. Aesres frowns slightly at first, but then smiles and says, "Making such a journey would be a pleasant diversion from all the tragedies and fears we have been experiencing. Yes, let us travel to this White Horse of Binn. The journey will give us a chance to learn of each other." He glances toward Sianna with a look of hesitation, but she smiles in return.

Fearghus has been listening to the exchange and adds, "A wonderful idea. The other drui and bards of Tomregan are most anxious to meet the people of Danu. I will travel with you to Tomregan, and then you can be off to the Horse of Binn. I will inform King Nuada and the others regarding the change in plans."

The rest of the evening passes pleasantly. Sianna arranges for a messenger to travel to Sligeach to inform Etain of the delay. Everyone retires to their sleeping skins, intending to make an early start.

* * *

The sun climbs over the slieves of red, illuminating a promise of warmth and clear skies for today's travels. King Nuada, accompanied by Ruairi, Flann, and Cairpre, are the initial group to depart. Ruairi has brought horses for each to ride. Their route to Tara will take them through Rathcroghan and from there they'll follow the main southern esker leading to Tara, the home of High King Cullainn.

We extend our farewells and wish them a speedy trip. With the horses, the journey will only take a few days. We do not have horses, but the trek to Tomregan is not far and the esker not well-suited for travel by horse even if we had them. We should arrive before nightfall.

Aislinn, Laragh, and I take the lead with Sianna, Father, and Aesres following behind as our adventure begins. The esker skirts the eastern and southern shores of Lough Aillionn, travelling through the forests of oak, birch, and ash. The new leaves of Beltane cover the trees. Many of the ash still hold their striking black buds, each ready to burst into new foliage. The excitement of the trip, the beauty of the trees, along with the pleasant, warm breeze gently nudges us along the esker. Aislinn ceaselessly asks questions regarding the system of eskers crisscrossing Inis Elga, the lough and landscape, Tomregan, and the White Horse of Binn.

Behind me, I discern our other three traveling companions awkwardly attempting to engage with each other. I hear Father telling Aesres and Sianna the ancient legends of how the people of Danu once left in their curaughs from the shores of this very lough.

Father is doing most of the talking. I peer back to see how they are doing. As I look back, I slip on the edge of the esker and slide into the gorse. Immediately, both Sianna and Aesres scramble down to help me up. I feel embarrassed by my inattention and fall, but note this accident brings Aesres and Sianna together to disentangle me from the spines of the foliage. As we begin again, we joke about my fall and the awkwardness between Aesres and Sianna appears dispelled.

Though the journey is long, the remainder of the day progresses swiftly. We advance up the steep path leading away from Lough Aillionn before descending into the rolling low hills near Tomregan. I note Aesres and Sianna have engaged continually in conversation since my fall. They act now as old friends who have not seen each other for a long time. Some of their conversation is light and airy, while at other times somber. I only catch small bits of their conversation, but do overhear Aesres speaking about his wife, Teagan. Perhaps Aesres and Sianna are two souls who were close in a past life and now are catching up.

The sky is darkening as we descend into Tomregan. Everyone greets us as we proceed to the central gathering area where the Beltane feast is being arranged. Though everybody is polite and respectful, there is keen interest regarding our Danann guests. They both possess fairer complexions than most of us and both have lighter-colored hair as well. Aislinn's is straw-colored while Aesres has light brown hair that falls to his shoulders. Aislinn is slightly built with fine features. Aesres is tall by Danann standards, but of average height to us. His features are also finer than those usually found among the natives of Inis Elga. The lightness of his complexion is in stark contrast to the darkness of Queen Sianna, whom he is accompanying through the village.

The elders are waiting at the central gathering area. We are led to our sitting area within the inner edges of the circle of tables holding the feast. In the excitement, I had nearly forgotten it was Beltane. The usual Beltane favorites of clay-roasted quail, boiled meats from the nearby fulacht fiadhs, and bread cover the tables. Flagons of mead dot the tables as well. Once we are settled, the other villagers come and take their places on the outside edges of the table circle. The space is especially crowded near where Aislinn and Aesres sit.

The sky transforms to darkness with spikes of light slicing through the blackness from Beltane fires on the hilltops around Tomregan. Far up on the high slieve of Cenn, the largest bonfire is piercing the horizon's black depths. The appearance of the bonfires and the presence of the Danann ignite the spirits of everyone at the feast. Aesres and Aislinn seem flushed with both excitement and sadness as they tell of their former homeland and their escape from its destruction. What they lost cannot be recovered, but they tell us the promise of this new land and the kindness of those around them fills them with hope.

Sianna listens intently to the stories told by Aesres and Aislinn. I, too, share with her the thoughts of what a wondrous land Aletea must have been and what powers these Danann once held. She especially listens to the stories told by Aesres. A slight smile appears on her face while she listens.

After a short while, Father interrupts, saying now is time to proceed to the stone circle to make our Beltane sacrifice. Torches are lit, and he leads everyone along the footpath toward the circle. We enter, the fire from our torches glinting off the gold covering of the central stone. Next to the golden stone is a young calf. Outside the circle, we hear the bellowing of our herd. They are nearby in a holding pen.

Once settled, Father draws near the young calf, softly stroking his head. This calms the calf and Father sits with it on the flat stone at the base of the central golden obelisk. He speaks pleasantries to the calf, continuing to caress his head, telling it of the sacred honor it is about to serve. Still talking to the calf, he reaches for his sgian, swiftly drawing the blade across the calf's throat. The calf lets out a small sound of surprise, but soon lies still on the stone with its blood draining down the stone to the base of the golden column.

Three new fires blaze up into the night. The central one near the golden pillar and two others, one on each side of the central flames, leave just enough room for paths. The lifeless calf is placed into a water-soaked wicker basket. This basket is hoisted onto supporting hooks just above the roaring flames of the central fire. The flames lick the edges of the basket, then begin to consume the body. While this takes place, our cattle are brought from their pen and driven between the flames along each path between the fires. The cattle are returned to their pen, the Beltane sacrifice to Cenn and the blessing of our cattle is now complete.

As the fires burn down, Father beckons us to sit and be comfortable. The time has come for the Beltane story talk. Father stands on the sacrificial stone at the base of the golden column to speak. The fires flicker, their light glancing off the gold as well as off each of the twelve smaller bronze-clad pillars surrounding the central one.

"This is a most festive and important Beltane for us all," Father begins. "It is the most significant Beltane since the coming of the cold so many years before. The prophecies told through the White Horse of Binn have come to fruition. The long-awaited arrival of the people of Danu has transpired. Life in Inis Elga is now forever changed.

"Tonight, to mark this occasion and to honor our special guests, I invite Laragh to recount for us her visions from the White Horse regarding the times when the people of Danu lived among us so long ago. In some ways, their arrival is a homecoming of long-lost relations. Our stories say many of us count as our ancestors the children born from the greenwood marriages on the Beltane night just before the people of Danu left for their new homeland."

Laragh takes her place on the stone where Father stood and recounts the legend told by Eachon. Everyone's attention is drawn to her. Most do not know this story in full and are eager to learn about the connection between themselves and the people of Danu. Knowing the story well, I look at the faces of my friends and neighbors as they listen. Their attention is fixed as Laragh recounts the tale of the bearded star that appeared so long ago and how Danu spoke through dreams to those who would travel with her to the new land. I believe no one else takes note of Aesres and Sianna slipping away into the dark.

After a while, I detect a small rustle nearby. The sound is Sianna and Aesres, their faces flushed. They come and sit near me, appearing to be listening intently to Laragh. I sense the Beltane magic occurring again, much like long ago when the Danann first left Inis Elga.

The night is long when Laragh finishes, and we all proceed back to Tomregan to sleep. Aesres walks with Laragh, Aislinn, Sianna, and myself. Aislinn is full of questions for Laragh regarding her story. The rest of us let them talk. Aesres and Sianna stay close to each other without speaking. I look at them and ponder on the events of the evening and the journey to the White Horse of Binn awaiting us in the morning.

* * *

The morning breaks clear with the promise of continued pleasant weather. Our small party swiftly eats, and we are soon on our way along the narrow esker leading north to the White Horse. The narrowness of the path and the closeness to the edge of the gorse and heather require us to proceed in single file. I am in the lead while Aesres brings up the rear. We settle into our walk, conversing little. I believe the others feel as I do, content to focus on the journey itself, the companionship, and enjoying the unfolding countryside.

By the time the sun is directly overhead, we reach the banks of the Claddagh river. We are now near the White Horse. I tell our companions that in some of the mussels found in this river are shiny, bright white, hardened tears legends say were left by the goddess Danu when she and Cenn parted so long ago.

As we ford the river, Aesres catches sight of an unusually large mussel lodged between two stones. He reaches down and retrieves it. Once on the far bank, he examines the mussel and asks me if this is of the type holding the tears of Danu. I nod yes, and Aislinn eagerly cajoles him to pry it open. "What do I do with it if there is one?" he asks. I tell him he should let the one daughter of Danu who is with us, Aislinn, receive this gift from the gods.

Aesres reaches for his sgian and soon the mussel is opened. To the surprise of us all, there are two tears of Danu in the mussel. One is brilliant white with a pinkish luster and the other a light, smoky color with the same luster. Aislinn gasps in surprise at seeing two tears saying, "It appears the goddess Danu wishes you to also receive one of her tears, Sianna. This tear," she says, reaching for the smoky-colored one "appears destined for you." Aesres looks toward Sianna to see her expression.

Sianna reaches for the tear, admiring its beauty. Looking at Aislinn, then toward Aesres, Sianna says, "Thank you. This tear of Danu is beautiful. And thank you, Aesres, for finding this gift. It will truly be treasured."

Aesres looks uncomfortable with this attention and declares we should be moving on.

I think to myself, *these are good signs from the gods.*

Before long, as we round a corner of the esker, the White Horse of Binn comes into full view. It stands crisply on the side of the slieve directly in front of us. We all halt and gaze at this extraordinary sight. I tell my companions the Horse has been visible on the slieve since the days of Eachon, many centuries before, and at Samhain, the Horse speaks to us through the spirit of Eachon, whose cairn lies near its mouth.

We leave the esker and proceed up the well-worn path toward the Horse. By late afternoon, we reach Eachon's cairn. The view from here is spectacular. Toward the south lies Slieve Roisin, and we can guess from its features about where Tomregan sits. To the right of

Slieve Roisin are the rolling low hills of Mag Senaig. These rolling hills form the base for Slieve Cenn, which is out of our view to the west, blocked by the ridge above us. To the north and east, we take in the expanse of a large lough.

In the pit near the cairn, we build our evening fire and prepare our evening meal. The setting is peaceful and the air warm. As night falls, we observe the Beltane fires come to life on the crests of many of the slieves nearby. A large blaze flames from the peak of Slieve Roisin with a smaller one near its base. This smaller one must be from Tomregan. We pass the evening in casual conversation. Sianna tells of her childhood in Sligeach, along with her many trips to visit her grandfather, King Ailill, in Rathcroghan. Aislinn and Aesres recount some of the history of their people and some of the extraordinary powers given to them by the goddess Danu. Laragh and I tell of the training we are undergoing to become druis and our life in Tomregan.

As our fire wanes, we wish each other good night and settle into our cloaks with each of us hoping for a visit from Eachon. I try to fall asleep, but the excitement of the past few days leaves me awake. Deciding to sit up to study the stars in the hopes of later falling asleep, I find, to my surprise, Laragh is also fully awake. Her arms are wrapped about her knees as she gazes out over the valley below. The Beltane fires are fading and barely discernible. The stars are bright, with an occasional shooting star streaking across the sky. I huddle close to my sister.

"He is being visited in his dreams," Laragh informs me as she motions her head toward the sleeping Aesres. I ask her if Eachon is visiting him and she shakes her head no. "The visiting spirit is his wife. She talks to him often. Tonight, they are discussing Sianna. Teagan is telling him Sianna is a good woman and Aesres will have a son coming from last night's Beltane magic, but she also warns of dangers.

"Those close to Sianna will notice her interest in Aesres and try to stop them. One is Trista, her long-trusted advisor. Trista wants what she regards as best for Sianna and for her people, the

Formorri, but views the situation only in black and white. Her ultimate loyalty is to her high king. She cannot perceive how Aesres or the Danann could ever be anything but adversarial. Trista will only see the Danann, and especially Aesres with his love for Sianna and her for him, as a threat to the Formorri.

"Teagan encourages Aesres to pursue his love of this young half-Formorri queen, but cautions of the extreme danger. They both must keep their public acknowledgments of love in check. Aesres must continue as the key representative of the Danann people and maintain a public distance in his dealings with Sianna. She must do the same. It is their only hope."

I ask Laragh if there is danger from anyone else besides Trista. She replies, "Yes, there is another who is also close to Sianna, but in a much different way. Teagan is telling Aesres that Sianna holds close to her heart another woman she has known since childhood. She is one of her companions who views the entering of Aesres into Sianna's life as a personal affront. This other devotes her life to Sianna and wishes to share her with no other. She cares nothing about the Danann. She is jealous of anyone who grows close to Sianna and through this self-absorbed jealousy comes danger. She desperately wants to keep Aesres away.

"Teagan cautions Aesres to be aware of what this person does and to be always on guard. Teagan also tells Aesres that what she has told him tonight is for his subconscious only and not for remembering when he awakes. She wants him to feel the danger from certain individuals, though not the specific details."

I consider Aesres as he sleeps. He makes no movements and appears content. I wonder if Sianna is also dreaming, and if in those dreams she is told she will be with child. My eyes drift back to the valley, then to the stars. Laragh is still holding onto me, but is now asleep. There has been no Eachon to tell us stories at the Horse of Binn this night, but there were stories nonetheless. Our future could be bright with this coming of the people of Danu, but it appears the road to this future includes dangers and pitfalls.

CHAPTER TWENTY-TWO

ONWARD TO SLIGEACH

As I wake, I find myself still holding Laragh. Nearby, Aesres is rescuing the remaining embers from our fire, soon bringing it back to life and providing welcoming warmth. We found several birds' eggs yesterday when near the river Claddagh. Previous visitors to Eachon's cairn had left a few cupped cooking stones and we place these in the edges of the fire to heat. Each of us crack open several bird eggs into these cupped stones and watch the clear egg gel turn white, then start to bubble. We sprinkle some dried herbs over the cooking eggs and soon we are eating.

Laragh asks, "Did anyone have a visit from Eachon last night?"

Aislinn responds, saying, "I slept soundly. Perhaps one day I will be able to return at Samhain and that will happen."

"Eachon would be excited to meet members of the long-awaited Danann at his funeral cairn," I tell her.

No one else claims they'd been visited by Eachon, nor does anyone share any strange or unusual dreams.

Aislinn asks, "Where do we go next on this journey?"

I glance at Laragh who looks at me to respond.

"We can begin our journey toward Sligeach. If we go up over the ridge above us, we will find ourselves halfway up the slieve of Cenn. The spot will provide an excellent view for Aesres and Aislinn to gain a better understanding of the surroundings, as much can be seen from this height. We should be able to identify Lough Aillionn, and estimate where the Danann encampment sits. The shoreline to the west should also be visible, and we can show where Sligeach lays. Once we finish surveying the landscape, we can drop down to the pool of the Sinann, which is the source of the mighty river Sinann. This pool was dedicated long ago to the goddess Danu. The spot is a good place to camp for the evening, as we can easily reach Sligeach the next day."

Aesres is excited to learn he will be able to survey the vast countryside surrounding the Danann encampment. In his first reconnaissance trip by eitilte, he had focused primarily on potential landing areas. The second trip during the landing of the fleet had limited visibility due to the shroud of fog. Aesres knows the Danann need to learn as much as possible about this new land to help ensure their safety. A trip to the heights of Slieve Cenn is an unexpected bonus.

We pack up our few travel belongings and move along a trail through the heather to the ridge above the White Horse. Reaching the edge of the ridge, I look back at the Horse, mentally wishing it goodbye.

Our party turns and moves forward along the well-worn trail leading to the heights of Slieve Cenn. The climb is steep, but not difficult. As we begin our ascent, we come across a giant elk grazing along the trail. It looks to be the same elk Laragh, Flann, and I saw last Samhain when we came to the Horse of Binn. The elk shuffles away from the edge of the trail as we go by, but does not flee. I interpret the elk's presence as a good omen.

Near midday, we reach the summit. There are several ancient cairns here but neither Laragh nor I know who they honor. As promised, the view is spectacular. The sky is a brilliant blue and Lough Aillionn is visible to the southeast.

Aesres gazes over the land, taking in the large loughs to the north and east and the mountains to the south and west. He asks me where I estimate the Danann encampment to be. I first point him to the south toward the western edge of Slieve Roisin and note with my finger where Tomregan lays. I then trace for him the route of our journey from Lough Aillionn to Tomregan. As I point to the southeast, most of Lough Aillionn is clearly visible. Blocking some of its view are slieves colored dark rust red. Their darkness practically blends them into the deep blue color of the lough. "On the other side of those dark red slieves, along the shore of Lough Aillionn, is where your encampment sets," I tell him.

Aesres gazes across this southern landscape for a long time. He asks, "Do many live in those flatter areas to the south of your village?" I tell him our village is the most important in the area, but several other smaller villages are nearby with these other villages under the domain of Rathcroghan. He then turns his focus to the north and the vast loughs covering much of the land. "What about the shores of this nearer lough?" he asks. I tell him there is a small village straight to the north where the lough curves, but the land is relatively un-peopled to the west. I also point out to him where Sligeach lies, not far to the west of the lough, on the edge of the sea.

Sianna has been with us all along, listening to my descriptions and taking in the landscapes. As I speak of Sligeach, she takes Aesres' arm, points it to the far northwest, and says, "Over there is where my village lies." Aesres gazes in that direction.

He finally breaks his gaze and sweeps his hand across the landscape from Sligeach to the north to the shores of the nearby lough and says, "This is an area worth exploring. Perhaps we will find this to be a good home for the Danann."

Aislinn, Laragh, and I leave Aesres and Sianna as they continue to survey the landscape, and wander about the meadow near the peak. Some early wildflowers have squeezed their way up through the dry grasses and daintily bend their purple, blue, and pink heads in the light breeze. Exclaiming at their beauty, we roam about the meadow, taking in the sights. Sianna and Aesres catch up to us and we make our way toward the pool of Sinann.

By late afternoon, we find the small brook that will become the river Sinann and follow this stream to its source at the pool of Sinann. The waters of the pool are nearly pitch black in color. Small strips of cloth hang from many of the branches of the trees hugging the shore. Many people visit this site, as there are clearly defined hearths, areas for bedding, and rock-lined cooking pits.

We settle around one of these hearths, start a fire, and arrange our bedding. Aislinn is taken with the area. "This place feels so magical, beautiful, and honored!" she exclaims. "It is comforting to find a place dedicated to Danu in this new land."

We pass the evening with small talk, enjoying our time together.

*   *   *

A light, misting fog greets us in the morning. We waste little time having our morning meal, packing our possessions, and preparing to leave. Before departing, we leave offerings to Danu. Last night, I fashioned a small wooden twig model of an eitilte. I place it near the edge of the pool.

The trail leading from the pool takes us up over a pass between two slieves, then down to the esker leading to Sligeach. Upon reaching the esker, the fog breaks and sunlight streams through the trees with the shadows dancing along in front of us. The sun cheers us and the anticipation of arriving at Sligeach soon grasps us.

Approaching the esker, Sianna tells us Sligeach is less than an hour away. We note a party of people approaching. Instinctively, we each reach down and ensure our sgians are at our hips. I can see from the darkness of their skins the approaching party are Formorri and soon Sianna tells us she recognizes Etain.

"My queen, I could wait no longer for your arrival," exclaims Etain as she reaches Sianna and bows before her.

"Enough formalities, Etain," replies Sianna as she moves to embrace Etain. "I have missed you as well. I'm sure you remember our new friends, Aislinn and Aesres of the Danann, and of course you know Keelen and Laragh."

Etain exchanges greetings with everyone and inquires how the trip has been.

Aesres exclaims about the beauty of Inis Elga, the hospitality shown them at Tomregan, the wonder of the White Horse of Binn, and the vast expanse seen from the summit of Slieve Cenn.

"What news of Sligeach?" asks Sianna.

Etain tells her, "Your cousins, Breas and Rayna, have settled and are comfortable. They have taken the guest quarters in your roundhouse, as you directed. Rayna feels much better. She finds the sea air reviving. Trista is spending much time with them. They talk about High King Elotha, Trista's brother, and their father. Are you sure you are well, my queen?"

Sianna assures her she is well and has taken pleasure in the trip. Sianna tells Etain of the wonders of the White Horse of Binn, as well as the sights from the summit of Slieve Cenn. From outward appearances, Etain appears to be happy to be with her queen again.

We are close to Sligeach, and it does not take long to enter the village. A runner had been sent ahead, and as we enter, Trista, Breas, and Rayna greet us.

Trista comes forward to personally greet Aesres and Aislinn. "Breas tells me much about you and your land of Aletea. I can understand your sadness in the loss of such a home. After so many years of turmoil and loss of life, the time is here for you and your people to be at peace."

Breas approaches Aislinn and Aesres saying, "It is so good to see the both of you again. I trust your trip was pleasant."

"Yes, most agreeable," replies Aesres.

Turning toward Rayna, Aesres says, "I'm sorry we did not have time to speak when we first met at the lough. Breas said you are his sister?"

"Yes," answers Breas, before Rayna has a chance to speak. "I first met Rayna during my stay with my father's people when I was sent from my mother's home in the cities of Danu to the Formorri home islands in my later youth. We have become fast friends and she has taught me many of the Formorri ways I did not learn as a child in Aletea. I can hardly think of being away from her."

Rayna bows her head toward Aesres, then to Aislinn. "Breas has told how much he loved Cairpre and the Danann people. I am honored to meet the esteemed Aesres, Cairpre's uncle, and his sister, Aislinn. From what I remember of Breas's stories, Aislinn, you were with Cairpre and Breas the night the tears from the bearded star came and destroyed the southern lands of Aletea."

Rayna then turns toward Aesres and says, "Aesres, the belief among the Formorri is you saved the sacred treasures of the Danann people from the final destruction of the cities of Danu. I do hope each of the four treasures arrived safely with you."

I can see Aesres pondering. He must be wondering if he should acknowledge that the four treasures are secure and in their possession.

"Yes," says Aesres, "we were fortunate to transport the sword, Claíomh Solai, the spear, Lúin, and the Caldron of Wisdom from the cities of Danu just before their destruction. Each, along with the Lia Fáil, is safely with us." I note a virtually imperceptible glance from Breas to Trista as the safe arrival of the four Danann treasures is confirmed.

The villagers crowd around to look at the fabled people of Danu though they part to allow the royal party and visitors to pass.

Queen Sianna appears tired from the long journey and she dispenses with any formal dinners or ceremonies. Aesres has told her he is anxious to return to the Danann encampment. He, Aislinn, Laragh, and I will leave early in the morning.

CHAPTER TWENTY-THREE

AT THE ENCAMPMENT

Morning comes, and I awake to find Aesres and Sianna in conversation on the far side of the hearth. Upon our arrival yesterday evening, Sianna arranged for us to stay within her rath in her council chamber roundhouse and had her servants prepare sleeping furs around the main hearth. Exhausted, I was thankful no formal dinners or ceremonies had been planned.

Laragh and I will accompany Aesres and Aislinn back to the Danann encampment. Seeing we are awake, Sianna greets us, telling us how sad she is that we are leaving. She says she and Aesres have been discussing the land along the lough to the north of Slieve Cenn. Aesres wishes to explore it to determine if it is a suitable place for the people of Danu to settle.

Aesres adds, "I am anxious to meet with my brother to learn about his trip to convene with High King Cullainn, as well as to discuss with him the lands we viewed from the mount of Slieve Cenn. Sianna tells me this area is outside of anyone's domain."

Sianna smiles and says, "This indeed may be a good land for the Danann." She turns toward my sister and me and says, "Keelen and

Laragh, thank you for letting me come along with you on this journey. Seeing the White Horse of Binn was an honor, and being able to survey all the lands around the flanks of Slieve Cenn was remarkable to behold. I know you must leave, but I am looking forward to your early return."

We eat quickly, gather our few belongings, and soon are bidding Sianna farewell. Aesres and Sianna linger off to the side to share some private moments. We do not see or speak with Trista, Breas, or Rayna before we leave, but we had told them the night before of our intent for an early start. Glancing out over the harbor waters, I notice a ship just coming into view. I point out the approaching ship to the others. Sianna says, "It is the Formorri trading vessel that comes about once a moon cycle. When you return to Sligeach, you must come down to the market. The Formorri trader often brings interesting and unusual items for trade. The vessel should be here for several days before loading the goods it traded in the market and moving to their next port of call."

We bid Sianna farewell and soon Sligeach is gone from view. As we leave, I see Aesres giving Sianna a final glance before turning to us and saying, "We need to make good time if we want to arrive at the Danann encampment before dark."

A light frost greets us as we begin our journey. Despite the cold, there is promise of a fine day. The sky is clear, and the emerging sun already warms my face.

The esker from Sligeach dips up and down through the rolling hills toward Lough Aillionn. We each keep our thoughts to ourselves and little conversation passes between us. Aesres appears deep in thought. I think to myself he must be weighing all that has happened since he and the Danann left Aletea. I'm sure he is unnerved. Despite the efforts of Father and all of us in Tomregan to welcome the Danann, King Ailill tried to block their coming. Then, there is the unexpected presence of Breas and the many questions he and Rayna ask.

By late afternoon, our party reaches the Danann encampment. Along the shores of Lough Aillionn, the Danann have created their temporary settlement. In the meadows to the north along the shore, I see the land is being prepared for planting. Along the south, pens are emerging for the cattle currently being procured in Rathcroghan. A crude, but still imposing roundhouse rises on the high ground in the center of the emerging village. The settlement itself is being surrounded by a rath for protection.

Aesres learns King Nuada is expected to return tomorrow. His intended visit with King Daire at Emain Macha has been postponed. Word reached him while with High King Cullainn that King Daire was away and not expected to return for a week or more.

Laragh and I will stay with Aislinn until Flann arrives with King Nuada. Aislinn takes the two of us to the part of the central roundhouse holding the four treasures of the Danann. I tell her I have seen these in my visions, but beholding and touching them is a remarkable experience. "We have no such treasures as those given your people by Danu," I tell her. "The way of Cenn is different. Instead of powerful treasures, he gives us guidance through the White Horse and our drui." After viewing the treasures, we explore the shores of Lough Aillionn, swimming, splashing, and picking flowers. The time feels surreal.

King Nuada and his party arrive the next day as expected. As they ride into camp, Flann and Cairpre are bantering between themselves. It appears the two have become friends during their journey. The five of us spend the rest of the day exploring the emerging village and the shores of the lough, much as Laragh, Aislinn, and I did the day before. We regale each other with the adventures of our respective journeys. As we talk about Breas and Rayna, Cairpre tells us, "Breas seems different. He is no longer my carefree, childhood friend, trying to fit in among the Danann. His years away from the cities of Danu have engrained the Formorri ways.

"His sister appears to hold much sway over him. I am not sure I trust her. She is guarded about herself and one must remember she is the daughter of High King Elotha. I am elated to see my old childhood friend again, but the timing seems odd."

Flann and I tell Aislinn and Cairpre we will travel back to

Sligeach the next morning. We want to see if we can learn why Breas and Rayna are here. Following a short stay, we will return to Tomregan. Laragh says she is returning directly to Tomregan with a small party of Danann who are traveling there tomorrow.

The sky is darkening as we return to the Danann encampment. Although the roundhouses and surrounding rath have not yet been finished, the main structure housing the four treasures is nearly complete and King Nuada insists we spend the night there.

As we are eating our evening meal, Aesres and Nuada come to wish us well on our journeys. Aesres reveals he intends to be in Sligeach shortly to further discuss with Queen Sianna the lands along the lough to the north. They excuse themselves and return to their nearby campsite.

Laragh, Flann, and I rise early and are greeted with a cold rain and dampening chill. We note only the sentries and the small party of Danann intending to travel to Tomregan are awake. Soon, we move toward the esker leading to Sligeach.

Aislinn and Cairpre walk with us for part of the way, with Cairpre expressing his desire to visit the fabled White Horse of Binn. "Aislinn," he says to his sister, "perhaps when Uncle Aesres goes to look upon the lands along the lough to the north, the two of us can go with him and include the Horse of Binn among our travels."

"I am not sure I can find my way to the White Horse on my own," answers Aislinn. "We would need Laragh, Flann, or Keelen to accompany us. Perhaps in the future, once we are settled."

Where the esker forks north toward Sligeach, Laragh, Aislinn, and Cairpre take their leave. We clasp each other close, saying goodbye and Cairpre makes one last statement. "Try and get to know Breas and Rayna while you are in Sligeach. Learn why they are here. Their arrival may be innocent, but I have found coincidences to be rare." I assure him we will do so. Laragh wishes us a speedy trip and says she hopes to see us soon. Flann and I bundle ourselves up against the chill and rain and proceed toward Sligeach.

CHAPTER TWENTY-FOUR

BREAS AND RAYNA

We arrive in Sligeach by midafternoon and make our way to Sianna's roundhouse. She is not there, but her attendants expected our arrival and show us to our chambers. The attendants also relay to us that Breas and Rayna wish to visit with us once we are settled. They are staying in Trista's roundhouse.

Although we are cold and wet from our journey, it takes Flann and I only a short time to arrange our sleeping furs and put away our travel belongings. We walk to Trista's roundhouse, which is next to Sianna's. Like Sianna's, Trista's roundhouse is aligned to provide a sweeping view of Sligeach and the harbor. Little can happen in the village or the harbor that cannot be seen from these two dwellings. Upon arrival, we are led to Breas' and Rayna's quarters and find them near a blazing hearth, enjoying a magnificent view of the harbor below. With the cold, rainy weather, there is a chill and the hearth provides a welcome, glowing warmth.

Rayna is the first to see us, and she rises to greet and embrace us. "I have been looking forward to your arrival," she says. "I find your land beautiful, though so different from my homeland. I hope you can tell us more about your country, your village of Tomregan, and perhaps even a little about the secrets of the White Horse of Binn. Trista attempted to describe these things, but I am afraid she is too much a Formorri and has travelled little around your lands." She smiles, leading us to where Breas is standing, waiting to greet us.

Rayna is not the shy, retiring figure as she first appeared. She actively engages us in conversation, first telling us much about her own homeland, which is an island to the south near the opening of a massive inland sea. "The climate is warm in our homeland and the waters about our island are also warm. Here, the climate and waters are cold. But your mountains and landscapes are breathtaking."

Breas engages in the conversation, though does not try to lead. Rayna asks us to describe our home village. With the conversation moving in this direction, I note Breas becoming attentive. Rayna still leads the conversation, but Breas asks probing questions now and then. We tell them how Tomregan is the leading learning center of Inis Elga; how all the people in our village are drui, bards, and apprentices learning the ways of the drui and bard; and how our father, Fearghus, is the foremost bard elder in Tomregan. We do not suppress any information regarding our home.

Breas asks about the prophesies from the White Horse of Binn and how they foretold of the coming of the Danann. Here, Flann and I are more guarded. Though appearing to tell all, we provide only a sketch of the prophesies and tell nothing regarding our ability to interact in spirit with some of the Danann, such as my spirit visitations with Aislinn.

Rayna inquires how the prophesies are given and we tell them that at Samhain, chosen people from our village spend the night near the mouth of the great White Horse. As the night becomes long, they fall into a trance and are visited by the apparition of an ancient elder as well as the White Horse. "Have either of you ever been one of these chosen?" asks Rayna.

"Yes," I reply, "both Flann and I, along with our younger sister, Laragh, were chosen to go to the White Horse this past Samhain."

This information perks Rayna's interest. "Please, tell us what it was like," she asks. "No such wonders exist in our homeland."

I look at Flann, giving a slight shrug to my shoulders. Flann catches this and recounts the night we spent at the Horse of Binn.

Rayna leans toward Flann. Breas sits back, his arms slightly folded across his chest. He is listening intently, though I perceive a sense of skepticism.

Flann relates how Eachon communicated that within a few moons, during the upcoming Beltane, strangers would be arriving near the reddish slieves by Lough Aillionn. They would arrive in strange craft soaring overhead.

I speak up. "Breas, of course you have already seen these strange craft. They are the eitilte, which brought the people of Danu across the sea from their destroyed homeland."

"Yes, those were remarkable craft. I understand the Danann destroyed them all after they arrived. Is this true? They didn't save even one?"

I nod my head in affirmation, telling Breas and Rayna all the eitiltes were burned shortly after the landing as a sacrifice to the goddess Danu and as a sign of their commitment to live in peace in this new land.

Breas nods thoughtfully.

The remainder of the afternoon passes swiftly. Trista's attendants inform us of Queen Sianna's and Trista's arrival. They are waiting to see us in the central chamber. We take our cups and proceed to meet them. There, a low oval-shaped table is arranged with food and drink. Trista and Sianna are in conversation when we enter, then turn to greet and welcome us. They bid us to sit as the two of them take their seats at opposite ends of the oval. Flann sits with Rayna on one side and I sit with Breas on the other. Arrayed before us is a feast of lobsters, fish, and clay-baked quail.

Sianna asks when we arrived and apologizes, saying both she and Trista needed to be away this afternoon.

"No need to apologize," I say. "The time gave us the opportunity to get to know Rayna and Breas. We were just talking about the White Horse of Binn when you arrived."

Rayna adds, "A fascinating encounter, don't you think Breas?"

Breas says, "Yes, a most interesting story."

I eat with relish. The journey and the long talk with Rayna and Breas made me hungry. When there is a pause in the eating, Flann asks, "Breas, I am curious, what brings you and Rayna to Inis Elga at the same time as the Danann?" One would never accuse Flann of being subtle!

Breas is quick in his response, as if anticipating such a question. "My father, High King Elotha, has a tradition of sending envoys to his outposts during the season of Beltane. Never having travelled to Inis Elga, I volunteered to make this journey. Rayna, too, was curious about this land to the north. Having my childhood friend here was a pleasant, though complete surprise.

"Our time here is being spent in council with our cousin, Queen Sianna, and our aunt, High Counselor Trista. I also had the pleasure of meeting Sianna's grandfather, King Ailill. It is a memorable and informative trip to-date. Both Rayna and I are enjoying the time thoroughly. Perhaps while we are still here, you can take us to your village of Tomregan to meet your father, as well as possibly allow us to visit this fabled White Horse of Binn. First, however, we promised King Ailill we would go again to Rathcroghan. We hope to leave tomorrow."

An interesting story, I muse to myself. The timing still seems much too coincidental.

Turning to Sianna I say, "Sianna, Aesres sends his regards and wants me to inform you of his intention to come for council late tomorrow. He advised his brother regarding the lands along the lough to the north and is keen to start discussions with you regarding this area, as you are the closest settlement to them."

As I expected, this news perks interest, not only with Sianna, but with Trista. I sense heightened interest from Breas and Rayna as well.

"What is this, my queen?" asks Trista. "What are these references to the lands along the lough to the north?"

Sianna shows no hesitation with her response. "This topic was to be among the agenda items for our meeting tomorrow. During my journey with Aesres, Keelen, and Laragh, we went to the summit of Slieve Cenn. From there, we viewed the lands just to the north along the large lough. Aesres asked about them and I agreed to talk further once he conferred with King Nuada."

Trista looks disturbed, though adds nothing more.

Breas interjects. "Aesres is coming tomorrow? I so want to visit with him. Rayna, lets delay our trip to Rathcroghan. Father would want to know about the plans of the Danann in Inis Elga."

Rayna nods agreement.

"Excellent!" says Sianna. "Rayna and Breas, please plan to spend tomorrow with Aesres when he arrives. This will give me time to council with Trista before I meet with him."

The remainder of the evening is spent in light conversation. I ask Rayna to tell me more about her homeland and swimming in the warm seawaters. It sounds nothing like the seawater here by Inis Elga. Flann asks Breas about his memories of Aletea and about his father, High King Elotha. Sianna and Trista listen, too, with Sianna seeming as fascinated as I am. Trista appears to be in good spirits, although she says little.

* * *

By the middle of the next afternoon, Aesres and his entourage arrive in Sligeach.

Sianna greets him, then informs him she cannot meet until tomorrow. For today, she tells him, he will be with Flann and me as well as Rayna and Breas. Breas clasps Aesres' shoulder and expresses his pleasure to see him again. "Come," he tells Aesres, "let us spend the remainder of the day visiting at Trista's roundhouse along with Rayna, Keelen, and Flann. Her home has a marvelous view of the harbor."

Both Flann and I express our gratitude regarding the invitation, saying we would love to hear about Aletea from Aesres. Aesres smiles, nods towards Queen Sianna, then our group is off to Trista's roundhouse. Everyone listens attentively to Aesres and Breas as they talk about Aletea, interspersing the conversation with questions.

Sianna and Trista have made their way toward Sianna's roundhouse. Part of my spirit can stay with Sianna and listen. Trista wastes little time in pointedly asking about the meaning of the reference to the lands along the north lough. "You're not intending to allow the Danann to permanently settle there, are you?" Trista questions.

Sianna forcefully replies that yes, she is considering granting the request should the Danann find the lands to their liking. She additionally reminds Trista the lands are beyond the realm of Sligeach anyway.

Trista fumes. "High King Elotha would not like so powerful a people this close to his areas of interest. Let them explore the wildlands to the west in the mountains. That area is remote, not only to the Formorri in Sligeach, but also to most of the northern kings of Inis Elga. A much more feasible solution."

Sianna is unmoved. "Let us hear how the council with Aesres unfolds before talking further on this subject." With that, Sianna moves to other topics.

The following day, Sianna provides us a morning meal in her council chambers. She invites Aesres to take his place at the position of high honor to her right with Trista taking the position of honor to her left. As we eat, Aesres asks Sianna if she would allow some of his entourage to travel to the lands along the lough to the north while he is in council with her. Aesres explains he would like firsthand accounts regarding the land. Those scouting would return by tomorrow and provide him needed insight. Without looking at Trista, Sianna provides her consent, and soon scouts leave Sligeach, heading northeast.

Breas and Rayna take their leave after the morning meal to prepare for their trip to Rathcroghan. Before long, they are off. Flann and I find ourselves alone after excusing ourselves from Sianna's roundhouse. We know the rest of the day will be filled with council between Aesres, Sianna, and Trista.

We remember the Formorri trading ship is still in port, and as Sianna had noted, the Sligeach village market should have many interesting trade goods. We have a few possessions that might be of interest to the traders. Both Flann and I carry an extra sgian, as we never want to be without one. They are finely crafted of bronze with intricate gold work around the handles.

Indeed, we find many interesting items at the market. Among the foods are a fruit from the warm homelands of the Formorri. They are brown, soft, and exceedingly sweet. We find them irresistible. The traders also have amber, like the amber of Laragh's necklace. Some pieces are a light brown and others orange and clear. A few include embedded insects. They are wondrous! Flann and I trade one of our sgians for some of the sweet fruit, along with pieces of the orange, clear stones. We select those with insects. One has a spider, another a fly, and a few bear mosquitoes entombed inside.

Darkness comes as we return to our sleeping areas within Sianna's roundhouse. Food is brought, the attendants extending Sianna's apologies for not being able to join us. They tell us she, Aesres, and Trista are still in council. We each indulge in one of our sweet, brown fruits, then pack the rest away to give our friends in Tomregan before retiring for the night.

* * *

Aesres rouses us from our sleep, saying it is time for the morning meal. The food is being laid out in the council chambers. We accompany him to the chambers and find Sianna alone, looking out over the harbor. She greets us, saying she hopes to spend more time with us now that the discussions with Aesres are nearly complete. "Trista has concerns, which I hope are now overcome," says Aesres. "I am anxious for my scouts to return. Their report could define where we finally settle."

Just as we are finishing, one of Sianna's attendants comes to inform her the scouts have arrived and are waiting. "Please send them in," replies Sianna, "we are all anxious to listen to their report."

The scouts enter, though before they provide their report, Trista is sent for so she, too, can listen. Their report takes the remainder of the morning, with Aesres and Sianna, and especially Trista asking many questions. Flann and I feel privileged to be allowed to stay and listen. We set ourselves off to the side, listening and observing the gestures and facial expressions of everyone. The scouts are excited by what they observed, saying there are meadows along the shores suitable for both crops and grazing, and stands of oaks nearby for acorns.

Trista, in particular, questions the scouts about the amount of suitable land and whether it is enough to not only satisfy the current population of Danann, but also satisfy the needs of future, larger populations. The scouts assure everyone there is ample land, and tell us they found no settlements of any kind in the immediate area. Trista's expressions and voice indicate her concern. Aesres, on the other hand, is enthused. Sianna tries to maintain an aura of neutrality, yet I can detect she is persuaded these are good lands for the Danann.

Food is brought for all at midday. The discussions and questions are drawing to a close. During the meal, Trista and Sianna confer to the side. I sense Trista is exasperated, judging from her arm and hand movements. It appears Sianna has made her decision. Though muted, I overhear Trista tell Sianna that High King Elotha will not be pleased. I cannot discern what Sianna says in reply, but by her facial expressions, I see she is not swayed by Trista.

After the meal, Sianna addresses us all. "Aesres," she begins, "it appears the lands along the north lough are promising. I give my approval for the Danann to settle there. Nonetheless, I believe it is important before this decision is finalized that you personally visit these lands and confirm all we heard this morning."

"Yes," replies Aesres, "I agree. Your approval is greatly appreciated, not only by me, but also by King Nuada and all the Danann. We must put our hard times behind us and move forward with our new lives. Tomorrow, I will return to our Moytura encampment and inform King Nuada of what transpired. I will then come back in a few days to explore."

He turns to Flann and me and asks, "Do the two of you wish to accompany me when I inspect these lands?"

I assure him it would be a pleasure and Flann adds his agreement.

Aesres says, "That's final then. I will leave tomorrow to consult with King Nuada. In a few days, I will return to Sligeach and have Flann and Keelen join me on my journey."

Turning toward Sianna, Aesres continues, saying, "For the remainder of this day, I am hoping Queen Sianna might show me the village and perhaps a view of the harbor from the nearby hill?"

Sianna smiles and the two of them leave us as they walk toward the village.

CHAPTER TWENTY-FIVE

BETRAYED

My brother and I decide to spend our afternoon cleaning and packing our supplies. We each seem to feel a need to be away from the others and just be among ourselves. As I look over my things, I think about all that has happened since the Danann arrival. I contemplate the growing bond between Sianna and Aesres. There is a strong connection, as witnessed by Aesres soaring his eitilte over Sligeach and seeing Sianna on his reconnaissance flight; Sianna secretly watching the landing of the Danann and Aesres seeing her; the dreams each have had about the other; the slipping away of the two of them in Tomregan while everyone listened to Laragh at the stone circle of Cenn; and the many close conversations they have had since then.

When Aesres arrived in Sligeach two days earlier, he lodged in Sianna's roundhouse. Sianna had the room just off her council chambers readied as his sleeping chamber. I noted Trista found this gesture of familiarity troubling and overheard her strongly advising Sianna this gesture was not in the best interest of Sligeach or the Formorri people. She pointed out the special powers of the Danann, saying no one could be certain they might not use these powers against the Formorri or against the native people of Inis Elga. She thought it inappropriate and dangerous, especially in these times of negotiation, to treat them as friends.

I wonder to myself, *does Trista's anger foreshadow difficult relations between the Formorri and the Danann? Will Sianna's grandfather accept the Danann presence?* My musings are broken when I hear voices approaching and see Aesres and Sianna return from their walk. Sianna catches sight of me and waves.

As Sianna and Aesres grow closer, Sianna says to me, "One of my attendants met us on the path to tell me the banquet is ready. I've sent word to Trista that it is time. We should all make our way to the banquet chambers."

The banquet is held in Sianna's council chamber, which is next to where Flann and I are staying. We enter the chamber and find the fire burning brightly, driving away the cold of the evening. Candlelight bathes the room in a warm, glowing yellow.

The banquet begins with toasts exchanged between the visitors, the Queen, and her counselors. The food is a mixture of Formorri and native Inis Elga dishes. Formorri seafood dishes are served alongside clay-encased quail, roasted pig, and blooded acorn and barley bread.

As the night grows late, Trista excuses herself from the banquet, saying there is much she still needs to do to prepare for the departure of the Formorri vessel that's sailing in the morning. Flann and I take this time to also excuse ourselves, as do Aesres's traveling companions. Sianna and Aesres wish us all a good night, then continue with their conversation.

Aesres is telling stories of Aletea and the wonders it once held. I take one last glance before leaving the chamber and see Sianna listening closely. She is asking many questions regarding the wonders of Aletea, the treachery of the Sons of Belial, and the Formorri traders Aesres had known in his homeland. From my sleeping chambers nearby, I can catch Aesres telling of the final months in

Aletea and the preparations made for their travel.

As I listen to Sianna and Aesres, I remember my last trip to Sligeach and how I had discovered Trista secretly listening to the information my family and I were providing to Queen Sianna regarding the prophesies from the White Horse of Binn. I wonder if she is listening again from the secret chamber beneath the council room. I try and see if I can reach her mind. I am able to locate her and, yes, she is in the secret chamber. But this time I cannot read her thoughts. Although Sianna and Aesres are speaking softly, I'm sure Trista hears them.

The tone of Aesres' voice is becoming more serious as the night deepens. I cannot keep myself from listening, particularly since I know Trista is doing so as well. Aesres tells of the dreams he experienced regarding Inis Elga. Sianna tells of her dreams about the coming of the Danann. Has Sianna ever told Trista about these dreams? My guess is she has not.

The talking becomes quieter, then comes the unmistaken sound of lovemaking. I'm certain this must incense Trista. What will Trista do now?

I sense Trista leaving the secret chamber and returning to her roundhouse. It is deep into the night. Feeling restless and curious, I step outside the roundhouse. I note someone with a torch leaving Trista's roundhouse, moving swiftly down into the village. What can this mean? Looking toward the village, I see lights near the shoreline. It is likely the crew of the Formorri vessel as they prepare to depart. The torch of light that came from Trista's roundhouse merges with these shoreline lights. Although it is chilly, I brought my cloak, so I wrap it tightly around me while I sit and wait to see if the light returns.

Before long, I note the torchlight again, this time coming up the hill. Whoever it is, they're retracing their footsteps. I am too far away to discern who is approaching, but can distinguish two people as they enter Trista's roundhouse. One must be from the ship. Again, I try to see if I can penetrate Trista's mind, but without success. The visitor does not stay long. Torchlight reappears with a single person moving rapidly back down the hillside. I notice no further movement within Trista's roundhouse and so return to my sleeping skins.

My brother and I are awakened by stirring both within and just outside the roundhouse. We dress to investigate and find Aesres and his companions making final preparations for their departure. The air is cold, and puffs of moist breath vaporize all about.

Sianna is standing with her arms folded, watching the men complete their preparations. She sees us and nods our way. Soon, Aesres and his companions are ready to leave. He gives Sianna a formal, somewhat awkward farewell, apparently believing no one suspects the relationship between the two. He then wishes the two of us farewell, reminding us he will return in a few days when we will join him to inspect the lands along the shores of the northern lough.

Sianna asks if Flann and I want to explore the shorelines near Sligeach. She says, "I have much work to do with Trista regarding the affairs of Sligeach. I can arrange to have a coracle made available for you." We immediately express our appreciation and voice excitement about exploring.

My brother and I follow Sianna's servant down toward the shoreline and the awaiting coracle. Although still cold, the sun shines brightly, and the air begins to warm. Arriving at the coracle, we look out over the harbor and spot the Formorri vessel at full sail, making its way from the village.

We place our supplies for the day inside and shove off, deciding to go toward the large island that protects the opening of the harbor from the sea. There is a small net in the coracle. Flann inspects it and says we should try our luck at various spots during the day.

We have a splendid day exploring the island and fishing. We catch a few fish, which pleases us both, as neither Flann nor I have ever tried fishing in open water. We also gather mussels from the rocks at low tide while on the island. As evening approaches, we take advantage of the incoming tidal surge to take us back to Sligeach.

We pull the coracle high up on the beach. The sun will soon set. Flann cords together our catch and I retrieve the net with the mussels. After giving the cooks our fish and mussels, which they say they will prepare for this evening's meal, we make it back to where we have been sleeping. A servant comes and tells us Sianna and Trista are still in council, so the evening meal will be a little later than usual. Flann and I take the opportunity to relax and rest by the fire.

The servant returns later and escorts us to the council chambers. Etain, who we had not seen since our arrival, also joins us. Sianna beckons us to sit near her.

Sianna, pointing to the platters of fish and steamed mussels, says, "Thank you so much for bringing us your catch. The fish is my favorite. I love its pink color and firm meat. The mussels provide an excellent complement to the fish."

Etain is particularly attentive to Sianna's needs. She engages us in conversation and we find her company most agreeable. Trista also participates in the conversations, yet looks remote, as if something is on her mind. Sianna inquires about our excursion in the coracle and what sights we saw.

We drink mead with our meal as well as another liquid I am not familiar with. It is deep purple in color with an unusual taste. Not sweet like the mead. Sianna explains the liquid is called wine and it came from the Formorri trading vessel we saw leave this morning. Thinking we may have never tried it, she thought we might find it pleasant. At first, I find the taste too tart, but soon become accustomed and find it much to my liking.

A gust of wind strikes the blanket covering the opening to the council chambers, briefly flapping it open. I sit nearest to the opening and feel a chill cross me. I wrap my cloak about me a little tighter.

I notice Flann is particularly enjoying the wine. He has never been shy, yet on this evening, he is notably engaging. He recounts to Sianna and Etain the adventures of our day and the several near mishaps we experienced. I add to Flann's stories by telling about how Flann almost fell out of the coracle trying to bring in the first fish we caught.

The hour is becoming late when I notice Trista looking solemn. Sianna also notices and asks, "Trista, is all well?"

Trista looks toward Flann and myself, then back to Sianna and says, "My queen. I hope you can understand what I am about to tell you and your friends from Tomregan. Etain is already aware. Forgive me for not telling you this earlier. I feared with your fondness of the Danann, you would disagree and try and stop me. Everything is now set in motion and nothing can prevent it. I kept your uncle, my brother, High King Elotha, apprised of the activities of the Danann, which is my duty as a Formorri. I fear you have become too close with these Danann and this closeness will be to the detriment of the Formorri people.

"Elotha, along with many warriors, are in ships nearby to protect Sligeach and maintain its neutrality in the upcoming battle between the combined forces of King Ailill and King Daire against the Danann. This battle comes with High King Cullinan's consent. The captain of the Formorri vessel that left this morning informed me these ships are now just offshore. I am to call upon them should Sligeach become endangered and I am to ensure no Formorri warriors from Sligeach are sent to the aid of the Danann.

"Since the landing of the Danann, King Ailill has been in contact with Elotha as well as King Daire of Emain Macha and High King Cullainn. Despite the council from Tomregan, we all concur the powers of the Danann cannot be ignored and danger exists with their presence. King Ailill recommended immediate action before the Danann can secure a strong foothold. King Daire agreed and approval was reached with High King Cullainn, but only if the Formorri remain uninvolved and no harm comes to Tomregan or its inhabitants."

Sianna tries to break in, but Trista continues speaking at now a higher pitch, seemingly determined to say what she wants to say without interruption.

"Yesterday, I sent word with Breas and Rayna to King Ailill, telling him High King Elotha agrees to these terms. King Ailill is unaware of the presence of our forces offshore. The warriors of both King Ailill and King Daire will attack the Danann early tomorrow morning at their camp in Moytura."

Flann and I, and especially Queen Sianna, are stunned. I see Etain try to soothe Sianna, but Sianna brushes her away, giving her a cold stare. Trista rises and says, "I am sorry for this, Sianna. I love you as a daughter, yet no other choice exists. I see you are in great pain and think it best for Etain and I to leave you."

With that, Trista sweeps from the council chambers with a weeping Etain not far behind. Turning to Flann, I say, "It's dark. Nevertheless, you must start your way to Tomregan. Father must know of this immediately. I will look after Queen Sianna." Flann nods agreement, goes and clasps Sianna's hand, then turns and leaves. I move and wrap my arms about Sianna.

CHAPTER TWENTY-SIX

THE MOYTURA BATTLE

Sianna and I travel throughout the night. The moon hangs low, full, and brilliant, lighting our way along the esker for much of our journey. Trista's duplicity still burns hotly in our minds. For Sianna, the apparent support for Trista from Etain must be a deep hurt. Sianna's face is lined with anger and sadness as well as fear.

As we descend the ridgeline toward Lough Aillionn, a deeply chilling, dense fog envelopes the landscape, making it difficult to proceed. We follow the esker path, continuing at a much slower pace. Dawn arrives soon. Even with our travel difficulties, we should reach the Danann shortly after midday. The cold fog penetrates our garments. My sense of fear heightens with each step.

We are each consumed by our own thoughts. Finally, Sianna speaks. "Keelen, I have been such a fool, letting my emotions sway my reasoning. I am Queen of Sligeach and should see the signs of danger. Greater care needed to be taken in my dealings with the Danann. I owe fealty to the High King of Inis Elga, yet I also hold allegiance to the Formorri people and my uncle, High King Elotha.

"Trista is Elotha's representative and she has not been subtle about voicing her concerns regarding the Danann. Why should I be hurt and surprised by her decision to turn against them? I was blinded by my dreams and visions and the strong connection I feel toward Aesres. Were these feelings wrong? My heart tells me no, yet what happened tells me perhaps I was wrong."

Sianna stops walking and looks to the ground at her feet. When I reach her, I wrap her in my arms. Her shoulders heave in silent sobs of pain. We sit on a nearby rock as I try to give comfort.

"Have I told you," Sianna begins again, "Teagan, Aesres' former wife, visits me in my dreams? She has told me of his character and strength and reminds my inner spirit he is no stranger to me. We loved in past lives and are destined to love in this one. How can I ignore such dreams and feelings?"

Bringing her in more tightly and gently rocking her, I assure her what the heart tells needs to be the guiding light. She has done the right thing. Finally, Sianna rises, her stance strong and determined.

"It's time we witness what has happened," she says.

Continuing our journey, I am no longer much aware of walking. The fog takes me deeper into thought. In a corner of my mind, I perceive the emerging figure of Aesres. Focusing intently on the image, he appears troubled. He now recognizes me as well and beckons to me. "Keelen," he says, "there is much you need to understand before you arrive. Let me tell you what has happened since I last saw you and Sianna. Use this knowledge to help soften the pain Sianna is enduring.

"After leaving Sligeach yesterday, I felt a compelling need to return as quickly as possible to our camp. I didn't understand why, though the sense to do so was overwhelming. Little did I know, forces led by King Daire were sweeping in from the north to join the warriors of King Ailill.

"Since our arrival in Inis Elga, King Ailill has shown his reluctance to have us here, believing even in our weakened state we pose a potential threat. This, despite our words of peace and the support of Tomregan. I am also sure Breas recounted to him the power of Aletea and our long history of dominance."

Aesres continues. "By day's end, my companions and I arrived and found all to be well. I met with my brother, reporting the progress made with Queen Sianna. He agrees the lands sound promising.

"Unable to shake my uneasiness, I wished I had a few of our flying eitilte to scout the esker trails, but all had been burned the night of our arrival in Inis Elga. My sleep last night began with dreams of contentment in the arms of Sianna and the sight of future sons and daughters. Those dreams became mixed, then replaced, by scenes of battle and blood. There was treachery in the air and through the mists of battle in my dreams, I began to recognize two faces. They were the faces of Trista and King Ailill.

"Awakening with a start and hastily dressing, I ran to my brother's shelter. Dawn would soon be upon us and I knew the battle scenes from my dreams were about to unfold. Waking my brother, I hurriedly relayed my premonition. Soon after, we roused everyone and prepared for the impending attack. My brother sent those who were not warriors up the esker leading to Tomregan for safety and protection. Those of us who remained readied ourselves. Before long, the attack came. It is taking place as we speak.

"The area known as Moytura is now covered with warriors in full battle. The forces of Emain Macha and Rathcroghan did not catch us by surprise as they had hoped, but they greatly outnumber us, and the fighting is fierce. Our superior skill, even against superior numbers, is evident. The plain above Lough Aillionn is becoming strewn with fallen warriors, the ground oozing their blood.

"Despite our superior skill, we are hard-pressed. The overwhelming numbers are pushing us back against the cliffs at the foot of the slieves of red. We are making our stand here.

"Swinging the Claíomh Solai with every ounce of strength, I slice through innumerable bodies. Wave after wave of warriors attack, though we are repelling them.

"Looking across the battlefield, I see King Ailill. He appears compelled to bring this battle to a victorious conclusion, as he himself is leading the next attack. He rides straight for me, but falls before reaching the sharp edge of Claíomh Solai.

"Despite the failure of King Ailill's charge and the mounting piles of dead, the attack keeps coming. I hope our energy maintains sufficiently to stop these constant surges of new warriors against us.

"Across the battlefield, I see a single warrior advancing through the bodies and dispatching any Danann challenging him. He appears focused on moving toward my brother. I shout a warning to Nuada."

Someone is shaking me, and I begin to faintly hear my name being called. The image of Aesres fades and is replaced by the panicked face of Sianna. She brings me back to reality, saying, "Keelen, can you hear me? You suddenly froze in your steps and have not moved for some time. At first, I waited, thinking you might be having a visitation, but you stood there so long. Are you all right?"

I touch my hand to my head to gain balance. "Sianna," I say, "I was with Aesres. The battle is in full progress."

I tell Sianna all Aesres relayed.

Sianna and I are still a few hours away and the battle may be finished by the time we arrive. "Let us make haste!" says Sianna.

The two of us push along the esker, despite the darkness and fog. At last, light begins to filter dimly through the fog, easing our way. We round what we know is the last curve in the esker near the camp of the Danann. My heart tightens and my stomach knots. The air is eerily quiet. There are neither sentries nor noise when the area should be teaming with people.

We begin to come upon discarded articles of armament. Then bodies and body parts begin to appear. Dismembered arms, legs, and even heads lie in growing number as we proceed. The cold fog is lifting and Sianna and I move toward high ground which will give us a clear view of the plain.

We reach this high ground just as the late midday sun burns through the fog. As we stare out over where the plain should be, the fog parts to reveal a vision of horror. The entire plain, for as far as we can make out, is covered with bodies in heaps. The battle must be finished, as any survivors from either side appear to be gone.

From the armament styles of the dead, we note most are warriors from King Ailill's and King Daire's army. Carrion crows have discovered the battlefield and are making themselves at home, feasting upon the dead. Their cawing fills the air, and more arrive by the minute.

Sianna crumples to her knees. A deep cry of anguish erupts from her, then she clutches her body, bending her head to the ground. Soft weeping follows.

After some moments, she stands full and straight, and an expression of determination is on her face. She turns to me, still with tears running down her cheeks, and says, "Let us acknowledge those who died by moving through the battlefield, remembering those we recognize and noting those we don't with honor.

"Afterwards, we must return to Sligeach to deal with this treachery. Word of survivors and details as to what happened may also await us there. I will dispatch a party of men to care for the dead."

I reach out and take her hand. I understand her greatest fear is not knowing if either her grandfather or Aesres survived.

The remaining daylight is used to review those now joined in the brotherhood of death. Sianna recognizes many of the fallen, though we do not find any sign of either King Ailill or Aesres.

With night falling, our exhaustion overwhelms us. We need to rest, but not near this place of horror. Finding the esker leading to Sligeach, we travel far enough away that we no longer hear the caws of the feasting crows. Sianna points to a flat area under an oak. We slump to the ground. I am instantly asleep.

With sunrise, we begin our journey again, moving along the esker in silence. I sense Sianna turning over many things in her mind, and I'm sure one of the things she worries about is how to deal with Trista and the complicity of Etain.

By midday, Sligeach is near and we are met by anxious members of Sianna's court. Settling onto a clearing near the esker, we partake in the food they brought and listen to their news.

A few of King Ailill's warriors from yesterday's battle became separated during their retreat and have wandered into Sligeach. They tell of the ferocious battle between the combined force of King Ailill and King Daire against the Danann. It had been both kings' hope to catch the Danann by surprise, but when the forces arrived at Moytura, the Danann were prepared and waiting.

The battle was fierce and many of King Ailill's and King Daire's warriors fell. The encounter raged for many hours with the ground, they say, becoming sticky from spilled blood.

They tell us with sheer numbers the Inis Elga warriors pushed the Danann back, despite their mounting losses. By late-morning, the Danann were trapped with their backs to the cliffs. Wave after wave of warriors were thrown against the entrapped Danann, yet they repelled them all. The bodies of dead grew into heaps.

Those telling the story now pause and look between themselves. Finally, one steps forward and says, "My queen, I am saddened to inform you, among those slain was your grandfather. He led one of the many unsuccessful attacks.

"With King Ailill dead and the situation looking hopeless, King Daire ordered a retreat and was able to secure your grandfather's body from the battlefield. It has been taken to Rathcroghan. We were also told King Ailill's champion, Sreng, managed to confront King Nuada of the Danann, severing part of Nuada's hand. However, Sreng needed to retreat before he could kill the Danann king."

Sianna maintains an appearance of calm as this story is told. Yet, I sense she endures deep pain as she hears of the death of her grandfather. I also believe she suffers from anxiety and fear from not knowing if Aesres has survived. Those telling of the battle say the Danann suffered few losses, but no mention is made regarding Aesres.

Sianna turns to me, her face etched in apparent pain, though I sense there is something additional she is pondering. Sianna asks those who met us why neither Trista or Etain are among them. They tell her Trista directed them to come and they have not seen Etain since early morning.

CHAPTER TWENTY-SEVEN

THE AFTERMATH

The day grows long as we listen to a detailed account of the battle. Sianna appears increasingly thoughtful as the story unfolds. She is asking fewer questions and looks to be weighing other matters.

I ask if anyone is aware of the fate of the Danann non-combatants. Aislinn had been staying with my father in Tomregan, learning our ways, yet I fear she may have returned to her home and been caught in this danger. Those telling of the battle say they learned nothing about the Danann non-combatants other than they were seen fleeing toward Tomregan.

Sianna stands, thanking everyone. We proceed to Sligeach, trying to arrive before dark.

Reaching the village does not take long and Sianna gazes toward Trista's roundhouse. I see there's only a faint light and there doesn't appear to be anyone around. I'd imagine that Trista is usually among the first to greet her, though with the recent events, I can understand why she is not.

We both proceed towards Trista's roundhouse. Entering, we find her handmaiden weeping. She gazes up at Sianna, then beckons us to follow her into Trista's bedchambers. There, we find Trista's body reposed on her sleeping skins, her hands still gripping a cup. Smelling the contents and seeing the open compartment of her ring, we know Trista took her own life.

Sianna kneels before Trista's body, holds her hand, and quietly weeps. The handmaiden touches Sianna's shoulder, saying she carries a message from Trista. She glances toward me with the question in her eyes that perhaps I should not be present. Sianna notes the look and informs the handmaiden I am her close friend, advisor, and confidant, and need to hear Trista's last words as much as she does.

The servant commences to tell us Trista's last words. "My mistress was overwhelmed by the necessity to fulfill her duty to her people and her king with the conflicting necessity to be disloyal to you. She told me to tell you she loved you as her own daughter and only wished you to have a life of happiness, yet duty to her people and the upholding of this ultimate commitment to the Formorri at the expense of personal loyalties and affections led to her actions. She ensured her duty was fulfilled, though once fulfilled, she could no longer live with the anguish and sorrow you were to experience. Confident all the Danann would be killed, she knew you would never forgive her. She also wanted to convey that High King Elotha knows nothing of your intimacy with Aesres of the Danann and he believes you continue to be a loyal Formorri Queen."

These words strike Sianna hard. She loved Trista as a daughter would her mother.

Sianna gazes at me with profound sorrow. "I was wrong to conceal my dreams and feelings from Trista. She was my chief advisor. I let emotions cloud my responsibilities. Trista would not have liked my dreams or feelings, yet she may have been able to advise how to accommodate them with my responsibilities. Perhaps all the killing was avoidable."

Sianna turns to the handmaiden and says, "Do you know if High King Elotha is still offshore or have he and his forces landed?"

The handmaiden nods. "Trista sent a dispatch to High King Elotha's vessel, informing him of the Danann victory. A messenger from his camp arrived just before you. The high king and his warriors landed a few miles west, along the coastline. They are prepared to engage the Danann if necessary."

"Thank you," answers Sianna. "In the morning, please send word to his camp informing him of his sister's death. We will make arrangements to honor her.

"Afterward, we will travel to Rathcroghan to prepare for King Ailill's funeral. He is welcome to join us.

"This evening, let us begin preparations for Trista's funeral. I wish to honor Trista's life and respect her final decision. The ceremonial cremation and internment will take place in Trista's roundhouse and we will build a cairn honoring her on the hill overlooking Sligeach near the cairn honoring the ancient champions."

Sianna directs a party of men to the battle site to intern and honor those who died. Because of the overwhelming devastation, Sianna sends most of the men in the village to perform this undertaking.

Etain abruptly enters the room. She appears to be desperately trying to maintain her composure, though she seems near collapsing. "Sianna, my dearest friend and queen," she gasps, "I am truly sorry for the recent events and tragedies. I was blinded and could not comprehend what tragedy would come from betraying you and the Danann. My own time is nearly finished.

"Trista wished for me to be with her at the end, helping her drink from the cup. She sipped half its contents before handing it to me. Holding the cup, I knew it held my fate as well.

"Wishing first to know you had safely returned, I waited until your arrival in the village before draining the remains and returning the cup to Trista's hands. Please forgive me. I am so sorry."

With these words, Etain collapses and Sianna catches her falling body. She holds onto Etain, rocking back and forth, crying. I can only stand back, taking in the sorrow Sianna bears. Long moments pass before Sianna gently lays Etain next to the body of Trista. Lingering a moment longer, she finally rises.

Frightened cries rise from outside. Sianna and I glance toward each other. Wide-eyed attendants storm into the roundhouse. "My queen," one of them exclaims. "The Danann are here, armed and in full force surrounding Sligeach! The one called Aesres bids a meeting with you!"

I detect a nearly imperceptible flash of relief in Sianna's eyes when she hears Aesres is nearby, soon to be before her. "Please inform the noble Aesres I await in my council chambers," Sianna instructs.

Sianna turns to me, now in full command of her emotions, and says, "Keelen, we have become close these past few days, enduring much pain and sorrow together and witnessing great tragedy. Somehow, we must stop this bloodshed. Come with me to my council chambers for the meeting with Aesres. Much work is needed to prevent further bloodshed."

Moving toward Sianna's council chambers, we indeed note what appears to be the entire army of the Danann surrounding Sligeach. The villagers are panicked, but those who spot Sianna stop to watch her reaction.

I can see that Sianna's presence calms the people. She moves deliberately toward her council chambers.

Scanning the far side of Sligeach, I see villagers scattering away from a body of men moving from the Danann encirclement. This must be Aesres and his entourage. Sianna pauses and looks toward the advancing Danann, then moves toward these approaching men and away from the council chambers.

As Sianna and I proceed toward the oncoming Danann, a path clears. We spot one man in front, moving swiftly towards us in full battle dress. There is no mistaking the strong profile of Aesres. At his side, brightly glinting in the sun, is the hilt of his sword, the

Claíomh Solai. Soon we are within feet of Aesres. His eyes search Sianna's face, and her eyes answer with the relief to see him. Aesres relaxes, appearing relieved.

Speaking first, Sianna says, "Trista and Etain are dead. Their treachery toward the Danann was revealed to me hours ago. I can only express sorrow and sadness, asking forgiveness for the betrayal by my family.

"We need to deliberate. Keelen should also join us in my council chambers to discuss the recent events and what steps to take next."

Aesres nods in agreement.

The entire population of Sligeach now surround us. All eyes are on Aesres, but he says nothing. He surveys Sianna and the crowd of villagers, seeming to appreciate the moment, and then together, we all walk toward the council chambers. Turning to his entourage, Aesres tells them, "Make yourself comfortable near here. Things appear to be as we hoped. I do not need your presence inside."

Sianna leads us into her council chambers. Aesres stays a step or two behind, glancing from side to side.

In the privacy of the council chambers Sianna momentarily breaks into tears. She rapidly recovers and looks toward Aesres. "How can you ever forgive me? My closest adviser, Trista, and dearest friend, Etain, betrayed you. Their actions helped lead to the attack. How can we go on together?"

Tears well in Aesres' eyes. "There is nothing to forgive! My heart cares only for you. My eyes show my trust in you is true and I know all is well. Still, we must talk. You do know your grandfather, King Ailill, was killed in the battle? It happened near me. He led one of the last charges and fell bravely."

"Yes, I knew he died. My grandfather is one of many of those close to me who are now dead. How cruel this treachery turns! I lose so many I hold dear." Sianna utters these words quietly and sadly, yet retains her composure.

I say, "We of Tomregan will endeavor to find peace and a home for the Danann. I see the two of you as key to achieving this. Hopefully, Flann will return to Sligeach today with Father to help in this matter."

Sianna nods, saying, "You speak truth, Keelen. I, too, am most anxious for Fearghus to arrive and provide his counsel."

Turning towards Aesres, she says, "I have not been a good queen for my people and I must make amends. Trista did indeed betray you and your people, yet if I had been a better queen, perhaps her death would have been avoided.

"I must warn you, my uncle, High King Elotha, and his army are nearby. They come to ensure the safety of Sligeach, though it is my understanding they, too, would have joined in the attack against you had High King Cullainn approved. He should be coming to the funerals for his sister, Trista, and King Ailill. Is King Nuada close by? We should include him as we discuss these matters."

Aesres considers the request, then turns saying, "My brother is with our forces on the hillside. We were uncertain what to expect and prepared to do battle if needed. I will signal him to come meet with us. Sunset is nearly here. We can all meet to discuss the issues at hand." Sianna agrees and all of us step outside. Aesres flashes a signal toward the hilltop near the edge of the village using the shining metal of the Claíomh Solai in the waning sunlight.

King Nuada and his entourage can be seen approaching. I notice his right arm is heavily bandaged. Although Sianna has become close to Aesres, she only met briefly with King Nuada at the initial meeting.

King Nuada approaches. "Queen Sianna, it is an honor. The high regard Aesres holds for you tells me there is much good in you. I am sorry for the losses you suffered these past few days, especially of your grandfather. The situation is unfortunate. His position at the head of the attack was brave.

"Keelen, I am glad to speak with you again. I met with your father not long ago when I returned from Tara.

"My scouts tell me King Ailill's forces separated from King Daire's, returning to Rathcroghan to mourn their fallen leader. King Daire and his forces retreated not far from Moytura to attend their wounded."

Aesres says, "Sianna just informed me her uncle and his army are camped nearby. Her advisor, Trista, who is High King Elotha's sister, was part of the instigation leading to the attack. She is now dead by her own hand.

"There will be funeral ceremonies soon for them both. Sianna expects Elotha will attend and believes these events may provide an opportunity for talks. Fearghus has been sent for and should be arriving soon. Perhaps he can serve as an arbiter for finding a means to end the bloodshed. I believe there is merit in continuing to listen."

Nuada pauses to consider his brother's words. I deduce from his expression he is feeling doubt. I see him touch his injured arm as if it is a reminder of potential treachery.

Turning to Sianna he says, "Queen Sianna, although I sympathize over your many losses these past few days, let me also express my distrust toward your uncle. Why is he here with forces of his own? Is he waiting for us to weaken so he can attack us himself? Does he intend to expand the Formorri presence here?"

"There is no reason for you to think otherwise," responds Sianna. "Nevertheless, he makes no move against you. He knows of your power, appreciating the difficulty he would have in attacking. But he also knows you are not strong enough to take on his Formorri forces. Agreements are possible, and your survival can be ensured."

King Nuada nods his head in concurrence. "You speak truth regarding a glimmer of opportunity for future peace. Let us determine if talks can be initiated and where the talks will lead."

Nuada turns to his lieutenants and issues an order for his warriors to prepare a battle-ready camp on the hill overlooking Sligeach and adds they should settle in for the night.

Nuada continues. "Then everything appears to be in motion to see if Fearghus can coordinate talks. Aesres, let us retire to our camp to await the arrival of Fearghus and any news of Elotha's intentions. This will give us time to tend our wounded and wait to see what evolves."

With this, both King Nuada and Aesres bow to Queen Sianna and depart.

Sianna regards Aesres and King Nuada as they leave. After some pause, she turns to me. "The time has come to build the funeral biers for Trista and Etain. Let us go to Trista's roundhouse to show where the biers are to be built. If you would help me, I want to wrap each of their bodies with esline cloth. Once they are prepared, I wish for us to place each of them on their biers. I want no one else involved."

I nod acceptance without saying a word.

CHAPTER TWENTY-EIGHT

ARRIVING IN RATHCROGHAN

Sianna and I work through most of the night and early morning preparing the funeral biers. After finishing, small groups of townsfolk take turns paying respects to both Trista and Etain. I assist by welcoming people at the entrance before leading them to where Sianna stands vigil. Sianna greets each person before allowing them to take time with Trista and Etain. As each group leaves, it is a signal for another group to come forward.

Late in the morning, Laragh, Flann, and Father arrive. Flann made good time reaching Tomregan in the dark.

By the time they arrive, almost everyone in the village has paid their respects. Father asks me to inform Queen Sianna of his arrival and his need to speak with her as soon as possible. I go to where Sianna is standing vigil and let her know of Father's wish. She nods, telling me to bring him to her.

Father enters the roundhouse and says, "Queen Sianna, please accept my condolences." After a pause, he continues. "The current circumstances are dire, and I am calling for an immediate Aslach to mediate the situation and dampen the chance of further bloodshed.

The Aslach will convene in Rathcroghan, following King Ailill's funeral. You need to be in attendance, as does High King Elotha."

"Thank you, Fearghus, for calling the Aslach," Sianna responds. "It may be the only remaining hope. A messenger from High King Elotha arrived just before you, saying High King Elotha intends to attend both King Ailill's and Trista's funerals. Shall I call for this messenger?"

"Please do," Father responds. Father tells the messenger to inform High King Elotha that he has declared an Aslach, to be presided over by the elders of Tomregan, and it is to occur the day after King Ailill's funeral.

"The funeral will be at sunset in three days, with the Aslach following at midday," Father continues. "High King Cullainn and King Daire of Inis Elga and King Nuada of the Danann are expected to also be in attendance. Tell the High King I wish for both him and Queen Sianna to attend." The messenger bows, taking his leave to return to Elotha's encampment.

Father asks if he, Laragh, and Flann could now offer their respects to Trista and Etain. Sianna nods, leading the way to their funeral biers.

After paying his respects, Father moves toward the Danann encampment. They are finishing their preparations to leave. I take up my position once more at the doorway of the roundhouse to again organize the remaining villagers who come to pay their respects.

By midafternoon, all who wish to honor the funeral biers have come. I enter Trista's roundhouse to join Sianna. She is standing silently between the two biers, a hand touching each. After an extended pause, she turns to me and says, "Now is the time to leave these sorrows behind and move forward. There is much to be done. I hope your father can lead us through the difficult times ahead."

We find Father, Flann, and Laragh waiting in Sianna's roundhouse. Sianna appears weary. I'm sure she feels drained from the intensity of the events and emotions flowing over all of us these past few days. She thanks Father for coming from Tomregan.

He nods and commences to address what needs to be resolved. "As the elder bard of Tomregan, I am duty-bound to convene the Aslach. I can't imagine the anguish you are feeling. Your strength to look beyond these tragic losses and confront the critical situation is remarkable. Your link to your uncle, High King Elotha, your grandfather, King Ailill, and to the newly arrived Danann will be vital toward finding a solution."

Father recounts his discussions with King Nuada and Aesres. He tells her they have agreed to attend the Aslach, despite misgivings about the other attendees.

He tells Sianna, that with immediate danger appearing low, both King Nuada and Aesres have judged it best to return to Moytura to tend to their injured. Father adds, "They do not believe attending the funeral of Trista and Etain is appropriate. They do not plan to attend King Ailill's funeral either, but will be in Rathcroghan for the Aslach."

Father also tells her he sent a messenger to High King Cullainn regarding the upcoming Aslach with the expectation he will attend.

The whereabouts of King Daire and his warriors is uncertain. King Nuada noted he thought they were tending their wounded near Moytura. Father sends another messenger to where Nuada believes their encampment to be to inform King Daire of the Aslach and his expected attendance.

The funeral for King Ailill is in a few days. Queen Sianna appears to be weighing many things in her mind and, despite looking fatigued, continues the conversation with Father. She says, "The arrangements to help intern the battlefield dead have been made and the funeral biers for Trista and Etain are in place.

"I must oversee the ceremony for my grandfather and prepare for the Aslach. I believe it is best to delay Trista and Etain's funeral until after my grandfather's and the Aslach. I assume that you, along with your family, will be proceeding to Rathcroghan tomorrow? If so, may I join you?"

"Of course, we welcome your company."

Sianna continues. "Now, if you will pardon me, the day has been long and trying. I need to rest before our journey and before the events in Rathcroghan. I am indebted to you for the council you provide and for your steady hand in these times of extreme difficulty. Your daughter is a blessing to me and I rely upon her for valuable support." Turning to leave, Sianna adds, "Sleeping arrangements have been made for your family. I bid you a good evening."

With these words, we all rise as she leaves, and proceed to our sleeping areas. As we walk, Father comes up next to me and pulls me close. Putting his hand on my head, he kisses my forehead softly. "Your mother would be proud," he whispers. I wrap my arm around him tightly, thinking how much I love and admire him and how privileged I feel having him compare me to Mother.

In the morning, little time is wasted before we all are ready to proceed toward Rathcroghan. Conversation is sparse. Time passes rapidly, and we do not stop for a midday meal.

By late afternoon, we reach Rathcroghan. Sentries alert the sons of King Ailill of our approach and Ruairi, King Ailill's oldest, meets us at the edge of the village. Though Sianna and Ruairi are not close, they embrace.

Fearghus asks, "May we offer our respects to King Ailill?"

"Of course," replies Ruairi. "Let me take you to his bier."

King Ailill's roundhouse is in the center of Rathcroghan with open space all about it. As we approach, Ruairi points to piles of kindling and wood being placed all about the roundhouse and the massive stones being carried into the structure.

He says, "The king's body will be interred into a cairn built in the center of the roundhouse under his bier. When the sun sets two nights from today, his roundhouse will be burned. The morning after, the ground will be cleared around the cairn and the site prepared for the Aslach.

"Tables forming a square about the cairn will be set with each of the parties taking one side. The ground to the south has a slight rise and will be the side for the emissaries from Tomregan who will serve as the judges. The Danann will be on the east side, the Formorri on the west, and High King Cullainn and King Daire will be on the north. As King Ailill's sons, Eoghan and I will not be part of the Aslach. We will sit on the edges to listen, along with all the villagers and visitors.

"Accommodations have been made for you and the other Tomregan elders."

We proceed to the entrance of King Ailill's roundhouse with Ruairi showing us in. In the central meeting area, a bier rises above a shallow scooping out of the roundhouse floor. The bier is a simple wooden frame and resting upon it, at about eye level, is the body of King Ailill. Within the room are mounds of stones to be used to create his cairn. Standing like a sentinel near the funeral bier is Eoghan, King Ailill's second son. Eoghan sees us enter and comes to greet us. First, he embraces Sianna, expressing sorrow for what has happened. He then embraces each of us.

Both Ruairi and Eoghan excuse themselves, leaving us alone with the body of King Ailill. Sianna gazes at the form of her grandfather. The moment is poignant, considering all that has happened recently. Despite her misgivings regarding his role in the conspiracy and battle against the Danann, I know she deeply loved him.

Sianna slowly walks to the funeral bier while my family and I keep a respectful distance. I hear soft, muffled crying as Sianna lays her hand on the wrapped shape on the bier. She stands especially upright with her hand on the body for an extended time. Then she bows down to kiss her grandfather before returning to where we stand. As a group, my family makes its way up to the bier, spending a few moments in respect.

After paying our respects, we move towards the entrance of King Ailill's roundhouse. Ruairi and Eoghan meet us near the entrance and Eoghan points to where our quarters will be, then informs

Sianna she will be staying in the vacant roundhouse of King Ailill's high advisor, Trevor, who has not been seen since the battle. He tells her it is not known if Trevor is dead, or if he escaped with King Daire's forces. Eoghan recounts how Trevor strongly influenced King Ailill to attack the Danann. Eoghan further admits both he and Ruairi were not opposed to this council.

Sianna glares at Eoghan coldly and says, "I know the way to Trevor's roundhouse."

Turning to us, she says, "It has been a long journey and I know we are all tired. Let us meet in the morning and talk about what the next few days will bring."

We agree, and with that, Sianna turns and moves toward Trevor's roundhouse.

Eoghan watches her go for a few moments, then says, "Follow me. A building just south of King Ailill's roundhouse is prepared for you and others from Tomregan. You will find several from Tomregan have already arrived." He guides us to the building, which appears to have been for storage, and is now modified into sleeping areas and a meeting area.

Laragh, Flann, and I excuse ourselves and retire to our sleeping areas. We are tired and wish to rest, knowing the next few days will be exceptionally intense. The bringing together of all these parties could prove explosive. Father, and the other elders of Tomregan, will need to use their vast knowledge of Brehon law as well as their innate ability to sense a properly balanced resolution for the Aslach to succeed.

CHAPTER TWENTY-NINE

KING AILILL'S FUNERAL

High King Elotha and his entourage of Formorri are the first to arrive for the funeral. They come just before midday and I see he has been careful not to bring any warriors. He has his high command, advisors, and assorted others. Curiously, among the others is Trevor, the former high advisor to King Ailill. He is indeed alive and seemingly serving a new master. Also of interest among the entourage are Breas and Rayna. Given all that has happened, I assume the two of them have been part of the conspiracy against the Danann. Their presence gives me an uneasy feeling.

Both Ruairi and Eoghan greet Elotha as he enters Rathcroghan, leading him to Trevor's roundhouse to join Queen Sianna. Elotha removes his traveling cloak and the sons of King Ailill escort him to their father's funereal bier. He enters the structure alone. I can only speculate as to what is happening inside. My guess is he is contemplating the upcoming Aslach and the opportunities it holds to strengthen the Formorri presence rather than pondering on the life of King Ailill. Upon concluding his visit, Ruairi and Eoghan escort him back to Trevor's dwelling. The sons of King Ailill appear intent to keep all parties separate during the time leading up to the funeral. I ask Father about this and he confirms he and the elders of Tomregan counseled Ruairi and Eoghan to follow this path.

Messengers soon appear, announcing the approach of High King Cullainn and King Daire. Despite the somberness of the upcoming funeral, there is excitement in the village over the pending arrival of two of the most important people of Inis Elga. By early afternoon, their entourages arrive, with Ruairi and Eoghan directing them to their accommodations. Ruairi attends to High King Cullainn, and Eoghan to King Daire. High King Cullainn wishes to proceed immediately to King Ailill's body to pay his respects.

I am standing near Father as the entourages arrive. He tells me High King Cullainn knew King Ailill since both were children. Though they lived a great distance from each other, they had become close friends. High King Cullainn was aware of King Ailill's apprehension toward the Danann and gave approval to the actions taken by him.

Father tells me he believes High King Cullainn is troubled by the inclusion of High King Elotha and the Formorri in this affair. To him and most of the other kings of Inis Elga, the Formorri are tolerated as a necessary intrusion into their world. The Formorri are skilled traders and the people of Inis Elga profit from their presence. The Formorri trading settlement of Sligeach is not considered a threat, especially since it's ruled by Queen Sianna. Father goes on to say he believes Cullainn views Sianna as having as much loyalty to the people of Inis Elga as to her Formorri uncle, High King Elotha.

Ruairi leads High King Cullainn to the entrance of King Ailill's roundhouse. Cullainn enters alone, spending considerable time inside. After exiting, he returns to his quarters. King Daire sees it is now time for him to pay his respects. Eoghan escorts him to the entrance. King Daire is much younger than either King Ailill or High King Cullainn. Though he and his fighters fought with Ailill against the Danann, he did not know King Ailill well. His visit to the funeral bier is relatively short and he, too, heads straight to his quarters.

Only a few hours remain before sunset and both Ruairi and Eoghan enter King Ailill's roundhouse to make the final preparations. Queen Sianna joins them.

I hear commotion from near the edge of the village. Danann messengers are announcing King Nuada and his brother, Aesres, will be arriving soon. I look at Father in surprise, as this is unexpected. Father appears concerned, and begins moving toward the edge of the village to await their arrival. I tag along.

Before long, the two Danann arrive. Upon seeing Fearghus, they ride to him and dismount. Nuada says, "Fearghus, I was hoping you would be the first person we encountered. After much discussion, Aesres and I both concluded we must honor those who have been integral to the present and past of this land. We hold anger toward King Ailill for his part in the treachery against our people, but as warriors and leaders, we fully understand the basis for his mistrust. We hope our presence will not cause difficulties."

Father nods. "It was my hope you would reach this conclusion and I welcome your arrival. King Ailill's sons and Queen Sianna are completing the final preparations for the funeral ceremony. The time for the observance draws near. Please follow Keelen to your quarters while I consult with High King Cullainn, King Daire, and the sons of King Ailill."

King Nuada and Aesres both acknowledge Father with a dip of their heads and follow me to the Danann quarters set aside for tomorrow's Aslach. Father proceeds towards where High King Cullainn is quartered.

A throng of villagers surround the roundhouse as sundown approaches and a full moon emerges on the horizon. They clear a pathway, whispering among themselves about the presence of the Danann.

King Nuada and Aesres arrive without an entourage. They are dressed in their finest robes. Each brings with them one of the Danann sacred treasures. Nuada carries the spear, Lúin, while Aesres wears Claíomh Solai, the Sword of Light. The end of Nuada's right arm is bandaged, covering the wound where part of his hand was severed.

Father and I join them, and we make our way into the structure set aside for the Danann, which lies on the east side of King Ailill's roundhouse. As with all the buildings housing the Aslach participants, a viewing area, which faces King Ailill's dwelling, has been prepared. Currently, this structure sits between the Danann residence and Trevor's, where the Formorri reside. After tonight's funeral fire, all parties of the Aslach will have clear views of each other.

Sunset will be within the hour. King Nuada and Aesres ask if I will stay with them for the funeral ceremony. I feel honored to do so. To the north, I note activity in the viewing areas in front of Ruairi's dwelling. I spot Father, Ruairi, Eoghan, High King Cullainn, and King Daire in deep conversation. To the south, I note many of my friends and the elders of Tomregan assembling within their viewing area. Catching the eyes of some, they nod acknowledgement.

From the corner of my eye, I glimpse activity coming from Ruairi's roundhouse. Turning to see, I note Queen Sianna joining the group. She and Ruairi converse and I sense they are discussing the Danann. Sianna glances our way. Nuada and Aesres are in deep conversation and do not appear to notice. Sianna notices me looking at her and smiles.

Soon Ruairi, Eoghan, and Sianna leave Ruairi's dwelling to enter the rear of King Ailill's roundhouse. The time has come for their final acknowledgement. His body now rests in the ground, covered by the stones of his cairn. All is silent in the village as we wait for the three to exit the front entrance. Many moments pass before they make their appearance. The three of them walk about the building perimeter, checking the stacks of wood and kindling to ensure all is properly in place.

Returning to the front entrance, with Queen Sianna between

Ruairi and Eoghan, they clasp their hands together and face the roundhouse entrance with heads bowed. The sun is nearing the sky's edge. They turn as one to face the structure holding the Tomregan delegation. Still clasping their hands together, they bow. They then move around the perimeter to where they face the Formorri delegation, but before they reach the Formorri viewing area, they stop and bow towards the villagers who are in place between the viewing areas.

Now they stand before High King Elotha and the Formorri entourage. Elotha bows to them, followed by Breas and Rayna, with Sianna, Ruairi, and Eoghan bowing in return. Moving toward where High King Cullainn and King Daire stand, the three heirs again, as they will at each point between all the viewing areas, stop and bow toward the assembled villagers. Upon reaching the High King, Cullainn bows, followed by King Daire. The three return their bows.

The final group is the Danann with King Nuada and Aesres. I stand by their side. As Sianna and the two sons of Ailill arrive, King Nuada salutes with the spear, Lúin, while Aesres draws and salutes with Claíomh Solai. King Nuada and Aesres hold their stance for several moments before drawing their weapons back and bowing toward Sianna, Ruairi, and Eoghan. The three take an extra moment before returning the bows.

The sun is just dipping below the horizon. Sianna and the sons of King Ailill return to King Ailill's roundhouse where a small fire burns near the entrance. Three torches lie on the ground and each takes one, lighting them in the fire. Queen Sianna, with her torch, stands near the entrance of the residence. Ruairi, with his, moves to a position about one-third around to the left and Eoghan with his to a position about one-third to the right. Each reaches their position and turns to face the gathering. Abruptly, from the darkness around the edges of the village, comes the long wail of bronze horns. It is an eerie reverberation, reminding me of our Samhain rituals for Cenn at Tomregan.

The wail persists several moments before ceasing. Quiet pervades the village. The three, torches in hand, turn to their right and begin igniting the kindling along the edge of the structure. Flames lick the walls, creeping upward toward the thatch. Tongues of fire penetrate the overhanging straw. Heat builds. The thatch bursts into an inferno, sending a hot shockwave against the faces staring into the firestorm.

Sianna returns to where the Formorri are gathered, while Ruairi and Eoghan return to Ruairi's roundhouse to be with High King Cullainn and King Daire.

The flame tips leap high into the sky. Glowing embers jump up each burning fork. The full moon over the village is speckled orange and yellow from the fire and embers. The funeral is a spectacle, one fitting for a king. The heat from the fire is intense, despite the distance each viewing area is from the fire itself. No one moves. Everyone is entranced by the display. Before long, the thatched roof collapses.

After some time, the walls begin to sag inward. From where we stand, the viewing area where the Formorri stand begins to come into view. I can make out each of them. Elotha stands in the middle, with Sianna at his right, Breas and Rayna to his left. Although difficult to tell from this distance, Elotha, Breas, and Rayna each appear to be staring into the now dying back flames. Sianna's eyes, however, appear to be gazing across the fire toward us. I glance over to King Nuada and note he is peering into the flames, but Aesres is gazing over the flames toward Sianna.

During this time, I have seen no movement from anyone in the crowd. However, with the flames now dying back and the structure in ruins, many of the villagers begin to stir and return to their homes. Those of us watching in the viewing stands linger. I spot High King Cullainn as he raises his arms and turns toward each viewing area, including that of High King Elotha, and bows. When finished, he turns and enters Ruairi's roundhouse, followed by Ruairi. King Daire and Eoghan move toward Eoghan's residence. I bid Nuada and Aesres a good evening and join Father, who is walking toward me. The ceremony for King Ailill is complete. Now the Aslach awaits us.

CHAPTER THIRTY

PREPARING FOR THE ASLACH

Sounds of activity from where King Ailill's roundhouse once stood awaken me. The sun has not risen, but the half-dark of pre-dawn signals it's coming. Looking outside, I see workers scurrying about the grounds, extinguishing the last of the hot embers and clearing away debris. King Ailill's cairn is clearly exposed in the center of the area. I notice initial stirrings from the other structures surrounding the cairn.

Ruairi and Eoghan are among the workers clearing away the debris. The two are working closest to the cairn to ensure the area is suitably cleared and the cairn undisturbed. The process of cleaning the grounds and preparing the tables for the Aslach will take several more hours. The preparations should be complete well before time for the Aslach to begin, which is when the sun is directly overhead.

Convening an Aslach is not common. Brehon law dictates the parties involved don't interact with each other before the Aslach commences. Retreating to the Tomregan compound, I find most everyone is awake. They are preparing food and drink and gathering about a central table that will later serve as the table where the

Tomregan delegation will sit. Flann and Laragh signal to me and together we sit at one corner of the table. Father and all the elders are in discussions about how the day will proceed. Father will moderate the Aslach and ensure the gathering proceeds without becoming mired in detail. The remaining elders will listen to what each party says and make inquiries as needed.

Laragh, Flann, and I can see we are not needed and decide to wander about the village. While walking, I detect two figures approaching the village from the north. Soon I recognize them as Aislinn and Cairpre. Flann and Laragh also spot them, and we rush over to greet them. Aislinn and Cairpre tell us their father had not wanted them to attend the funeral, but believed it important that they witness the Aslach. Aislinn and Cairpre ask lots of questions regarding the funeral.

We proceed to where King Nuada and Aesres are quartered and find the two of them polishing the spear, Lúin, and the sword, Claíomh Solai, and speculating about the upcoming events. Upon seeing us, they rise to greet Aislinn and Cairpre. Both Nuada and Aesres seem to be in good spirits. We leave them and continue to walk about the village.

The remnants from King Ailill's roundhouse are almost removed. Several people sweep the ashes into baskets to carry away. King Ailill's cairn prominently rises above the remnants of last night's inferno. As we walk around the grounds, I tell Aislinn and Cairpre about the soaring flames and sparkling embers. As we pass the quarters for the Formorri, I see Queen Sianna is standing alone in the viewing area. She appears deep in thought, staring at her grandfather's cairn. I call out in greeting as we approach. She acknowledges us, but appears to be weighing serious matters. As we pass, she says, "Keelen, do you have time to spend with me?" This catches me by surprise, but I quickly tell her yes and join her. The others wave goodbye and continue their walk.

Sianna welcomes me and says, "Brehon law states that parties cannot discuss issues between themselves before an Aslach begins. I know you are not technically part of the proceedings, but your father will play a pivotal role, so I cannot discuss specifics with you. Let us walk toward the edge of the village. I need to be with someone I trust."

There are several hours remaining before the Aslach commences, giving ample time for Sianna and me to talk. "As I said, I cannot discuss specifics with you," continues Sianna, "but please keep anything I do tell you in confidence." She pauses, again looking deep in thought, then says, "My uncle does not intend to sail away from Inis Elga without achieving at least some of his goal to create a greater Formorri presence. As the local Formorri Queen, I must support him, though I may not agree. He wishes me to be the Formorri Aslach representative who suggests his ideas for solving the Danann situation. These ideas will be couched to make them at least minimally acceptable to the Danann and they will seem even more acceptable if coming from me. My grandfather's former high advisor, Trevor, informed my uncle of my friendly relations with the Danann, advising him to exploit those relations. As the Formorri Queen of Sligeach and the Aslach representative, I will not be able to openly tell Nuada or Aesres of his true intent. I am hoping that after the Aslach, you can inform them why I did his bidding and the true purpose of what he wants."

This news alarms me. My first instinct is to say I cannot keep this kind of information from my father and others, but, I refrain. We walk a while in silence as I consider this revelation.

Then Sianna declares, "I've put too much burden on you and cannot hold you to keeping the information confidential, though I must still advise you to do so. I believe there is an advantage to the Danann agreeing to Elotha's plan. Doing so would provide the Danann time to establish themselves and grow strong. This is the primary reason I agreed to help my uncle. Come, we need to return to the Aslach site. It is time to make the last preparations."

I look at Sianna, feeling her pervading sadness. We proceed back toward King Ailill's cairn. Sianna gives me much to weigh and consider. Somehow, this information needs to be given to others, but who?

I leave Sianna and head back toward Father. Around the cairn, four tables are being arranged for the Aslach. I am still considering what I should do, and am glad Sianna released me from keeping the information confidential. She did not reveal Elotha's plan, only that the plan is designed to favor the Formorri.

At our quarters, I spot Father still in discussions with the other elders. Divulging to him what Sianna revealed would be inappropriate. He and the other elders need to be impartial arbitrators. Hearing this would stain their objectivity.

I conclude King Nuada and Aesres must be informed. They need to know so they can participate in the Aslach on even footing with the Formorri. The Aslach outcome could depend on their knowing.

Looking about the grounds, I spot Laragh, Flann, Aislinn, and Cairpre near Ruairi's dwelling. To reach them, I need to pass the Danann viewing area. Both Nuada and Aesres are standing in their viewing area, surveying the activity about them. This could be my opportunity.

They greet me as I come close. Moving towards them, I smile and say in a low voice, "I carry news regarding Queen Sianna." Their eyes tell me they understand the need to act as though nothing more than common conversation is occurring.

Hurriedly, I divulge the information. We each maintain appropriate composure, though they nod acknowledgement.

I note Laragh, Flann, Aislinn, and Cairpre approaching and turn to greet them as though nothing unusual has happened. They ask why Queen Sianna wished to walk with me and I only say she wanted quiet time with a friend before the Aslach begins. Flann indicates it is time for us to return to our own viewing area as the Aslach will soon start. We wish the Danann farewell. Laragh peers at me with knowing eyes, but says nothing.

CHAPTER THIRTY-ONE

THE ASLACH

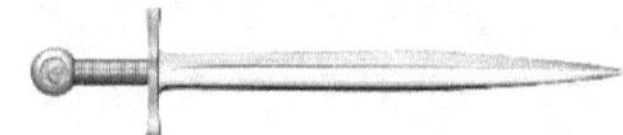

We arrive at our quarters just as Father and the other elders are preparing to leave. Only Aslach participants are allowed at the tables surrounding King Ailill's cairn, however anyone is free to listen and watch at a distance. The three of us take our seats in the viewing area. The day is crystal clear and warming to a comfortable temperature. One can smell the burnt wood and ash from the fire. A light, warm breeze pleasantly stirs the air.

The elders from Tomregan are the first to take their position at the Aslach tables. Father moves to a spot inside the arrangement of tables to stand next to King Ailill's cairn. Once he's there, the Formorri and the Danann take their appointed places.

With everyone settled, Father looks toward each of the parties, then, facing High King Cullainn, he begins to speak. "Great King, King Ailill's cairn lies before us. His death is the unfortunate consequence of the battle between the Danann and the combined forces of King Ailill and King Daire. The Danann are refugees from their land, which was recently destroyed, and is now lying under the sea to our west. Their coming has been expected for many years from the prophecies given at Samhain by the White Horse. We of Tomregan, as well as Queen Sianna of Sligeach, welcomed them to our lands since the prophecies told they'd come in peace and the lands of Inis Elga would prosper with their presence. From our reports of the prophecies to you and to King Daire each year, you too were aware of their expected coming. The Danann arrived peacefully not long ago along the shores of Lough Aillionn. They burned their formidable eitiltes as an offering to the gods, Cenn and Danu, in thanks for their safe passage and as a sign to you of their peaceful intentions.

"Although I am one of the arbitrators for this Aslach, I cannot but be surprised by the actions taken by King Ailill and King Daire. Your approval of their attack particularly confounds me. Despite these misgivings, I can assure you, High King Cullainn, we will listen to all that is said with open minds, trying to understand the situation from perspectives different from our own. The arbitrated outcome of the Aslach will consider all that is heard, with its conclusion binding under Brehon law."

After finishing his opening remarks, Fearghus continues to stand near Ailill's cairn, holding his staff for support.

High King Cullainn stands and begins to address the Aslach. "Fearghus, you are correct in your observation that you kept not only me, but all the kings of Inis Elga aware of the prophecies from the White Horse of Binn. However, we are not druids or bards, but men with responsibilities for the people we lead. We take the information from prophecies and advice from our advisors and weigh that information against what would happen if the information were wrong. Part of the weighing includes our regard of the sources. My fellow kings and I have the highest regard for what you of Tomregan tell us, but this high esteem is not a regard that considers your counsel infallible.

"King Ailill discussed with me many times the prophecies from the White Horse. It is well known the Danann, even in reduced numbers, are formidable. Ailill's concerns regarding their proximity were well-founded. King Daire shared these same concerns. King Ailill also reached out to the Formorri regarding these apprehensions. He had a long history of contact with the Formorri and trusted them. His own daughter married High King Elotha's brother. His granddaughter from that union is Queen Sianna of Sligeach. The Formorri know well of the Danann through their extensive trading network. King Ailill was more aware than any of us of the true power held by the Danann. I relied heavily on his counsel before approving the attack. My approval was only given under the conditions the Formorri not be included in the attacking forces and no harm come to the people of Tomregan. I am uncertain what led to King Ailill's final decision to attack. Regrettably, he is dead and cannot provide us his reasoning. However, both of his sons are here. If Fearghus approves, I would like Ruairi to relate to us what he knows."

Fearghus nods his acceptance and Ruairi begins to speak. "My father had, as do we all in Rathcroghan, the highest respect for the elders of Tomregan and consider all information and counsel from them with utmost seriousness. We also regard the Formorri as our friends and they, too, tell us stories of the Danann. They have described a commanding people whose lands were destroyed because they thought their powers to be as great as, or superior to, their goddess, Danu. The Danann became a divided people, the worst of whom were destroyed thirteen Samhains past. Even with the destruction of the most wicked elements, the goddess Danu was still troubled by their actions. The most recent appearance of the bearded star portended their end was near. Given this history, how could we be certain the Danann, who were prophesized to come to the shores of Lough Aillionn, would not carry some elements of this evil? Father and the drui of Rathcroghan tried to discourage their landing near Lough Aillionn by creating a dense fog. But this effort was thwarted by the drui of Tomregan and the Danann successfully arrived. It appeared they burned their powerful flying eitiltes, but we could not be certain some had not been hidden away. The Danann came armed, evident even last night at Father's funeral, with the appearance of the spear, Lúin, and the sword, Claíomh Solai, in the hands of King Nuada and his brother, Aesres.

Trevor, our high counselor, recommended we discuss the Danann situation with the Formorri. We felt their extended contact with the Danann would be insightful. These discussions led to the decision to attack. We relayed this decision to King Daire and High King Cullainn, asking High King Cullainn for his approval of the attack and if we could enlist the services of the Formorri. King Daire joined the attack with his forces, but the Formorri followed High King Cullainn' s condition that they not participate.

We were not successful, a testament to the strength of the Danann. As a result, Father lies before us encased by his cairn. Father concluded the best path to take for the long-term good of our people was to destroy the Danann."

As he spoke, Ruairi focused his attention straight ahead in the direction of the Tomregan representatives. He never glanced either to his left, toward the Danann, nor to his right, toward the Formorri. His voice sounded bitter, but was this bitterness toward the Danann for killing his father or some other factor?

Ruairi sits after finishing and Father speaks again. "We have listened to the reasoning behind the attack. King Nuada, I invite you to address us."

King Nuada rises from his seat, but before speaking, he gazes slowly at each person assembled around the cairn for the Aslach. His focus then turns to Father and the elders of Tomregan, and he begins. "My people experienced difficult times for many years and those of us who arrived here represent only a small handful of the multitude we once were. Ruairi is correct in his account of the divisions within our people and the destruction of many of them thirteen Samhains past. Unfortunately, remnants of those opposed to our goddess Danu survived the destruction and their thoughts continued to infect our people. We of the northern lands of Aletea stayed true to the goddess Danu. As a reward, she provided us the opportunity to escape to Inis Elga while she began the final destruction of our homeland.

"Prophecies foretold this could occur, and the prophecies also identified where we would go. Through visions, she revealed to us the land of Inis Elga, along the shores of Lough Aillionn. When the bearded star appeared, the visions, as seen through my daughter, Aislinn, became stronger. In spirit, Fearghus's daughter, Keelen, visited our lands to learn about us and to help us in our journey. We were warned not everyone on Inis Elga would welcome us, but the kings of Inis Elga were aware of the prophecies and these prophecies foretold we'd come in peace."

Flan, Laragh, and I exchange glances. I appreciate that King Nuada's referenced our help.

He continues. "Although an effort was made to prevent our landing, it appeared we would be welcomed and allowed a place to live. I met personally with you, High King Cullainn, as well as King Ailill. Through our contacts with Queen Sianna, suitable lands for settlement were identified along the large lough northeast of Sligeach. My brother, Aesres, was in discussions with Queen Sianna regarding this land and he returned to our camp the night before the attack. If not for my brother's dream that night foretelling treachery, we would not have been prepared to defend ourselves and it is likely the goal of King Ailill and King Daire would have been accomplished.

"The collusion between the kings of Inis Elga, including you, High King Cullainn, ended in your defeat. The Danann people claim the right to rule and entreat the Aslach to recognize this assertion. Banish High King Cullainn, King Daire, and the sons of King Ailill from their positions of power. They must depart to another region of Inis Elga, perhaps the wilds to the west."

Shouts of anger erupt from the contingency of High King Cullainn and King Daire. Sreng, their champion, leaps onto their table, brandishing his sword and shouting a challenge to King Nuada. "Let us settle this now in single combat. I will finish what I started when I took off your hand!"

Aesres jumps to his feet, taking a defensive stance beside King Nuada with Claíomh Solai drawn.

Father moves between the two delegations to defuse the situation.

Nuada holds up his injured right arm, proclaiming, "I would be happy to avenge the loss of part of my hand against Sreng in single combat. But only if the combatants are equally handicapped. Sreng, shall someone remove part of your right hand so we may proceed with the contest?"

Sreng glares toward Nuada, hate etched across his face. Tense moments pass before he lowers his sword and returns to his place at the table.

Nuada continues. "We are not a vengeful people, but we do expect justice. We call for no deaths or the removal of anyone outside of High King Cullainn, King Daire, and the sons of King Ailill. Communal society must continue if peace is to be maintained. Rulers need be selected to replace King Daire and King Ailill, but no one should be named High King. We will place the Lia Fáil, the Stone of Destiny, which selected our Aletea kings through the ages, at Tara. During the next Beltane festival, the Lia Fáil should select the next High King."

Turning his focus to the Formorri contingent, Nuada says, "Since the attack, I learned of the possible complicity of the Formorri. From my understanding, only High King Cullainn's directive prevented the Formorri from being part of the attack. I am familiar with Elotha, knowing him from our time in Aletea. One of his wives was the daughter of our Danann High King, and his son, Breas, is a close friend of my own son. Breas and Cairpre were together, along with Aislinn, the night the southern portion of Aletea was destroyed by the mighty tear sent by the goddess Danu from the bearded star."

King Nuada pauses, looking over toward the Formorri contingent.

"To my surprise, Breas is here, among your delegation. Thankfully, I know of no direct involvement by him in the attack.

Also among your delegation is Queen Sianna, who is an ally we trust. My hope, High King Elotha, is for you and your warriors to leave Inis Elga. With the help of Queen Sianna, and possibly Breas, should he wish to stay, we can build at least a tolerant, if not friendly relationship."

Now facing Father and the delegation from Tomregan, Nuada continues. "Claiming kingship should be my right. However, as you can see from my disfigured hand, all I have left is my thumb and short stubs of the remaining fingers. Danann tradition requires a Danann king be a whole person with all appendages and senses. Because of this injury, I can no longer serve as king of the Danann, nor assume any other kingship. My brother, along with the elders of our people, deliberated on this situation. We intend, for the immediate time, to be ruled by our council of elders, of which Aesres and I are part. We wish to settle on the lands along the northern loughs that Aesres located. Further, we wish to include the area ruled by King Daire as part of our domain.

"There are too few Danann to consider including the realm of Rathcroghan as well. Identifying the new Rathcroghan king is a sensitive matter. No one involved in the attack against us would be an acceptable choice. Finding a proper candidate not involved in the attack will be difficult."

As King Nuada speaks, I regard the expressions of those around the Aslach tables. Neither Father nor any of the Tomregan elders betray their emotions. Each is listening closely.

High King Elotha leans forward from his seat, listening with keen interest. Once King Nuada's talk turns to the issue of his severed fingers and his inability to continue serving as king, a nearly imperceptible smile crosses his face.

Sianna stoically watches King Nuada as he speaks.

Breas and Rayna attempt to display little emotion, but when Nuada describes his hand and the need to identify a new Rathcroghan king, they exchanged a glance.

The delegation for High King Cullainn and King Daire continues to exhibit agitation.

While observing everyone, I detect movement from Eoghan's nearby roundhouse. Glancing over, I spot a large bird perched on the roofline peak. Peering closely, I discover it is a crane. The presence of a crane portends much. We consider them messengers to the kings. They counsel toward paths of accommodation to avoid war. Is the bird's presence a sign or mere chance?

King Nuada finishes and all eyes shift toward High King Elotha. Father again addresses the Aslach, asking if the Formorri wish to speak. To everyone's surprise but my own, Queen Sianna rises as the Formorri representative. Sweeping her gaze across all in attendance, she begins.

"High King Elotha believes it best for only those who live in Inis Elga to speak at this Aslach, as it is their future being decided. With my father being his brother and my mother being the daughter of King Ailill, he believed I should represent the Formorri. The High King personally expressed to me his regret for supporting King Ailill's decision to attack the Danann.

"His long personal contact with the Danann, his marriage to the daughter of the Danann High King, and his personal familiarity with King Nuada and his brother, Aesres, should have assuaged his fears. His own son, Breas, is a close friend of Cairpre, King Nuada's son.

"My uncle believes the path King Ailill pursued against the Danann was one of several available to ensure stability. However, this path is now withered and gone.

"A new path must be found and followed. I respect the Danann and was distressed with the actions taken by my grandfather. I also have much respect for my uncle and my Formorri blood. The Formorri presence in Inis Elga has been long, prosperous, and peaceful, one my uncle wishes to ensure continues."

I see Sianna moving her gaze toward the Danann delegation.

"A new king is needed for Rathcroghan, but as King Nuada stated, this is not an easy task. There is merit to King Nuada's argument that it would be difficult from the Danann perspective to have anyone involved in the attack as king. This argument plays against considering either of King Ailill's sons. Have a Danann king? The logical selection would be King Nuada, but that is impossible given his injury.

"My uncle suggested an idea for my consideration, which I first thought unseemly. The idea being to have a king who is a stranger to these lands, but who by birth holds strong ties both to the Danann and the Formorri. This kingship does not need to be permanent, but only put in place until a suitable candidate is agreed upon. The best choice is Breas. He, like myself, is half Formorri, being the son of High King Elotha, but he is also half Danann, as his mother is Fiona, daughter of the Danann High King Conall. Even saying this now, the idea appears unseemly, but I can comprehend no other clear alternative. This proposal is perhaps one that can be accepted by all parties and bring peace to the land."

With this statement, Queen Sianna returns to her seat. I note High King Cullainn staring at the Formorri viewing area, taking in the sight of Breas. Nuada and Aesres do not appear surprised. My message regarding Sianna's warning that something unusual would be offered must have taken hold with them.

All eyes turn to Fearghus, who still stands next to King Ailill's cairn. Fearghus glances toward the Danann and to High King Cullainn to determine if they have any further words to offer, but neither party makes a move to speak. Seeing no further words are to be spoken, Fearghus bows to each of the three viewing areas and returns to sit with the other elders of Tomregan.

It is time for them to discuss what has been said so they can decide the outcome of the Aslach. The elders stand as Fearghus approaches, but before they return to their quarters, a loud squawk comes from the roofline of Eoghan's dwelling. Rising above the roundhouse, unfolding its wings for flight, is the crane. The bird squawks again as it flies over those assembled and then flies away to the west. Everyone gazes at the bird until it can no longer be seen.

Fearghus and the Tomregan elders retire to their quarters. Uncertainty pervades as to how long the ruling will take or what decisions will be made as part of this ruling. The issues are complex, and the alternatives voiced by the involved parties each have points of merit and elements of difficulty.

To me, the idea of Breas as king of Rathcroghan, even if only temporary, is absurd. Breas is not of Inis Elga and Rathcroghan must only be ruled by someone who has lived in this land.

CHAPTER THIRTY-TWO

THE DECISION

No one knows how long it will take Father and the Tomregan elders to deliver their decision. The Aslach itself only lasted until mid-afternoon.

The parties to the Aslach have retired to their quarters. Flann and I spot Aislinn and Cairpre leaving the Danann quarters and we move towards them. "Can you believe the idea of Breas as King of Rathcroghan?" exclaims Cairpre as we meet up with them. "That would be too strange. But Father believes the concept may be the only solution in the short run and he's prepared to accept it. I wonder if Ruairi, Eoghan, King Daire, and High King Cullainn will really be banished."

"What of your father?" I ask. "Does he really intend to step down as king?"

"As he stated in the Aslach, he convened a meeting of elders and their decision is to rule by council, delaying consideration of who should be the Danann King. Father believes our skilled silversmiths can create artificial fingers. Having stubs remaining of each finger provides hope he can regain full finger mobility again."

"If a functioning hand can be crafted, would this new ability allow him to be king again?"

"He hopes this will be true. There is too much flux in the current situation to not have a strong Danann leader."

Walking about Rathcroghan, we see anxious villagers, huddled in groups, engaged in animated conversation. I sense their fear of having an outsider be their king. I share their fear. Breas is not familiar with our ways. I question Cairpre and Aislinn about Breas. Aislinn says she only knew him for the brief period when they were together in the cities of Danu.

Cairpre says, "As children, we were virtually inseparable, exploring every cranny within the cities of Danu. As we grew older, Breas's father sent him away to their home islands with greater frequency until, a few years ago, he never came back. I am happy to see him again, but, as I've said before, he is different now, more Formorri than Danann. He also appears to be close to his half-sister, Rayna. She seems to have influence and power over him. I know nothing of her."

I ask if Nuada and Aesres have contingencies based on what the decision may bring. Aislinn looks at me and says, "Father thanks you for the information you brought before the Aslach. He and Aesres deduced Breas might be involved as part of the solution, and Father crafted his words before the Aslach based on this deduction. They tell me Breas is a better alternative than having Ruairi as King of Rathcroghan. The Formorri are formidable and he wishes not to war with them. He believes they will be consolidating their new power for several years, giving the Danann time to grow stronger. Inevitably, war will come. Father hopes to buy time."

Cairpre nods his head in agreement. Flann asks me what information I gave to King Nuada and Aesres after my walk with Sianna. I catch him up and he agrees having Breas as ruler is the optimal decision for the Danann, though having an outsider will not be well accepted by the villagers.

"The kingship should not be given to an outsider," I say. "Breas may be half Danann, but he is also half Formorri. I believe his heart is with the Formorri and will never be for Inis Elga or the Danann. Ruairi may have agreed to attack, but he is King Ailill's son and of Inis Elga. Given the options, I believe he would agree to peaceful relations with the Danann."

We walk to the far eastern side of the village where an ancient wall stands. Legend tells us this wall once surrounded Rathcroghan, but peace in the land had diminished its importance. Now all that is left is the eastern section. The other portions are gone, but the people of Rathcroghan continue to maintain the eastern section in respect for the old times. The battlement is unique in its double-walled construction, with the space between the two walls stretching about twenty paces. The structure appears impenetrable, extending the full length of the village.

Near the middle portion of the wall grows an ancient and knurled sacred oak. Its branches sweep down to the wall's edge, covering some of its exterior. As the tree is considered sacred, no one has entered its foliage for several generations. Approaching the tree, Laragh is particularly drawn to it. She beckons us to come along towards its branches. I, too, sense an energy emanating, but Laragh appears to be communicating with the tree. Laragh is silent as we stand near the tree, staring into the foliage. Several moments pass before Laragh swiftly turns with panicked eyes and says, "We must return without delay to warn Nuada and Aesres. Their lives are in danger!"

Startled by this sudden pronouncement, we race towards the village. As we scramble, a bronze horn blares, proclaiming the Aslach decision will soon be announced. Reaching the Danann quarters, we spot King Nuada and Aesres. Laragh beckons them to come listen. We cannot catch what Laragh is saying but hear the urgency in her voice and note the rapt attention being given by Nuada and Aesres.

King Nuada turns towards us. "There is treachery in the air. Aislinn and Cairpre, quickly gather your things. We must leave now and follow Laragh to an escape point. Our lives are in danger. Keelen and Flann, there is no time to explain, but all will be evident soon. It is important the two of you return to where Fearghus is about to make his announcement. Laragh will come with us as we escape to the northern loughs. She will rejoin you later."

Looking at Flann in amazement, I move hastily to say goodbye to our friends and to wish our sister well. Laragh assures us all will be fine. The sacred oak told her as much and has shown her the way to lead the Danann to safety. Flann and I exit the compound and move toward where Father and the other Tomregan elders are assembling. While approaching Father's location, I glance toward the Formorri enclave and see Elotha already in place, surrounded by his armed entourage. Queen Sianna is standing off to the side. I sense from her a high level of anxiety and note she is staring out toward the cairn of her grandfather, doubtlessly continuing her gaze across to where the Danann viewing area lies. I am certain she is anxious to understand why the Danann are not there.

Fearghus steps up to King Ailill's cairn and all eyes center on him. "High King Cullainn," begins Father, "the events of the past week have been troubling. We of Tomregan are of the unified opinion the Danann came in peace. King Ailill, in concert with King Daire, did not serve to benefit the lands of Inis Elga with their attack on the Danann. King Ailill paid the price for this error and we wish to condemn King Daire for his participation in this attack.

"In our judgment, the Danann are granted the lands along the shores of the northern loughs as a new home, living there as an independent people. They will also have domain of the lands controlled by King Daire. For their complicity in the attack, High King Cullainn and King Daire forfeit their crowns and are banished to the western lands of Inis Elga. Rathcroghan is of vital importance. The kingship of Rathcroghan must be held by a native son of Inis Elga. We concur its logical new king to be King Ailill's oldest son, Ruairi. With these pronouncements, we conclude this Aslach."

As Father finishes the Aslach pronouncements, I see many

pointing to the empty Danann viewing area, puzzled by the Danann absence. Looking over toward the Formorri, I note Elotha appears not at all upset or concerned with the Aslach findings, though they are not in his favor.

Elotha rises. As he does, armed Formorri warriors come forward, taking positions around the Aslach area. He begins to speak. "Elders of Tomregan, we of the Formorri respect your traditions and ways, but they are not our traditions. You are making a grave error in your judgment of the Danann. Yes, they are friendly and peaceful now, but my people have known the Danann since we can remember, and they have always ruled and always been the most powerful people of all the lands of the earth. They speak of egalitarianism, but their own goddess slew most of them as punishment for taking advantage of others and wanting to rule as gods themselves. We must finish the job their own goddess began and wipe their memory from this earth forever.

"You will note they are absent. I am sure King Nuada and Aesres are on the run. They likely plan for a new clash, but they are trapped. My forces have surrounded Rathcroghan up to the edges of its mighty eastern wall and there is no escape. Even after we find King Nuada and his brother and kill them, the remaining Danann will still be imposing. It will take time to completely eradicate them.

"I accept the ruling that Ruairi will one day be King of Rathcroghan, but not until we Formorri eradicate the Danann. Until such time, my son Breas will rule as the military commander of Rathcroghan with a contingent of Formorri and Rathcroghan fighters. They will hunt down the Danann.

"I welcome Ruairi and his brother, Eoghan, to serve as commanders of the Rathcroghan warriors until this issue is settled. Once settled, Breas will relinquish his position as military commander and Ruairi will be crowned. High King Cullainn and King Daire, we have no quarrel with you. Continue with your positions and depart Rathcroghan in peace."

Near chaos is now enveloping Rathcroghan. I see High King

Elotha talking in earnest with Queen Sianna. He is pointing in our direction.

Sianna comes over to us, and says, "The move by my uncle to take power caught me by surprise and now I feel trapped into staying with the Formorri contingent as we must leave soon to attend Trista's and Etain's funeral. My uncle instructed me to inform you he wishes no harm to come to those of Tomregan and hopes soon you will understand and agree with his decision. You are free to leave and return to Tomregan whenever you want."

Sianna turns to me and asks, "Have you word on the fate of Aesres and Nuada? They evidently made their escape, as Elotha's warriors cannot find them."

I recount to Sianna all that has happened with Laragh and the sacred oak and how she is guiding Aesres, Nuada, and his children to safety over the eastern wall. I say, "Yes, it does appear Laragh was successful. The five of them must be well along in their trip back to the Danann encampment. Sianna, won't you stay with us? Although Father wishes to proceed at once to Tomregan, I'm sure Flann and I could accompany you to Sligeach."

Sianna takes my hand. With emotion, she says, "That is kind, my dear friend, but this is a burden I must face myself. Perhaps I can be a voice of reason with Elotha, Breas, and Rayna. I must try."

With that, Sianna departs. I accompany her for a short distance as she returns to the Formorri contingent. Turning to me one last time she says, "You and your family must leave. It is dangerous here. Promise that as you learn about the fate of Aesres and King Nuada, you will somehow get word to me." She gives a wan smile, then departs.

High King Cullainn, King Daire, and their contingents are the first to exit Rathcroghan. My family and I finish our preparations to depart. We will not be going to Sligeach for Trista's funeral but instead will return to Tomregan.

As we leave, I observe Ruairi's roundhouse is now occupied by Breas and his entourage. Rayna is directing where items should be placed. Breas is strutting about, apparently pleased with the day's outcome. Eoghan's residence is being transformed into a military headquarters for the Formorri commanders. The villagers appear stunned by the developments. Their faces reflect disdain for the Formorri, but they act with the timidity of a conquered people. The Formorri roam about the village, treating it as their own, with minimal regard for the inhabitants.

High King Elotha and Queen Sianna mount horses for their trip to Sligeach. Trista's and Etain's funerals are to be tomorrow evening. Looking toward Sianna one last time, we nod acknowledgement to each other. Then they are gone.

CHAPTER THIRTY-THREE

THE ESCAPE

Two moon cycles have passed since we last saw Laragh. We arrived in Tomregan without incident, but have received no word from anyone regarding the activities of Breas and the Formorri. Whether High King Elotha left Inis Elga or not is unknown. We also have no news concerning High King Cullainn or King Daire, but assume no news means they returned safely to their raths.

I know Laragh and the Danann are safe. Ravens visit me often and I understand through their cawing that all is well. I did send word to Sianna regarding the news the ravens provided, but she did not respond.

The latest ravens are more excited than the earlier ones. Through their cawing, I understand Laragh is on her way to Tomregan.

Father appears in good spirits despite the outcome of the Aslach. He confides to Flann and me he believes the Formorri made a grave mistake with their power-play in Rathcroghan. They may hold the upper hand now but, as noted by High King Elotha, the Danann are a formidable foe, even with their small numbers. Calling them out as enemies is a dangerous step, and the Danann are gaining allies.

Travelers from the area say Ruairi and Eoghan were incensed by the actions of the Formorri. They refused the offer from Elotha to join forces against the Danann. They left Rathcroghan, along with many followers, and moved to the west. Here they intend to bide their time. Ruairi sent emissaries to the Danann to say he supports the Aslach decisions, offering to join with the Danann to fight the Formorri.

Other warriors from King Ailill's army who did not go with Ruairi and Eoghan have made their way to the new Danann encampment, also offering to support the Danann. Many from King Daire's forces have joined them as well. They support the Aslach decisions, believing they are now subjects of the Danann.

* * *

Flann and I walk along the path leading to the stone circle. The day is beautiful, with crystal clear blue skies. As we approach the circle, a conspiracy of ravens spirals down from the sky, coming to roost on the standing stones. Does this portend danger, or do they bring news? We enter the circle and the ravens repeatedly jump from one standing stone to another, cawing raucously. "This is a good sign," I tell Flann. "They are telling us Laragh will be arriving soon and she brings traveling companions with her. We must return to the village at once."

Indeed, as we arrive at the settlement we spot figures approaching along the esker from the north. Racing towards them, we are heartened to recognize Laragh, accompanied by several armed Danann. I embrace her, and Flann and I both express our joy at seeing her again. Standing nearby is the smiling presence of Aesres, the Claíomh Solai strapped firmly to his side. Flann and I turn to Aesres, thanking him for escorting our sister back to Tomregan.

"It is my brother and I who are indebted to Laragh for warning us and leading us to safety in Rathcroghan," replies Aesres. "Without her help, my brother, his children, and I would be dead, the fate of my people uncertain."

We catch shouts of greetings coming from the village and I spot Father making his way towards us. Though he never let on he was concerned about Laragh's safety, I can see he is overjoyed by the presence of his youngest daughter. Reaching us, Father says, "Before you regale us with your exploits, please, let us get you food and drink."

Aesres says, "Let's have Laragh and I recount our adventures at the circle of Cenn so all in the community can listen." Father nods in agreement.

Following the meal, the bronze horn sounds, informing all in Tomregan to meet at the stone circle. Father, Flann, and I join Aesres and Laragh for the walk through the trees. Others in the village surround us, anxious to learn about the Danann's adventurous escape from Rathcroghan.

When we arrive at the circle, Flann and I stand to the side while Father, Laragh, and Aesres move to the central stone. Everyone quiets. Father turns to the gathering. "We are all anxious to know what happened to Laragh after the Rathcroghan events. Fortunately, our friends the ravens have been informing Keelen all has been well with Laragh and with the Danann. Nevertheless, having her here warms my soul. I am, as are all of you, most anxious to learn the story of their escape and the events since then."

Laragh is a skilled speaker, able to draw all who listen into what she says. She moves forward and begins. "My friends, I can only say how gladdened I am to be among you again. The events that began at Rathcroghan have been more of an adventure than an ordeal. I am certain Keelen and Flann told you of our experience when we found the sacred oak along Rathcroghan's eastern wall. The tree communicated a sense of eminent danger, and I had an instinctive urge to act at once.

"I was uncertain why the tree was sending me these feelings but, more importantly, what I was supposed to do. Sensing my reaction, the tree took power over my face and drew my eyes deep into its thickest branches. I stared into these branches before finally noting an opening in the wall, camouflaged by the branches. Then I understood what the tree was telling me. There was intense danger in the air and those in danger needed to escape. Further, I understood the tree was referring to the Danann, with the menace coming from the Formorri.

"The group of us promptly returned to Rathcroghan, where I relayed this information to King Nuada and Aesres. They agreed with my interpretation and asked if one of us could lead them to the tree. I told Keelen and Flann it should be me as it was me to whom the tree revealed the opening.

"Aesres, Nuada, Cairpre, and Aislinn followed me as we quickly returned to the tree. I peered into the branches to determine the best way to proceed and then we climbed in. We struggled to squeeze through the tight escape route up into the branches and through the wall. Once on the other side, we found the area between the two walls to be brushy and nearly impenetrable. The second wall was about twenty steps away. Peering through the brush, I spotted another ancient, barely alive, sacred oak clinging against the side of the second wall. Making our way through the brush, we found the gnarled old oak easy to climb. Soon we were on the other side.

"On the village side of the walls, we heard the shouting and scuffling of what we knew to be Formorri warriors. The two trees had saved us! We knew we needed to go to the Danann encampment as swiftly as possible, but dared not proceed along the wall toward the proper esker, as it would likely be manned by Formorri soldiers. Our only choice was to advance into the forest and hope we found the esker before darkness fell."

There is a murmuring of low voices in the crowd. I hear expressions of astonishment. Laragh hears the murmuring as well and pauses before continuing.

"We caught the sound of rustling in the brush near the forest edge. Ducking low for cover and fearing somehow the Formorri had found us, we heard another rustle. Peering through the brush, I recognized the outline of a mighty elk. The elk snorted noisily, making its way into the forest. Here was more providence! We moved toward where the elk had been grazing and found a game path winding into the forest. King Nuada suggested that with luck this path would lead to the esker heading to the shores of Lough Aillionn. He told us the curaugh he, Aesres, Cairpre, and Aislinn had used earlier to cross the lough from their camp to come to the Aslach had been hidden along the bank. He assured us if we could reach that curaugh, we would have no trouble returning to the Danann encampment before the arrival of any possible Formorri force.

"Good fortune truly came our way. By dusk, we reached the shoreline of Lough Aillionn. Soon, we found the curaugh and were sailing across the lough under a bright, virtually full moon. Upon reaching his people, Nuada quickly convened a meeting of all the Danann. He recounted the Formorri treachery and the need to abandon the encampment by dawn. He told them they needed to travel to the lands along the northern loughs. There, they should build defenses, plant crops, and settle. Nuada told the assemblage he doubted the Formorri would attack a strongly-held Danann position. Rather, they would concentrate on gaining a strong foothold in and around Rathcroghan. The remainder of the night was spent preparing for the move. Scouting parties were sent along the shores of the lough, both to the east and west, to avoid a surprise attack by the Formorri.

"During our preparations, Aesres informed me the northern loughs include two separate bodies of water, connected by a small river. The most defensible spot is an area between the two. Here, a narrow strip of land hugs the southern shoreline leading east. Rugged terrain lies to the south, protecting it from attack. It is this narrow strip of land along the eastern lough where the Danann wished to create their settlement and set up their defenses.

"At dawn, the people of Danu gathered once again to escape, but this time without eitiltes. King Nuada left several trailing scouting parties to make sure the Formorri did not follow. He also sent scouting parties ahead to safeguard their path.

"A full day was taken to reach the choke-point of land for the new encampment. Nuada, upon examining the terrain for the first time, named the area Learga for the rising ground emerging from the narrow shoreline.

"The Danann were exhausted. They created temporary, defensive barricades across the choke-point from the shoreline to the rugged terrain immediately to the south. The remainder of the Danann made camp, prepared food, and settled for the night. Patrols scouted each end of the encampment, but particularly to the west, the likely direction if a Formorri force were to come."

Laragh pauses again, this time looking toward Aesres to see if he wants to add anything. He nods his head towards her, indicating she should continue.

"Many days passed with the Danann establishing fortifications, building roundhouses, and planting crops. Scouting patrols constantly kept lookout for any suspicious activity. Then, a general alarm was raised.

"Danann fighters hastily assembled near the center of the new settlement with Aesres and Nuada joining them in full battledress. A scout, still breathing hard from his race, recounted how his scouting party heard voices coming from near the pool of Sinann. Investigating, they found six men camped at the pool who wore the battledress worn by those who serve King Ailill. The scout decided they must be a scouting party searching for the whereabouts of the Danann.

"Nuada and Aesres wasted no time sending scouts forward and proceeded with a full contingent of Danann warriors towards the pool of Sinann. I, of course, stayed in the settlement. All of us were anxious as we waited. The fighters who remained in the village sent the children and a few women to the east where they could proceed to Tomregan if an attack occurred. The remainder of us, both the women and non-combatant men, armed ourselves, steeling for the worst.

"Dusk came, and still we had no word. Throughout the night, all eyes stared into the blackness."

Again, the crowd murmurs among themselves. I suspect they are expressing their anticipation for what is to come next. I, too, am filled with eagerness.

"Pre-dawn light began to illuminate the landscape. From high on the ridge, a shout came down. A Danann runner was approaching. The runner arrived, out of breath, but he signaled with his hands that all was well. A great weight lifted off all of us and we clasped each other in joy."

The crowd lets out a sigh of relief that all was well.

"Nuada, Aesres, and their armed contingent arrived a few hours later. Walking among them, still armed, were six warriors dressed in the garb of King Ailill.

"Nuada, knowing we were all eager to learn of what happened, found a high point to stand and recount the events. 'Leaving our village yesterday, I feared we had encountered advance scouts from Rathcroghan with forces moving against us. We spotted the six warriors moving up the esker from the pool of Sinann. Ducking from sight until they were close, we confronted them. All dropped their weapons, declaring they came to join us. I sent scouts far down the trails beyond the pool, both toward Sligeach and Rathcroghan, to determine if any forces were advancing. No signs were seen. Once satisfied, I sent the runner to you to declare our safety.'

"Weeks passed with no Formorri activity spotted, but vigilance was maintained. Both Nuada and Aesres longed to fly in their old eitiltes for scouting, but those belonged to the past. I conversed with the ravens, telling them to take messages to Keelen to inform her all was well.

"Two days ago, Aesres concluded it was safe for me to return home. We left the new Danann village, proceeding east along the shores of the lough, then along the esker leading past the White Horse of Binn to Tomregan. It is good to be home again."

With this last account, Laragh finishes her story.

Aesres turns toward those assembled to speak. "My brother and I and all the Danann people owe a great debt to you of Tomregan. You helped with our arrival along the shores of Lough Aillionn and led the welcoming to your land. The unfortunate treachery of King Ailill and, later, the Formorri, brought new dangers. Again, you came to our assistance. Without Laragh's help at Rathcroghan, my brother, his children, and I would be dead, our people could have been annihilated. Instead, we have found a secure home along the shores of the northern loughs.

"The Formorri will remain a danger, but it appears unlikely they will attack in the near future. Former soldiers of King Ailill are joining us and we continue to send scouting parties toward Sligeach and Rathcroghan. There is much Formorri activity, but their actions appear limited to solidifying their hold on the lands of Rathcroghan and Sligeach. They, too, are building defenses and do not appear to be readying for an offensive strike. Many Rathcroghan villagers are sympathetic to our plight. Through our communications with them, they informed us High King Elotha returned to his homeland, but left almost all his Formorri warriors. Before leaving, he personally crowned Breas as the Formorri king of Rathcroghan. It is still too early to determine their long-term strategy.

"Informants tell us Queen Sianna is in seclusion. We have been able to communicate with some of the villagers of Sligeach and they reveal she rarely leaves her roundhouse.

"There is a large contingent of Formorri fighters in Sligeach. It appears High King Elotha wishes to ensure Sligeach is securely part of his new, expanded Formorri presence in Inis Elga. The villagers of both Rathcroghan and Sligeach also convey rumors that Formorri settlers are expected by the next Beltane. Such action makes it apparent the Formorri do not intend to give Rathcroghan back to the peoples of Inis Elga or to King Ailill's sons.

"Tomorrow, I leave with my contingent of warriors to perform my own reconnaissance of Rathcroghan. I hope to utilize the same secret entrance over the eastern wall Laragh took us through in our escape. I want to observe and listen to Breas and Rayna and determine for myself what preparations they are making."

Aesres peers across the gathering to see if there are questions. Hearing none, he turns to Father and together they begin walking back toward Tomregan, engaged in conversation.

I hear Aesres ask Father what he learned concerning the Formorri, as well as request news regarding High King Cullainn and King Daire. Father can provide no more detail about the Formorri than what is already known by Aesres. He says there has been no word from High King Cullainn or King Daire. Father speculates the Aslach rulings against the two likely made them wary of contact with Tomregan.

Aesres and his party of warriors prepare to depart early the next morning. He invites Flann and me to visit the new Danann settlement, saying Aislinn and Cairpre are most anxious to see us again. We look to Father, who readily agrees. Aesres tells us that once he returns to the new Danann village, he will send an escort of soldiers to accompany us to the settlement.

CHAPTER THIRTY-FOUR

SIANNA

I am in Learga visiting Aislinn and preparing for the Beltane festivities. It has been just about a Beltane since the Danann settled in Learga. The name pays homage to the pinch point and rising ground that provided easy defense for the Danann when they first arrived.

During this Beltane cycle, Aesres has confided to me his longing to see Sianna. He sent messengers who secretly entered Sligeach to deliver word to Queen Sianna from him. However, he received no communication in reply. Inexplicitly, the messengers reported the Queen refused to receive them and they were instructed to relay their messages through her servants. The messengers reported the presence of many Formorri warriors in Sligeach, which dashed thoughts by Aesres to sneak into Sligeach himself.

There is commotion near the sentry station at the edge of the village. A runner is approaching. As he comes closer, I realize he is Formorri. Aislinn notes this as well and she sends a messenger to find Aesres and Nuada. Soon, Aesres is at the sentry station, talking with the runner. Both Aislinn and I are now at the station and able to hear him saying, "I bring word from Sligeach for Aesres of the Danann."

Aesres identifies himself and the runner continues speaking. "Queen Sianna requests you come without delay. She has important information you must hear. Tomorrow morning a contingent of Formorri soldiers will arrive. They will provide escort and protection. These warriors are loyal to Sianna and not to Breas of Rathcroghan. Please allow them to come unharmed. Those loyal to Breas have been drugged and secured."

I see Aesres is heartened to finally learn about Sianna. He asks, "How is your queen? In good health?"

"My queen is not well. She informed me to have you make haste, and says you must come alone."

Aesres appears stunned. He has tried to contact her all this time with no success, and now to hear this news? Nuada now arrives and Aesres informs him about Sianna, saying, "I know it appears foolhardy to put myself into the hands of Formorri warriors and go to Sligeach alone, but there is no other choice. I must leave now. I cannot wait for the contingent to arrive. I will meet up with them on the esker."

Nuada considers what Aesres is saying for only a few moments before stepping forward and clasping him within his arms. "Of course, you must go," replies Nuada. "I have but one request. I know Sianna asked you to come alone, but I would prefer if Keelen were to travel with you in spirit so I will know if you are in danger."

Aesres agrees. Turning to me he says, "I have never felt comfortable sharing my thoughts with others. However, Nuada is correct. I will welcome your presence."

I, too, am shaken by the news of Sianna's illness and had first hoped to accompany Aesres to Sligeach until the runner dispelled that thought with his words, *Aesres is to come alone.* "Yes!" I exclaim. "Of course, I want to come. Sianna is my dear friend."

"Good," replies Aesres. "I will leave now with the runner to find the Formorri escorts and then continue to Sligeach. Aislinn, take Keelen to your father's roundhouse and make her comfortable. Bring her food and drink. She may need to stay with me for many days. Keelen, once you have eaten and become comfortable, come join me." With that, Aesres bids his brother goodbye and leaves Learga with the runner.

Aislinn grips my hand and off we run to Nuada's residence. We gather food and eat, then lay out soft skins for me to recline on for the time I will be with Aesres. I tell Aislinn, "Do not worry about your uncle. Sianna would never place him in danger. You will be able to know what is happening through me. I am ready to join him."

Nuada joins us and thanks me for agreeing to be with Aesres. I settle onto the skins and commence to concentrate. The faces of Aislinn and Nuada begin to fade away. Now, I am with Aesres. He is talking to the contingent of Formorri warriors, asking about Sianna. They give no more information other than that she is sick. Aesres notes my presence and welcomes me. The contingent moves out, heading for Sligeach.

Sligeach is normally a long day's journey from Learga. Aesres left Learga at mid-morning and with the fast pace we are taking, we should arrive in Sligeach by dark. I feel the deep worry he is experiencing as we walk. He does not communicate with me directly and he doesn't speak with his Formorri escorts. All his thoughts are focused on Sianna.

Just after dusk, we arrive in Sligeach and straightaway proceed to Sianna's roundhouse. Torches are burning at the entrance where an attendant awaits. Aesres is promptly escorted inside. As he enters, he hears a baby crying and momentarily thinks such a sound seems out of place. But that thought is lost when he sees Sianna. She is lying on fur bedding near the fire. The air is not cold, but she is bundled for warmth. As he approaches, Sianna's handmaiden whispers to her, saying Aesres is present. Sianna opens her eyes and in a barely audible tone, tells the handmaiden to bring the child. She gazes toward Aesres with a weak smile and reaches out her hand.

Aesres goes to her, kisses her hand, then wraps his arms about her. I sense the joy of seeing her replaced by the sadness of realizing she is weak and frail. Sianna hoarsely whispers, "Aesres, you don't know how much I longed to see you. I am sorry I cannot present myself better." Aesres peers down at her. His heartache chokes and constricts his throat. He can say nothing and just brings her hand up for a kiss.

"Do you remember our first journey to Tomregan, soon after your arrival, for the Beltane ceremony at the stone circle of Cenn?" she asks. "We slipped away for our greenwood marriage?"

"Of course," answers Aesres.

The handmaiden reappears, holding a baby. Sianna tenderly takes the child, showing its fair-skinned face to Aesres. "Lugh," she says, "this is your father. One day you will be a mighty leader like him. He is going to raise you among the Danann and perhaps you can help end these bitter times." She hands the child to Aesres, who is too awestruck for words.

Sianna continues. "After the Aslach, I became aware of being with child. Times were difficult. My uncle lectured me on how I had forgotten my responsibilities as a Formorri, with Trista's death being the result. He forbade me to have any further contact with the Danann and said any disobedience would not be tolerated. I was to attend to the needs of Sligeach. Breas and Rayna would attend to Rathcroghan and the elimination of the Danann. Soon after Trista's funeral, he returned to his home islands.

"I heard little from Breas and Rayna, but stories reached me of their struggles and Breas' paranoia regarding the Danann. He is certain you will soon attack and is devoting his efforts toward fortifying Rathcroghan. I know several of the soldiers in Sligeach are tasked with monitoring my activities and reporting back to him.

"Realizing I was with your child filled me with fear. This needed to be kept secret from everyone, including you. If Breas were to learn I carried your child, he would use this knowledge against you and the Danann. Fortunately, he was unaware of our closeness. To avoid discovery of my pregnancy from those he sent to monitor me, I kept to myself, feigning mourning for all those I've lost. I mostly stayed in the roundhouse, only venturing out occasionally to visit the cairns of Etain and Trista. Despite everything, I miss them both."

Weakened further by the conversation, Sianna pauses to regain strength before beginning again. "The pregnancy and birth were difficult. I fear my time in this place is soon ending. I needed you to come. To visit you one last time and to give you the gift of our child."

Feeling awkward staying with Aesres in these poignant moments, I ask if I should leave. He replies no, saying my presence helps ease the pain. He asks if I want Sianna to know I am with him. I consider, but say Sianna needs to focus solely on him.

Smiling weakly, Sianna hands the baby to Aesres, saying, "He looks much like you. My heart is lightened seeing you are here with our child. But please forgive me, I need to rest."

Aesres devotes the remainder of the evening to holding Sianna, the child sleeping peacefully nearby. Sianna awakens for short periods and they talk about their times together and events since Rathcroghan. She wants to learn about the new settlement of Learga, and Aesres provides the details, starting with the escape from Rathcroghan. By first light, the dawn of Beltane, Sianna wakes again, squeezing Aesres's hand tightly. She looks up into his eyes, her tears streaking down. As he bends for a kiss, her eyes close. She is gone.

He holds her close and clutches their son, while rocking back and forth. Muffled sobs shake his body. Many moments pass before Aesres calls for Sianna's entourage, informing them of her death. He tells them her funeral will be tonight, and he declares he will build the funeral bier here in the roundhouse. Like her grandfather, King Ailill, the structure will be burned and Sianna's cairn built where the dwelling now stands. Stones are ordered to be brought for the cairn.

Aesres gently gives Lugh to the handmaiden and asks for esline cloth to wrap Sianna's body and material to build the funeral bier. He further tells the entourage to inform the people of Sligeach of her death, but also instructs them that no word is to be sent to Breas at Rathcroghan or to High King Elotha. This funeral will only be for the people of Sligeach, for himself, and for his new son.

A somber air hangs over the village. Everyone in the community comes to pay their respects for Sianna, Aesres, and Lugh. Aesres posts himself by the roundhouse entrance the entire day, often holding his son, as he greets the villagers. As dusk approaches, Aesres and Sianna's entourage enter the structure, take her body from the bier, lay her to rest in the shallow trenching in the floor, and cover her remains with the cairn stones. With darkness falling, Aesres walks about the roundhouse, lighting each bundle of kindling stacked against its walls. Flames soon are soaring. On the hill overlooking Sligeach, where the cairns of Trista and Etain stand, a Beltane fire comes to life. Soon, more Beltane fires erupt across the countryside. The fires seem like the spirits of the ancestors coming to greet their friend and daughter, Queen Sianna. I am sure among the first are Etain, Trista, and King Ailill.

None of the usual Beltane festivities occur in Sligeach this night. Rather, the blazes emulate both a sense of sadness for the passing of Queen Sianna and hope for the future, symbolized by her son, Lugh.

Before departing the next morning, Aesres makes sure the grounds where Sianna's dwelling once stood and the site of her cairn are in order. He gazes about the village, remembering the brief moments he shared with her.

The same contingent of warriors who escorted him to Sligeach, along with a wet nurse for the baby and Sianna's handmaiden, now accompany him and Lugh back to Learga. With the late midday start, their journey spans into the next day. It is time for me to return to my body.

Stunned by the experience of the past two days, I have trouble concentrating on my surroundings, but ultimately see the faces of Aislinn and Nuada coming into focus. Aislinn holds me close. Nuada thanks me for staying with Aesres and for keeping him apprised of the developments and activities of the trip. I nod, but am unable to speak in my own voice yet. Aislinn helps me to a sitting position. "You are weak from not eating or drinking these past two days," she says. "Here is some food and drink. First, regain your strength, then recount all of the events."

While I was with Aesres, I kept Aislinn and Nuada apprised of Aesres's safety and a general description of what was happening. Now, being recovered, I provide them detail on the occurrences. Many hours pass as I recount what took place. We hear a commotion coming from near the edge of the village. "It must be Aesres," I say. We quickly join the crowd to see who's approaching and, yes, it is Aesres and his contingent of Formorri.

The entire village of Learga welcomes Aesres as he arrives. Aislinn takes Lugh, showing him to the gathered people. Lugh is unique with his heritage, one-half Danann, one-quarter Formorri, and one-quarter a native of Inis Elga. At a meeting of Danann elders, where Fearghus and the rest of my family are invited, Lugh's special status is recognized, and a plan made for his education. He will be taught not only the ways of the Danann, but also the ways of the Formorri and of the native people of Inis Elga. Sianna's handmaiden will help care for the child. She will stay in Learga, at Aesres' request, to help keep the memory of Sianna alive.

CHAPTER THIRTY-FIVE

RETURNING TO THE WHITE HORSE

Seven Beltanes have passed since Sianna's death. The strength of Brehon Law and the acceptance of the Aslach findings by all but the Formorri led to the banishment of High King Cullainn and King Daire to the wilds of the western lands. The Danann established hegemony over the regions of Tara and Emain Macha. Nuada regained his crown. After many unsuccessful efforts, the Danann silversmiths crafted a functional, artificial hand. Nuada can now grasp objects and even wield a sword or spear. The council of elders met and agreed his silver hand is of sufficient functionality to meet the guidelines of Danann kingship. King Nuada now spends most of his time near Tara. The Lia Fáil was moved to the summit of the Hill of Tara, but has not yet been used to select a high king.

Lugh grows strong and can defeat most combatants, despite his youth. He is learning the traditions and history of the Danann and receives schooling at Tomregan. His Formorri training is limited to what Sianna's former handmaiden can teach. She also recounts stories to Lugh about his mother, King Ailill, and his mother's legendary relationship with his father, Aesres. Aesres, too, spends much time with Lugh. He continues to grieve for Sianna but smiles when watching Lugh at play or in training. Both Sianna and his first wife, Teagan, often together, come to him in his dreams, comforting him and foretelling of the future greatness of Lugh.

Samhain is approaching and the seven years since the Rathcroghan treachery portend change.

Aislinn and Cairpre are coming to Tomregan at Father's request. He sent for them, saying he carried important news. I have not seen my friends for some time and am most anxious to see them again. My studies keep me fully occupied with little time to travel.

"Aislinn, Cairpre," I shout as they enter the village. I run to embrace them. "It has been far too long. Come, Father wishes to talk to you. He is in the council chambers, preparing for Samhain with Flann and Laragh."

As we move toward the council chambers, Aislinn and Cairpre shower me with questions regarding why they were summoned. I smile, but only say, "You will be pleased."

Hearing our approach, Father looks up from his work. "Ah! Aislinn, Cairpre, you are here. Come, sit by the fire. I expected you would arrive about now. I have some food and drink for us all."

Flann and Laragh embrace our Danann friends and we all settle by the fire. Father takes a bite of food, then a drink of mead. He says, "I know you are most anxious to hear why I summoned you." Aislinn and Cairpre put down their food and look intently at Father. "As you know, each Samhain, the elders of Tomregan select who will visit the cairn of Eachon at the White Horse of Binn. This year, it will be Flann, Keelen, and Laragh. We elders also thought representatives of the Danann should be invited. Would the two of you like to go?"

"Of course!" they reply. "We are honored."

The next morning, the five of us depart, hiking along the esker leading to the White Horse. Laragh, Flann, and I want to know all that has happened in Learga since we last saw them. How is Aesres?

Is Lugh getting stronger? Is there news about the Formorri or about Sligeach?

Aislinn replies to my questions, saying, "There is much talk of war. These past seven years have treated my people well. Nuada is our king again. Our weapons are superior to those of the Formorri and we have crafted a full arsenal. Our warriors are well-trained, and have swelled to include many warriors formally allegiant to King Daire and High King Cullainn."

She tells us that Breas expanded the defenses of Rathcroghan and has many defenders at the ready. "Father and Aesres believe we should make our move soon, perhaps by the next Beltane.

"King Ailill's sons, Ruairi and Eoghan, visited Learga. They made amends for the last attack and are now allied with us. Father and Aesres pledged support for Ruairi's claim to kingship of Rathcroghan. Ruairi and Eoghan related interesting stories they have heard about Breas and Rayna and the conditions in Rathcroghan. Sligeach is much as it was under Queen Sianna. The Formorri power is centralized in Rathcroghan with Sligeach an outpost."

Cairpre interjects. "Yes, their stories are most interesting. They learned one of High King Elotha's motives for wanting to increase the Formorri presence in Inis Elga was to relieve strains within the Formorri homelands resulting from their increased numbers. The Formorri are a trading and pillaging people, and under Elotha they have been highly successful. Despite their wealth, the ability to meet the basic needs for food has become difficult. The Formorri homeland is hot and dry and not conducive to significant levels of agriculture or herding. Inis Elga, in contrast, has a long tradition of successful agriculture and herding. To High King Elotha, expanding his kingdom to include parts of Inis Elga was logical and justifiable. The coming of the Danann was the excuse to make the move."

We reach the banks of the Claddagh. While fording, we peer into the water, looking for any large mussels, but only see small ones. It appears we will not find any tears of Danu this trip.

Resuming our trek, Cairpre continues sharing news. "Little

coaxing was needed to convince King Ailill that the Danann, despite all their words of peace and assurances from the elders of Tomregan, were a serious threat. King Ailill agreed to allow Elotha to expand the Formorri area of control around Sligeach in exchange for their assistance in dealing with the Danann. Unfortunately for King Ailill, High King Cullainn would not allow Formorri participation in the Danann attack. Elotha still believed there would be little trouble in overwhelming and destroying the Danann, especially as they were newly arrived and unsettled. To his surprise, the efforts to destroy them failed.

"After crowning Breas the King of Rathcroghan, Elotha returned to the Formorri home islands, assembling a group of his people to colonize Inis Elga. He left most of his warriors behind to ensure they maintained control of the freshly acquired territory. The colonists arrived by late summer, which was too late to establish new farms and herds before winter. Therefore, Breas forcibly had many existing farms and herds forfeited to the freshly arrived Formorri. Breas provided compensation, but that did little to quell the anger erupting from this action.

"Despite receiving the richest farmlands and the most prized herds of cattle, the Formorri settler's lack of skill and dislike of the climate has led to many difficulties. Crops have not been properly attended and the quality and health of the herds has suffered. Breas attempted to resolve these difficulties by forcing many of the former landowners and herdsmen to assist the Formorri settlers. They have become little more than slaves. These moves helped improve the quality of the crops and livestock over the years, but only aggravated the growing resentment among the native inhabitants."

"It's hard to believe Elotha thought Formorri, who know nothing of farming or herding, could now become stewards of such," I say. "Their efforts must have appeared comical to those they replaced."

"Yes," replies Cairpre. "Ruari told us how the former landowners easily hid much of their harvest without the Formorri ever being aware.

"High King Elotha encouraged Breas to extend friendship to the other kings of Inis Elga who held power to the south of the area now controlled by the Danann. He reasoned that they, too, must have concerns regarding the Danann strength. He urged a marriage between Breas and a daughter of one of these kings. But Breas insisted his desire was to have his half-sister, Rayna, as his queen. High King Elotha reluctantly agreed. Upon their marriage, Breas commissioned the building of an elaborate roundhouse in Rathcroghan for the two of them. He razed many of the buildings on the east side of the village for the site of this new residence and had the old east wall extended to surround the community. He ensured the cairn of King Ailill was given a spot of prominence within these walls, but the new roundhouse would be the centerpiece of the rath fortification."

Staring at Laragh and Flann, I shake my head in disbelief. How could Breas act so foolishly?

At Eachon's cairn, we make camp, then view the night sky. Waiting in anticipation of Eachon's visit, I am nervous, since this is the first time any Danann has participated. The sky sparkles brilliantly with light, but the bearded star is no longer present. The star disappeared shortly after the Danann arrival.

A trance creeps upon me and soon I discern Eachon and the White Horse emerging from a mist. The White Horse approaches both Aislinn and Cairpre, nuzzling them kindly. Eachon begins, "The White Horse is pleased to see the two Danann with you on this Samhain evening. After the many years of speaking of their coming, then their struggles to find a secure home, it is good to take in the reality of their presence firsthand. The White Horse wishes me to tell all of you the difficulties with the Formorri will soon be over. There will be another battle, this time between the Danann and the Formorri, with the Formorri driven from Inis Elga. Once Breas and his forces are defeated, there will dawn a golden age of peace and prosperity. The knowledge the Danann bring with them will benefit everyone of Inis Elga.

"Aesres's son, Lugh, will become a mighty leader. Following Nuada's death, when Lugh takes his turn and climbs onto the Lia Fáil, the stone will cry so deafeningly with joy that all the people of Inis Elga will know of his greatness. This cry from the stone is not only to confirm him as King of the Danann, but also, as High King of all Inis Elga.

"Lugh will assign the kingship of Learga to Cairpre, and of Sligeach to Flann. The Lia Fáil will confirm these decisions with another cry of joy."

Eachon pauses, appearing to be conferring with the White Horse. He begins speaking again. "The White Horse reminds me there is more to tell you beyond the fate of the Formorri or the future greatness of Lugh."

Turning toward me, Eachon continues. "Keelen, you will become the greatest druis Inis Elga has ever known. Your counsel will be sought by all, but most specifically by Lugh, the future High King. With your counsel, not only will peace be maintained, but the new ways and new teachings provided by the Danann will be embraced by the people of Inis Elga."

Now facing the others, Eachon states, "Laragh, Flann, Aislinn, and Cairpre, the four of you will represent the first union between the people of Danu and the peoples of Inis Elga. Cairpre will marry Laragh and Aislinn will marry Flann. Your lives will be examples for all and your rule of Sligeach and Learga will lead to the uniting of the peoples of Inis Elga with the people of Danu."

This final revelation from Eachon is the last any of us remember from this Samhain visit. I feel dazed. Looking towards the others, they too appear stunned and wide-eyed. The revelations portend great changes in all our lives.

We must hurry back to Learga to tell Father, Nuada, and Aesres all the Horse of Binn revealed. They will be most anxious to hear these new revelations.

Once we relate these prophecies, they are stirred, especially over the revelations regarding Lugh. The three believe it best not to reveal these insights. Prophecies provide a window on what is likely to happen given current and expected circumstances; they are never guaranteed. Revealing what was said concerning Lugh may place him in danger and change the future path.

Given the expectations provided by the White Horse, Nuada and Aesres conclude it is time to drive the Formorri from Inis Elga. They resolve to use the winter cycle to make final preparations. By Beltane, everything should be in place to move against Breas's forces.

A messenger is sent to Ruairi and Eoghan regarding this plan and requesting a meeting. Both Ruairi and Eoghan accompany the return messenger. Each is anxious to regain their life in Rathcroghan to reclaim their family's heritage. The plan is for Ruairi and his forces to attack Sligeach just after Beltane. In coordination, King Nuada will lead his forces against Breas and his stronghold in Rathcroghan.

Ruairi and Eoghan brought with them a villager who has lived in Rathcroghan from the days of King Ailill. He provides insights to Nuada and Aesres regarding activities within the village since King Ailill's funeral.

He tells them, "Since Breas and Rayna have ruled Rathcroghan, they have made substantial modifications. The walled enclosure, along with their roundhouse, has grown, both in size and splendor. The walls now wholly encircle the settlement and are higher, due to the deep trench dug around the outer portion. Inside the village, the materials excavated from the trench were used to create a central high ground on which a new residence for Breas and Rayna was constructed."

Laragh asks, "Do you know if the sacred oak between the old, eastern walls still stands?"

"Yes," replies the villager. Outside of trenching around the outer wall, the eastern walls are much as they always have been.

"Before the new residence was erected, the workers created an underground chamber to be used as a refuge should an attack come against them. Above that chamber, a new roundhouse provides a commanding view of the countryside, unobstructed by the walls. From this vantage point, Breas and Rayna hope to witness the Danann warriors advancing against Rathcroghan and watch them destroyed in combat."

The final words of the messenger send a chill through me.

"An attack from the Danann is expected. Breas has devoted all his efforts towards fortifying Rathcroghan to make it practically impenetrable. He does not wish to face the Danann outside of Rathcroghan."

CHAPTER THIRTY-SIX

THE SECOND BATTLE

Winter passes and the Danann grow increasingly confident. Beltane fires begin to blaze from the heights surrounding Learga. Every resident is anxiously preparing for the upcoming clash. The village is swelling with the arrival of warriors accompanying King Nuada from Tara and Emain Macha. Pent-up energy drives the battle preparations and festival celebrations. The mood of those assembled is one of relief, tinged with the knowledge many will soon die. The protracted quest to achieve peace and stability is within grasp.

My brother, sister and I are in Learga to witness this momentous juncture. Although not a fighter, Flann trained with Cairpre throughout the winter on the arts of a warrior. He will serve as a runner for King Nuada to deliver messages to his commanders. Cairpre will serve as a field commander.

Aislinn and I appeal to King Nuada to permit us to accompany the army as part of the rear supply entourage. Laragh says she has no wish to witness so much bloodshed and will return to Tomregan once the army deploys. Nuada hesitates and appears uncertain it is wise for Aislinn and myself to accompany the army, before saying,

"The White Horse of Binn foretells that the two of you will be in positions of power soon. Those who possess power need to know the terrors war holds. I consent."

Lugh has grown tall and strong. He is exceptionally skilled as a fighter, given his age of eight Beltanes. He, too, will accompany the army, serving as a runner for Aesres. Aesres reasons it is time for Lugh to begin his emergence as a Danann leader.

Following the Beltane ceremonies, the Danann army advances toward Rathcroghan. Along the route, we skirt the pool of Sinann. Stopping briefly, King Nuada places an offering to Danu.

Our first night, we camp at Moytura, the site of the Danann's original encampment along the shores of Lough Aillionn. Many years have passed since I was last in Moytura, but memories of Sianna and I walking among the dead flood back to me. Being here again makes me think, *the time has finally come to make right the wrongs committed here.*

Rathcroghan is not far.

Nuada sends Flann to where Ruairi's forces are believed to be massed to inform him all is ready. Our attack is to be in the morning, as should Ruairi's be against Sligeach.

The army moves from Moytura well before dawn. King Nuada wishes to have Breas awaken to the vision of the Danann army massed against him.

With the rising sun, we are on the plain facing the walls of Rathcroghan. Our warriors angle their shields to reflect the sun onto Breas's roundhouse, which is clearly visible on the high ground.

Frantic commotion breaks out within the walls, but Breas sends no combatants forward. It appears he believes the war will be won at the walls and inner walls. Aislinn and I find a safe vantage point from which to survey the upcoming fight.

King Nuada orders his fighters onward. Scaling ladders are brought forward. Fighters mass behind and follow the scaling ladders with their shields, protecting both those carrying the ladders and themselves. A rain of arrows darkens the sky, directed toward the advancing Danann, but few find a target. Most clatter harmlessly off the protective layer of shields. The advance continues, as does the showers of arrows.

The scaling ladders are against the outer wall and soon combatants from both sides are engaged in fierce hand-to-hand combat. From our viewpoint, we watch as many fighters fall, but cannot distinguish if most are Formorri or Danann. King Nuada joins us. With him is the viewing crystal Aesres used in his reconnaissance flights from long ago. He hands it to Flann, who has just returned from Ruairi's forces, asking him to describe the battlefield proceedings.

Flann dismounts and finds a clear viewing position near Nuada.

Flann recounts the action along the outer wall as the crystal brings the battle scene into focus. "The fighting is brutal along the rim of the wall. We appear to be gaining the upper hand, but as yet have not succeeded. Many Rathcroghan warriors lie slain."

Nuada asks Flann to move the viewing crystal up the hill toward Breas's roundhouse. Flann says, "I see Breas and Rayna. They are watching the fighting from a vantage point just below their roundhouse, acting as if it is a play being performed for their pleasure."

Flann soon lowers the crystal back down to the fighting and informs King Nuada, "The outer wall now appears controlled by the Danann. The outer gate is being swung open and Danann fighters are flooding through. They are fanning out on both sides of the gate between the two walls, dispatching each enemy they encounter. Regrettably, I cannot view what is happening on the other side of the inner wall."

Nuada informs us he is going to join Aesres in the struggle to break through the inner gate. Flann hands me the crystal, as he will be accompanying Nuada.

I watch them through the viewing crystal and they are soon amid the fray, near the inner wall gate.

Taking my eyes off them, I focus on the mass of soldiers ramming the inner gate. Nuada joins the ramming party and I note that Aesres and Lugh are engaged in hand-to-hand struggles against the few remaining Formorri.

Abruptly, the inner gate pivots open. Masses of Formorri fighters empty out, throwing themselves against the Danann. Nuada's forces are staggered, being pushed back by the sheer numbers. Flann stumbles, but Nuada takes hold of him, shoving him away from the immediate fighting.

I hand the crystal to Aislinn so she can see her father in battle. She gasps at what she sees. "Keelen, at the front of the Formorri outpouring is a massive fighter who is slaughtering all who oppose him. Do you think this is their champion, Balor, of whom legends are told? I thought he never left High King Elotha's side, but this warrior can be no other. Father sees him and is moving to confront the giant. Balor appears to have spotted Father as well and he, too, is moving toward a confrontation."

The sound of a bellowing roar sweeps across the battlefield. I strain to see as much as I can when Aislinn screams in terror. Looking at her, I see she has dropped the viewing glass and her hands clasp each side of her mouth as she continues to scream. Her eyes are wide, filled with horror.

"Father is dead! Balor cut him down with a single slash of his sword."

Aislinn hands me the crystal. "Keelen, you must watch. I cannot. Tell me Aesres, Lugh, and our brothers are safe. Father is dead! How could this have happened?"

I wrap my arms about Aislinn, trying to provide comfort before taking up the crystal and telling her, "I see Balor leading the surge of Formorri. The fight appears to be turning their way." I search for Aesres, Lugh, and our brothers. "There is Aesres! He is raising his sword and rallying men around him. They are pushing toward Balor. I've just caught sight of Lugh. He is off to one side, near Aesres. He appears to be loading a stone into his sling. I see Aesres beginning to engage Balor, and Lugh swinging his sling. Balor is rising to full height with his sword held high, preparing to swipe at Aesres. Lugh has let his sling fly."

I jump in excitement. "Lugh's stone has struck Balor in the eye." Even at this distance, Aislinn and I both hear Balor bellow in pain and rage. "Aesres is moving toward Balor." I stop for a moment and hold my breath as I watch. "Aesres has buried Claíomh Solai in Balor's chest. Balor is dead!"

I move the crystal around the battle scene. Both armies look stunned and stop fighting for a moment. "Keelen, it appears the death of Balor has renewed the Danann confidence and they are surging forward again. Both walls are now breached and Danann soldiers are flooding through the inner gate.

"I can't see the struggle behind the inner wall, but I can see Breas and Rayna. They seem panicked and are retreating into their roundhouse. They must be heading to their inner sanctum. The Danann fighters are swarming over the vantage point recently vacated by Breas and Rayna. Aesres is leading them. They are entering the roundhouse. I imagine Breas and Rayna are hearing the feet of the Danann trampling the floor above."

Desperately wishing to know what is happening inside the structure, I hand the crystal back to Keelen, who is crying softly. I sit and meditate, trying to direct my spirit into Aesres. I succeed!

Aesres, gripping the Claíomh Solai, is leading the way down the torch-lit passageway toward the inner sanctum. Coming to its entrance, he peers inside and sees the lifeless bodies of both Breas and Rayna. Aesres pauses, reflecting on the two dead Formorri as well as his dead brother.

It is over!

No one enters the room. The party of Danann warriors returns to the surface and seals the passageway. Aesres orders bundles of wood brought into the enclosure, stacking them along the walls. He commands his fighters to leave. Aesres lights each of the bundles. As the fires take hold, he exits as flames erupt through the thatched roof.

Fighting ceases. All the Formorri are either dead or wounded. The villagers emerge from hiding, gazing at the burning roundhouse and destruction from the battle.

Aesres orders his men to vacate Rathcroghan, closing the inner gate once all have left. He finds Lugh, Flann, and Cairpre standing guard over King Nuada's body. The four wrap Nuada's lifeless form in a cloak, preparing to take the body with them back to Learga.

I come out of my trance and see Keelen peering through the crystal, tears still streaking down her cheeks. She utters, "It's done. The Formorri are beaten, but Father is dead. I will grieve long over this loss."

She hands me back the crystal, saying, "Come. Let us join our families and honor my father's death as well as this great, though bittersweet, victory."

Runners arrive from Sligeach, informing Aesres the Formorri have been routed from there as well. Ruairi and his warriors are moving toward Rathcroghan to reclaim dominion. Aesres dispatches Flann with a message for Ruairi, stating Rathcroghan is secured, awaiting his arrival. The message also reports the death of King Nuada and the departure of the main body of the Danann forces to Learga.

Word is sent to Learga, proclaiming the great victory as well as the death of their king. With Ruari's taking of Sligeach, the victory is complete.

* * *

Riding his horse, Aesres clings to the body of his brother as the Danann forces return home. Nearing the village, the path becomes lined with villagers. They clap as the soldiers enter the village, but no one cheers. As Aesres passes with King Nuada's body, each villager kneels and bows.

Keelen and Cairpre take their father's body from Aesres, placing it on a bier in the central gathering area of Learga. Over the next few days, everyone in the settlement will come to pay their homage. Ruairi and his brother send word they are coming from Rathcroghan, as do the elders from Tomregan.

The day after arriving back home, Aesres calls a council of elders. He invites Flann and myself to attend. As we enter the council chambers, I see Lugh, Aislinn, and Cairpre sitting next to Aesres. Aesres rises and addresses the gathering. "Under my brother's kingship, we achieved a great victory over the Formorri. We waited long for this opportunity and now I can safely say we are secure in the lands of Inis Elga. The price was high with many of our fellow Danann killed, including our king. But this cost was necessary.

"In two days, myself, Lugh, Aislinn, and Cairpre will take our king to the summit of Slieve Cenn, the highest point in this region. Here, at a spot overlooking Lough Aillionn and Tomregan to the south, Learga to the north, and Sligeach to the west, we will build a burial chamber where my brother, your king, will rest. He will sleep knowing that peace covers all the lands he can sight from his resting place.

"To ensure long-term security, I have decreed that all remaining Formorri in this land must leave or be slain. This must occur before the next full moon. Messengers have been dispatched to inform all Formorri of this ultimatum. I am arranging to have ships in Sligeach harbor to take them back to their homeland. There will be no exceptions.

With this, the meeting ends. Aislinn and Cairpre join their uncle to finalize what they need to bring for their trip up Slieve Cenn. Flann and I return to our quarters and prepare for our journey home to Tomregan tomorrow.

* * *

Several moons have passed since the victory over the Formorri. Messengers from Learga have relayed that some resistance to the Formorri expulsion was met in Sligeach. Aesres personally slew those who would not board the ships. The messengers also said the mood is still somber in their village from the death of King Nuada.

From other travelers, we hear both Rathcroghan and Sligeach are secure. Ruari has re-established his family's control in Rathcroghan and a contingent of Danann oversee Sligeach. Sligeach itself is nearly empty, as there are no longer any Formorri present.

The weather is hot. I am not accustomed to such heat. Since the coming of the Danann so many Beltanes ago, our weather has gradually warmed. Now, we at times experience periods of heat, like we are having now. We never knew such heat in the days before the Danann. The Samhain festival will be in another moon, and with the new moon, the welcome cool of fall will arrive.

I am tending to our fields of grain when I see four figures approaching. By their clothing, I know they are Danann. Peering closely, I recognize Aesres, Lugh, Cairpre, and Aislinn. I wave to them and cry out, "It's so good to see you!" They run up to me and I embrace each one in turn.

"I have come to seek council with your father," says Aesres. "It is time for Lugh to know the prophesies provided last Samhain by the White Horse." We walk down to the village and find Father.

We all gather in the council chambers, along with Laragh and Flann. Father initiates the meeting.

"All who visited with Eachon and the White Horse last Samhain are present. I must caution that the prophesies given by the White Horse only identify a most likely path and not a definitive track to what the future holds. Care must be taken to not use the knowledge to create advantage. This knowledge is like the powers provided to the Danann by Danu. Abusing the power can lead to catastrophic results.

"Perhaps Cairpre can start by telling what he learned last Samhain. Others may add to his account."

Cairpre rises and begins. "Cousin Lugh, last Samhain, Aislinn and I were given the honor to visit the White Horse of Binn, along with Keelen, Laragh, and Flann. The White Horse told us we would drive the Formorri from this land and this victory would mark the beginning of a golden age of peace and prosperity. This golden age has begun.

"The White Horse talked of you, saying the son of Aesres would become a mighty leader. Following King Nuada's death, a ceremony would be held at Tara to determine the next High King of Inis Elga. Adhering to Danann tradition, the Lia Fáil will confirm who this king will be."

Lugh appears stunned. Turning to Aesres, he says, "Father, can this be? You should be our High King. If not you, surely Cairpre. Not me!"

Aislinn interjects. "Lugh, your bloodline is exceptional. Mostly you are Danann, but you also have the blood from the natives of Inis Elga and of the Formorri. No one ever born has your heritage. The White Horse foresees you as the unifying force, bringing together the people of Inis Elga."

Aesres holds his son close. "Lugh, the White Horse has seen this. You will be a mighty king. A compassionate king. All of us in this chamber will be there to help you. The blood of kings and queens flows through your veins. Your mother would be so proud, as would your grandfather. I have watched you grow in wisdom as well as strength, and my pride swells with each passing moon. Your quick thinking at Rathcroghan saved our people. I don't know if we could have stopped Balor otherwise."

Turning to Father, Aesres continues. "Fearghus, our council of elders believes a High King for Inis Elga should be decreed at the next Beltane. The Lia Fáil is at the crest of the Hill of Tara. Tara is the traditional home of the Inis Elga High King, and the Lia Fáil is our traditional selector of a High King. We wish both traditions to continue, but we desire agreement with this plan from you and the elders of Tomregan."

Still holding his son close, Aesres smiles down at him while waiting for Father to answer.

"Since learning the latest prophesies from the White Horse," Father replies, "we elders have discussed how we might help enable Lugh to be recognized as High King of all of Inis Elga. Your victory over the Formorri is known by all, as is the banishment of High King Cullainn and King Daire. A vacuum of cohesion amongst the kings of Inis Elga now exists because we have no High King. If this continues, war amongst the kings may break out."

Father smiles at him as he says, "Stories about the sacred treasures you carried from Aleta and their powers are well known across the land. There is skepticism that a stone would 'cry out' when the rightful High King stands upon it. However, I believe that if each king, along with the Danann representative, is given a chance to stand on the Lia Fáil and if the stone does 'cry out', the decision will be accepted. Having all the kings meet at Tara next Beltane to determine the next High King is a good plan."

I note smiles from all in the council chambers. Even Lugh looks convinced.

Father tells Aesres, "I will dispatch messengers to all the kings throughout Inis Elga, telling each that we will convene at Tara on Beltane to select a new High King. The powers of the Lia Fáil will be used to make this selection."

* * *

Little Radha splashes water on me as I dangle my toes in the cool of the Claddagh river. "Radha, please, I don't want to get wet. We are only half way to Learga." She laughs, glancing at me over her shoulder, then chucks another wave of water my way. "Okay little one, just for that, into the river you go."

She squeals in delight, running just out of my reach, but soon I have her. I whip her around, threatening to let her go into the river.

"That's enough fun. It's time to go. We don't want to arrive in Learga after dark. Your mother would be worried. Besides, soon we will be able to see the White Horse of Binn."

Radha settles down and we start to move away from the Claddagh. Glancing back, I can visualize Aesres prying open the mussel and finding the two tears of Danu; one for Aislinn and one for Sianna.

So much has happened these past Beltanes since the Formorri were driven from Inis Elga. Father died a few Beltanes ago and his cairn lies next to King Nuada's on the peak of Slieve Cenn.

"Look, Radha, the Horse of Binn." Seeing the White Horse brings back many memories. As foretold, Cairpre and Laragh rule over Learga with Flann and Aislinn ruling Sligeach.

Radha, Laragh's first child, is named after our mother. It means, *a vision*, acknowledging the gift of sight that both she and Laragh possess. Aislinn has just become pregnant, causing great excitement among us all.

Tomorrow will be Beltane, the seventh since Lugh became High King of Inis Elga. So many events have occurred on Beltane over the years, including the arrival of the Danann, but watching the kingship ceremony, when Lugh became High King, is one of the most memorable. As I walk along the esker below the towering figure of the White Horse, I can picture it all again. There was Lugh, all but ten Beltanes old, standing with his father on the crest of the hill of Tara. The two of them watched as one by one, each of the kings took turns standing on the Lia Fáil. Each king's face glowed in excitement, hoping the Lia Fáil would proclaim him High King. But each stepped off, disappointed. Finally, Fearghus turned to Aesres and Lugh and asked, "Who of the Danann will step on the Lia Fáil?"

With a pat on his shoulder from Aesres, Lugh stepped forward, proclaiming, "It will be I." Lugh stepped up on the stone and from it came a load roar, signaling the High King had been found. All the kings of Inis Elga bent to one knee, acknowledging fealty to their new High King.

I can only imagine the roar reached as far as Sianna in her place in the heavens.

For a free 21-page compilation of pictures and descriptions of the
sites included in the novel and how they look today go to
www.danannconquest.com to see those images.

Story Characters and Terms

Aesres (Ah-rish): The brother of King Nuada, and the keeper of the four treasures from Aletea. He is from the Danann city of Fáilas.

Ailill (AL-yil): The King of Connacht, one of the northern kingdoms of Inis Elga. His kingdom included the northwestern area of Inis Elga and he ruled from Rathcroghan. King Ailill is also the grandfather of the half Formorri Queen of Sligeach, Sianna.

Aislinn (Ās-lin): The daughter of King Nuada, and sister of Cairpre. She is from the Danann city of Fáilas.

Aletea (ah_leh_Tay_uh): The homeland from which the Tuatha de Danann came. It consists of a northern island and a southern island. It was located to the west of Inis Elga, and was destroyed by the goddess Danu.

An Scairp (AN_Scarp): Name for the astrological constellation, Scorpio

An Trogan (AN_Trowgan): Name for the astrological constellation, Cancer.

Aracos (Ah_Ra_Co): Eitilte pilots skilled at the craft of soaring and gliding.

Artgal (AHR-dahl): A warrior from the Danann city of Fáilas. He leads one of the search parties looking for King Nuada when Nuada is feared lost during the destruction of Slieve Danu.

Báire (Ba_reh): The goalkeeper in the game of Iomáint, a game similar to modern hurley.

Bard (BĀrd): The bards were a class of learned individuals steeped in the history and traditions of the people and country and were trained storytellers, reciters of poetry, and musicians. It took many years of training to become a bard.

Belial (BEL-ee-EL): The southern king of the Danann. His actions lead to the breaking of the covenant with the goddess Danu and the eventual destruction of Aletea. He enslaves a people to the west known as the Brahm and conducts a war against them. He and all the southern lands are destroyed by a comet. The destruction of the southern lands triggers the times of the cold that gripped Inis Elga when Laragh of Tomregan was born.

Beltane (BAWL_tuh_nuh): The Beltane festival marked the beginning of the pastoral summer season when the herds of livestock were driven out to their summer pastures and mountain grazing lands. One of the chief ritual acts is the kindling of bonfires. Sacrifices were often burned in the bonfires. Celebrated near the first of May.

Binn (Bhinn): Short name for the mountain Benaughlin, where the mountain figure of the White Horse lies. Currently, the figure is overgrown and cannot be seen. Benaughlin is near the present-day town of Swanlinbar.

Brahm (B r uh m - m ah): A people from the far east who were under the subjugation of King Belial of the Danann.

Breas (BRI-es): The son of the Formorri High King Elotha. His mother was Fiona, the daughter of the High King of the Danann, Conall. Breas becomes one of the northern Kings of Inis Elga as part of a negotiated peace among the Danann, the Formorri, and the kings of Inis Elga.

Brehon Law: Based on oral tradition, the laws were concerned with the payment of compensation for harm done and the regulation of property, inheritance and contracts; the concept of state-administered punishment for crime was foreign during this time.

Cairn (CAR_n): A pile of stones placed in a conical shape. They are used to mark a burial site or to commemorate any sort of event, such as the site of a battle.

Cairpre (KAHR-bra): The son of King Nuada and older brother of Aislinn. He is from the Danann city of Fáilas.

Caoimhe (KEE-va): Sianna's mother. Daughter of King Ailill.

Capall (KA-pall): The horse that Aislinn rides in her search for her father, King Nuada, when he is feared lost during the destruction of Slieve Danu.

Ceili (Kay_lee): Traditional group set dances. Each dance is comprised of several defined movements set to music. The footwork ranges from simple stepping to fast tapping steps, but generally the foot is held relatively flat. In ceili dancing you dance with a partner, yet in each movement, the couples also dance with one or more of the other couples in the set.

Cenn (Sen): A male god within the novel. Patterned after the ancient Irish god Crom Cruach.

Claddagh River (Klah-dah): A small river in present day Fermanagh and Cavan; it means "the washing river." The Claddagh travels both above and underground and is near the White Horse of Binn.

Claíomh Solai (Kli_av_Sali): The Sword of Light. Brought to Ireland by the Tuatha de Danann from the city of Finias. It had the power to cut through any armament and was unstoppable in battle.

Conall (CON-AL): The High King of the Danann. He is killed during the destruction of Slieve Danu.

Coracle (KOR_uh_kul): An ancient Irish boat that was oval in shape with a structure made of a framework of split and interwoven wooden rods, tied with bark. The wood and bark was often hazel or willow. The outer layer was composed from animal skins.

Cullainn (Cah-Lin): High King of Inis Elga. He rules from his rath at the hill of Tara.

Curaugh (Kurr_ah): A larger version of a coracle. It could be taken into the open sea.

Dagda (Dahg_duh): The planet Mars.

Daire (DAW-ra): One of the northern kings of Inis Elga. His kingdom included the north central area of Inis Elga known as Uliad (Ulster) and he ruled from the city of Emain Macha.

Danann: (see Tuatha de Danann.)

Danu (Day'-noo): A female god of the Danann. The goddess of fertility.

Dillat (Dill_at): A horse blanket used by the Tuatha de Danann.

Drui (Dree): The priests and scholars of Inis Elga. In the novel, they have their college at Tomregan.

Eachon (EACH-in): Eachon lived many years before and was one of the greatest bards ever to live in Inis Elga. To honor him, his cairn was placed near the mouth of the oracle, Horse of Binn. His spirit is released during Samhain when a bonfire is set near his cairn, and it is through his spirit that the oracle speaks to those who tend his fire.

Eitilte (Ehl_tyeh): Flying craft made of wicker and leather that became weightless by using the liquid geal leacht and crystals. The eitilte were designed to maximize the craft's range by having wings to allow soaring and gliding.

Elotha (YEOL-a-ha): The High King of the Formorri. He is the brother of Trista, the father of Breas, and the uncle of Queen Sianna.

Emain Macha (Ewin_Maha): A site now known as Navan Fort, situated in the North of Ireland, a few miles west of Armagh. This spot was the prehistoric capital of the Ulaidh (Ulster).

Eoghan (YEO-gan): The second son of King Ailill of Rathcroghan.

Esker (Es_Ker): Long, winding ridges of sand and gravel, often left at the edges of retreating glaciers. In Ireland, these formed the ancient footpaths across the land and, along with rivers, were the main means of travel.

Etain (AY-teen): A close confidant of Queen Sianna who grew up with Sianna. She was jealous of the attention given to Sianna by Aesres and participated in the conspiracy to attack the Danann.

Fáilas (FAL_lee_us): The northern city of the Tuatha de Danann in the homeland of Aletea. It was near this city that the Tuatha de Danann first came to their homeland. The Lia Fáil was originally in this city.

Fearghus (FUR-gus): A native Tomregan, Fearghus is the leading elder of the bards in Tomregan. He is the father of Keelen, Flann, and Laragh.

Finias (Fin_nee_us): One of the three cities in the southern part of the northern island of Aletea. Finias faced toward the sea to the south and from it came Claíomh Solai, the sword of light. Finias, along with Gorias and Murias, surrounded the base of the Slieve of Danu. A circular network of interconnected, interior waterways surrounded the entire Slieve of Danu and connected the three cities.

Fiona (fee-O-na): The daughter of the Danann High King Conall. She is the wife of the Formorri High King Elotha. Her son, Breas, is a friend of King Nuada's children, Aislinn and Cairpre. Breas becomes one of the northern Kings of Inis Elga as part of a negotiated peace among the Danann, the Formorri, and the kings of Inis Elga.

Flann (Flan): A native Tomregan, Flann is a bard in training and is the son of Fearghus. He is the older brother of Laragh, and the twin brother of Keelen.

Formorri (F'_MOR_ee): A dark-skinned sea people that specialize in trade. They have their origins on islands somewhere near North Africa. They established a trading center in the sea coast village of Sligeach.

Fulacht Fiadh (Full_Oct_fee_ah): Cooking pits filled with water. Stones are heated in a fire and once the stones are red-hot, they are dropped into the fulacht fiadh. After a short while, the water begins to boil. When the water warms to boiling, meats that have been rolled tightly in a cooking skin are weighted and placed in the fulacht fiadh to cook.

Geal Leacht (Gyal_Lacht): A metallic, silver-colored liquid (similar to mercury) found in pools in the caverns within Slieve Danu. Geal leacht, in conjunction with special crystals, caused objects to become weightless.

Gorias (GOR_ree_us): One of the three cities in the southern part of the northern island of Aletea, facing the sea to the west. From Gorias came the Spear of Lúin. Gorias, along with Murias and Finias, surrounded the base of the Slieve of Danu. A circular network of interconnected, interior waterways surrounded the entire Slieve of Danu and connected the three cities.

Hurley (Hur_lee): The stick used to hit the leather ball in the game of Iomáint.

Inis Elga (Inish_El_ga): Ancient name for the Irish Island. Means "The Noble Island."

Iomáint (Um_int): A game that uses a stick and a leather ball filled with compacted hair. Played on a field with two standing poles with a crossbar at each end of the field. Much like the modern game of hurley.

Keelen (KEE-lin): A native Tomregan, Keelen is a drui in training and is the daughter of Fearghus. She is the older sister of Laragh and the twin sister of Flann.

Laragh (LAR-ah): A native Tomregan, Laragh is a drui in training and is the daughter of Fearghus. She is the younger sister of Keelen and Flann. She is known to be able to see the future.

Learga (Larg Ah): The village founded by the Danann along the northern loughs. It is near present day Blacklion between Upper Lough MacNean and Lower Lough MacNean.

Lia Fáil (Lee_ah_foyl): The Stone of Destiny, brought from Aletea to Ireland by the Tuatha de Danann. In legend, it originated in the Tuatha de Danann city of Fáilas. The stone cries out in joy when the rightful king stands upon it.

Lár (LAR): A midfielder in the game of Iomáint. A game similar to modern hurley.

Lolair (LUH_lar): Gaelic word for an eagle.

Lough (Loh): A lake or inlet from the sea.

Lough Aillionn (Loh Al_in): Modern day Lough Allen in the county of Leitrim. The Shannon river flows into and out of it.

Lugh (Lú): The son of Queen Sianna and Aesres. It is predicted that he will one day be High King of Inis Elga. Also, the name for the planet Venus.

Mag Senaig (Maw_shlaykht): Is the name of an historic plain that comprises an area of about three square miles, situated in the southeastern part of the Parish of Templeport, in the county of Cavan. It is mentioned in The Metrical Dindshenchas (Poem 25 Ailech III) in the story of the Dagda, Corrgenn and Ailech, wherein it states the Corrgenn travelled from Tara to Lough Foyle in the Inishowen peninsula via Mag Senaig. In Pre-Christian times the small area where the Crom Cruaich (Cenn is the name for Crom Cruach used in the novel) idol stood at Kilnavert was originally named Fossa Slécht or Rath Slécht, and it is from this small location that the wider Magh Slécht area received its name. The plain is not flat, but consists of little drumlin hills. However, as it is surrounded by mountains, it is a plain in comparison. Tomregan lies at the edge of Mag Senaig.

Morca (More Ka): Queen Sianna's father, who was King of

Sligeach. He married the daughter of King Ailill.

Moytura (moy-toor-a): In the first Battle of Moytura, site of the battle between the Danann and the High King of Inis Elga. In the second Battle of Moytura, site of the battle between the Danann and the Formorri.

Murias (Mure_ree_us): One of the three cities in the southern part of the northern island of Aletea. Murias faced toward the sea to the east and from this city came the cauldron of wisdom. Murias, along with Gorias and Finias, surrounded the base of the Slieve of Danu. A circular network of interconnected, interior waterways surrounded the entire Slieve of Danu and connected the three cities.

Nuada (Nu-ah): The northern king of the Danann from the city of Fáilas. He is the father of Aislinn, and the brother of Aesres. He leads his small band of Danann from Aletea, the homeland of the Danann, the people of Danu, to Inis Elga.

Rath (RAH): A home of importance. A fortress.

Rathcroghan (RAH_Cre_han_ee): An ancient ritual center in Ireland where, according to ancient lore, the kingdom of Connacht was ruled from. It is located in the county of Roscommon. In the novel, it is the home of one of the northern kings of Inis Elga, King Ailill, who is also the grandfather of the half Formorri Queen of Sligeach, Sianna.

Rayna (Rein Ah): The half-sister of Breas, and his constant companion. She marries Breas and they briefly rule Rathcroghan.

Ruairi (ROR-ee): The eldest son of King Ailill of Rathcroghan.

Samhain (Saoe'en): The Festival of Samhain is a celebration of the end of the harvest season and is generally regarded as ancient New Year. It occurred toward the end of October and went into early November. There was much celebrating and feasting.

Sianna (SEE-a-na): The Formorri queen of the trading village of Sligeach, seaside trading village of the Formorri located at the modern city of Sligo. She is half Formorri and half Inis Elgan. Her mother was the daughter of King Ailill of Rathcroghan. Her father was the brother of the Formorri High King Elotha.

Sinann (Shan_nin): The modern day river Shannon.

Sgian (Skeen): Small, single-edged knife. The Sgian is normally worn on the right leg, but can also be worn on the left, depending on whether the wearer is right or left handed.

Slieve (Shleeve): A mountain.

Slieve Benaughlin (Shleeve Binn augh lin): A mountain on the border of present day Fermanagh and Cavan. It means "peak of the speaking horse" and on it was the Horse of Binn.

Slieve Cenn (Shleeve_Sen): The mountain to the north of Mag Senaig, now known as Slieve Cuilcagh, dedicated to the god Cenn.

Slieve of Danu (Shleeve Ah nue): The central mountain of Aletea around which the cities of Danu were built. These cities were connected by canals. These cities were Finias, Gorias, and Murias.

Slieve Ruisen (Shleeve_Rusheen): A mountain to the east of Mag Senaig, now known as Slieve Russell.

Sligeach (SHLIG_ahk): A seaside trading village of the Formorri, located at the modern city of Sligo in County Sligo.

Spear of Lúin (Loo_in): A spear that was another of the four treasures brought to Ireland by the Tuatha de Danann. In legend, it originated in the Tuatha de Danann city of Gorias.

Sreng (shreng): The champion of High King Cullainn. Fought King Nuada at the first battle of Moytura and severed Nuada's fingers.

Tadgh (TIEg): A warrior from the Danann city of Fáilas. He leads one of the search parties looking for King Nuada when he is feared lost during the destruction of Slieve Danu.

Tara (Tah_re): The hill of the king and the location of the rath of the high king of Inis Elga. Near the modern-day village of Tara.

Teagan (Té Gueun): The deceased wife of Aesres.

Torc (TORK): A neck-ring piece of jewelry made of intertwined metal, usually gold or silver.

Tomregan (Toome_Dree_gun): A village in the northern county of Cavan, near the modern town of Bally Connell and at the edge of Mag Sehaig. It was the site of a legendary druid college. The stone "Tom Regan" found in a church in Bally Connell, is from this site.

Tragan (Tra_gun): Name for the astrological constellation Pisces.

Trista (TRIS-ta): The aunt of Queen Sianna and her high counselor. She also represents the interests of the Formorri High King Elotha, who is her brother and Queen Sianna's uncle.

Trevor (TRE-vur): The closest advisor of King Ailill of Rathcroghan.

Tuatha de Danann (TOO_'hada_Dah_n'n): Are the people of the goddess Danu who come to Inis Elga in their flying craft under the leadership of King Nuada.

Ulaidh (Oola): Ancient name for Ulster.

Una (OO-na): An older friend of Keelen's.

Vailixi (Val_lixi): Large lifting platforms used by the Danann in Aletea. The platforms became weightless by using the liquid geal leacht and crystal.

ABOUT THE AUTHOR

Gary Cullen was born in St. Louis and grew up in Virginia, Montana, and Oregon as his family moved. He joined the navy during the Vietnam war, serving on an oil tanker that supplied fuel to the fleet off the coast of Vietnam. Much of his free time on the ship was spent reading Michener, Dostoyevsky, Leon Uris, Tolstoy, and Clavell, among others.

His experience in the navy gave Gary a strong appreciation for education. He began his lifelong career as an energy efficiency policy analyst while still in graduate school.

During family vacations to Ireland, Gary became taken by the country and sought out his roots. His efforts brought him to a small stone cottage just south of Swanlinbar where an old man in his 90s lived by himself. He was born in the cottage and lived there all his life. Records showed that this cottage remained in the Cullen family until 1904. Willie's parents, the old gentleman still living in the cottage, must have acquired it shortly after this. He met Willie's neighbors, who were applying a whitewash to the cottage, and they told him that it had a dirt floor and no electricity until just a few years before.

In a latter visit to Ireland, A Swanlinbar gentleman named Michael told Gary and his wife Kathleen about a white horse hill figure that once could be seen on Benaughlin mountain just north of Swanlinbar. He and Kathleen hiked up the mountain to the area where they were told it once existed. At first, no sign of it could be found and Gary decided to climb to the top for a wider look. Kathleen stayed behind to wait and as she waited, a giant Irish hare popped up within feet of her and surveyed her for a while. Then the hare slowly moved off and Kathleen followed. Soon, she was in a field of white stones covered in grass.

Gary stayed in Ireland another week after Kathleen returned home to do more exploration. A local man showed him the sites of many small stone circles not seen by tourists, and then took him to the site of some very large stones lying on their sides in a wood. This, he said, was the stone circle for Crom Cruaich and legend has it that St. Patrick himself had the stones pushed over. The Killycluggin stone, once part of this circle, was found near this site. The gentleman also told me about the ancient druid college of Tom Reagan (Tomregan), the site of which was partially destroyed during the building of the Slieve Russell hotel. The Tom Reagan stone is in the church entryway in BallyConnell.

Gary came to realize that many of the ancient legends he had been reading took place in this part of Ireland. With this realization came the idea of writing this novel. He tried to pin an actual historical timeframe for the novel when there was likely significant change and upheaval. Looking through old tree ring records showed a very significant event that caused the climate to dramatically cool occurred in the spring/early summer of the year 1159 BCE. This became the starting point for the tale.